Adventures with
DANGEROUS
WOMEN

ALSO BY PHILIP GURIN

THE JAMES BOND TRIVIA QUIZ BOOK

Adventures with
DANGEROUS
WOMEN

by
PHILIP GURIN

DONALD I. FINE, INC.

New York

Library of Congress Cataloging in Publication Data

Gurin, Philip.
Adventures with dangerous women.

I. Title.
PS3557.U815A65   1989   813′.54   88-45849
ISBN 1-55611-123-1
Manufactured in the United States of America
10 9 8 7 6 5 4 3 2 1

Designed by Irving Perkins Associates

FOR CHERYL AND DANIEL

And I find more bitter than death the woman,
whose heart is snares and nets,
and her hands as bands.

Ecclesiastes 7:26

Contents

PART ONE:
Being of Sound Mind

11

PART TWO:
Paranoia on $30 a Day

75

PART THREE:
The Sun Also Comes in From the Cold

203

PART ONE
Being of Sound Mind

ONE

Yeah, right.

See, the scary thing is I was starting to understand Van Gogh and Hemingway and what led them to do it. I don't generally like dwelling on the negative, and those who know me will vouch for my abnormally high degree of optimism. But the cliche of being a struggling artist was beginning to make me sick.

So while I was sitting in the rear balcony of the Broadway Theatre, watching one of the latest British-import musicals, it became suddenly clear that the desire to mutilate oneself out of extreme commitment to one's art was something I could relate to.

The show unfolded apace and I applauded in all the right places, but if a gun were held to my head I couldn't tell you how it all ended. I was too preoccupied with the notion of artistic martyrdom. My date, a doe-eyed redhead from Quogue who worked as the personal assistant to a junior options trader, was riveted, clutching my hand and a tissue, crying for all she was worth. She was cute, energetic, a bit shy, and as I looked at her weeping for the unhappy lovers on stage, I couldn't wait to get her home and in bed.

Look, this is how things were going for me then, so if I really have a place to start, it was there, that night, as Jean Valjean

13

was being chased by Inspector Javert. It was during this production of *Les Misérables* that I felt my life on the verge of change.

The idealistic, severely dedicated public policeman Javert, doggedly pursuing the not-so-innocent yet ever-so-noble man who stole bread for his family, had all the scope and dimension one would want in an epic. I should have been sympathizing with Valjean but instead couldn't help but root for Javert. Maybe it's because like most people I root for the underdog. Maybe it's because Valjean seemed too pious for my tastes. Or maybe it was because I wanted to see another good guy *get it*. I am, was, always hope to be, a good guy, but have been *getting it* (read shafted) for the past number of years. And I'm fucking sick of it.

I've spent my life as a writer. More precisely, a television writer, which, as cliches go, is not quite the same thing. A television writer works for hire, and hence, is a well-paid wage slave. His work belongs to the people who buy it. That person, inevitably a producer, may cut, paste, edit, delete, rewrite or completely throw out the writer's labor of love without the slightest hesitation or guilt. Spend months of your life pouring your soul into something, anything, even a moderately successful syndicated adventure series called *The Underground Force,* and watch what happens when a smartass executive, a "suit," a twit who looks too young to shave, tells you it doesn't send a "chill up my spine" and subsequently brings in a team of freshly scrubbed hacks to "punch it up," you'll see. You'll quickly understand the literary equivalent of the rabbit punch.

So there I was, feeling shitty, used, abused, artistically spent. Eight years in television, with a brief stint doing an animated Saturday-morning kids' show, with nothing to show for it except a collection of toy miniatures from the series' successful merchandising line, and a collection of friends and memories that were increasingly getting on my nerves. I was clearly facing a midlife crisis, though I was only thirty-two.

I had dreamed of writing the great American screenplay, but somehow that experience had eluded me. Sure, I'd sold a number of scripts, been hired to write a few more "assignments," but none of these were getting produced. A writer can live on the income from unproduced material for years, and I once saw a picture in the New York *Times* of a well-paid screenwriter concealed behind a life-sized stack of shelved scripts. But there's no satisfaction in that.

For that matter, there was no satisfaction in my *life*. I'd been out of college ten years, drifted from romance to romance, never quite finding my dream girl in the white T-Bird anywhere near Columbus Avenue, and was generally feeling disappointed with everything I did.

I'd been a native of New York for far too long, and *something* had to give.

There's a remarkable clarity that comes with sudden, profound insight. All at once the issues that cloud your mind vanish, and the world opens up before you with newfound understanding. This is especially true if, after a night of delightful sex, you wake up, smack your forehead and say "Wow." I didn't quite want a glass of vegetable juice, but I couldn't continue as I had been. Seven months between gigs was a trifle too long for my liking.

A week after I'd seen *Les Miserables,* Danette Riley from Quogue phoned to see if I was busy. It was Monday night, the football game on TV didn't interest me, so I asked her over for popcorn and a flick. I suggested she bring over whatever she wanted from the Video Shack, so she arrived with a copy of *9½ Weeks.* I took this as the hint it was, and we bedded down right on the kitchen floor, cold linoleum and all. Danette was clearly into it from the start, and after I ran an ice cube around each nipple, down her stomach, around her pubis and gently inside her, she shuddered with a loud moan, dragging her long nails down my back deep enough to draw blood. We continued our culinary experiments with chocolate syrup, ice cream and champagne, making a mess with everything, but enjoying our childish selves nonetheless.

In the middle of this I began drifting. I was still horny, a fact which was rather evident to Danette and to which she lowered her mouth with delicious abandon, but my mind was caught thinking about a recent article I'd read in New York magazine.

Now, New York magazine is a terrible dishrag that no right-minded New Yorker who cares about his cache can live without. My subscription had been steady for years, even before I lived in Manhattan. It was filled with self-serving articles that made you want to scream and throw up and accost people on the street to see if they felt the same way. The articles about people living hi-ho the glamorous life, about young couples working eighty-seven hours a day and still finding time to play with their kids in the spacious apartment they bought "before Koch" for no money whatsoever—who were these people? I'd never met them. No one I knew had ever met them. I was sure they couldn't possibly exist.

I'd been conditioned to read New York just like everyone else for fear of not being properly informed on all the kitschy new trends, concepts and possibilities of life at the vortex of civilization. Especially since so many of their feature stories were bought by film production companies and used as the bases of movies. The most infamous of these was a brief report on preening Brooklyn youths who journeyed to Manhattan to boogie with the babes every weekend. It became the period piece *Saturday Night Fever*, and woe unto the young film company story editor—or "D-Girl," in the vernacular—who missed the chance to buy the next article about the life and rituals of the evolving Baby Boomers.

So there I was, being fellated by an expert, when all I could think of was how much I hated New York magazine.

This was not the sign of a well-adjusted individual.

Danette sensed my distraction, stuck a finger in my ass and throated me till I shot all over her face.

She seemed to enjoy it.

Later, in bed, after a more mundane missionary encounter, Danette complained about not being able to spend more time together. She lived in Murray Hill now, I on the Yupper West Side, and her boss was making her work extra hours. She wanted to go out more, do more things on the town, take advantage of the restaurants, nightclubs, museums, but seven months sans remuneration is seven months, and though I was expecting a paltry residual, I could no more afford a night at Indochine than I could a pair of hot dogs at Gray's Papaya on Broadway and Seventy-second. Those fifty-cent beauties have more often than not been all that stood between me and starvation, but tonight I couldn't even spring for a full-course meal there with fresh papayas, and this beautiful, sexy, kinky, redhead with porcelain skin and eyes to break hearts wanted to do the town. I had to remind her that the "Les Miz" tix were comps from a friend.

Anyway, we cuddled like spoons and my mind continued to drift. I was scared. I was losing focus. I couldn't concentrate on any one thing too long. My writing of late had been scattershot, I spent more time reading newspapers than at the word processor, and everything in the world was a welcomed distraction. I wasn't yet having Walter Mitty–like spells of out-of-body experiences, but I wouldn't have been surprised if the next time I fell asleep I woke up to find myself a human sacrifice in some ancient Mayan ritual. Mental stability was fast becoming a memory.

As we held each other close, inhaling each other's animal smells, it occurred to me that I hated going to the movies. (How's that for a non sequitur?) Not only because I hated the long lines, the uncomfortable seats, the stale popcorn. I hated movies as a form, a concept. I wanted to write them, make my living and reputation from them, yet since I currently wasn't, I had no time to enjoy them. I simply *resented* them too much.

What a startling revelation that was! It clearly indicated I was on the road to some kind of disaster.

Tuesday morning and Danette was up early, eagerly making breakfast. I usually suffer the morning meal with a cup of coffee and Stella D'Oro Breakfast Treats, but there she was, whisking up eggs and bacon. The dishes were all set. There were even little half-moons of orange slices garnishing each plate. Danette looked at me with her doe-eyes all sad and sleepy, and she smiled. She seemed so happy. I wanted to cry. I wanted to sit right down on the floor and weep like a baby. Since when did I deserve such a nice young thing like Danette?

And then the phone rang.

It was Rick. He desperately needed to see me at the Whitney. Rick didn't work at the Whitney, he worked in a large office building on Sixth near Rockefeller Plaza, but every now and then he'd get rushes and feel the need to visit an art gallery, "just to touch base." Rick was a lawyer who once dreamed of being an artist. More precisely, he was an artist who sold out for the quick bucks of jurisprudence. He lived in a beautiful one-bedroom overlooking Central Park West, but he never seemed to enjoy it because he was always working. Six days a week, eleven hours a day. He worked so much he had no discernible sex life, either. This was something we usually commiserated about over brews, but since I was currently "blessed with Ms. Riley" (Rick's phraseology), the rules had changed, and the subject was less overtly broached.

Rick was jabbering over the phone as I watched Danette lovingly scoop eggs onto each plate. "There's this new photo exhibit they got, I think Cindy Sherman or someone. I really want to see it before lunch."

"How about one? I'll meet you by the door."

"Listen Cliff," he said, "I'm under a lot of stress. The partners got me working on this fucked-up case, I been here all night. They bought me a cot so I could sleep here. Generous goddamned cocksuckers. A nice idea at the time, but I actually used it last night, and today I feel like I slept in a paper shredder. I can't stand straight. If you see someone slide up to you at the museum wearing a power suit who looks like Quasimodo, promise you won't scream." He yawned on the other end of the phone. "I gotta get me some aspirin."

"One o'clock, Rick. By the door. We'll grab lunch first."

"Goddamn it!"

"What?"

"Cliff, you still there?"

"No, it's Klaus Barbie, how may I serve you?"

"I got a note here my secretary called in sick. How the fuck am I gonna finish my work? I oughta fire her."

"We'll look at the nice Allie Sherman pictures and relax. We'll have a good time."

"It's *Cindy.* Not Allie. Cindy Sherman took the photos. Who's Allie Sherman?"

"He used to coach the Giants." I didn't really share Rick's interest in art, but could watch a mud-drenched football game between the worst teams in the league with thorough delight. I prided myself on having had season tickets to the defunct United States Football League, and saw every Jersey Generals game played in the Meadowlands before Donald Trump came in and screwed everything up trying to turn that league into competition for the senior circuit.

Danette sat down at the kitchen counter, actually an island that separated the kitchen from the living room, I hung up and we ate.

"Eggs are delicious," I said, chewing.

"Glad you like them." Chew, chew. "Who are you going with to the museum?"

"Rick Partridge. Buddy from high school. He's a lawyer by profession but an artist by temperament."

"He wants to have lunch at the museum?"

I saw which way this was going but could do nothing about it. "Every now and then he feels the need to see the newest exhibits. And since he's currently without a girl friend, I have the misfortune of being dragged along. I don't mind though. I willingly suffer for my friends."

Danette seemed to weigh this in some sort of Solomon-like judgment. "Do you talk about art, or the lack of women in his life?"

"Both, depending on the mood. One subject will take precedence over the other."

She paused, considering this response. She resumed eating, then put down her fork and looked directly at me. "I have a half day coming up this Friday. Do you think we can spend it at the Met? I haven't been there in years."

Manipulative little vixen, isn't she?

"Danette, I'd never refuse you anything."

I got to the museum early. It was a gorgeous autumn day, bright, sunny, not too cool. I took the crosstown bus at Seventy-ninth Street and walked down Madison toward the museum. It never ceased to amaze me what a different world the Upper East Side was from the Upper West. The East had more provincial, quasi-Gaulish charms. There were art galleries and antique galleries and designer boutiques of every description. The Hotel Carlyle was a block north of the Whitney, and I'd always wanted to take a girl to the club there one night and listen to Bobby Short sing and play piano. Other friends had done that already, some enjoyed him, others less so, but for me, not having made the pilgrimage, Bobby Short was nothing more than a black singer who used to plug perfume on television. ("There's a fragrance that's here today, and they call it . . .")

Sitting on the concrete fence that surrounded the Whitney's courtyard at street level were a group of construction workers. Mostly wearing denim blue, they looked like a pack of bored Chinese Communists. A few beautiful young secretaries floated by on their way somewhere, and like construction workers the world over, these men shifted their concentration accordingly.

"Hey, chickee-babe."

"Want to climb my flagpole?"

"My tubesteak of love wants you bad, girl!"

"What the fuck are you looking at?" It was Rick. "I thought you were happy with Danette."

"I didn't realize I was looking anywhere," I said.

"Come on, Cliff. Let's chow down before we look at the art." Rick was wearing a wrinkled blue pinstriped suit, yellow power tie, wing tips, a badly-stained white shirt. Everything looked like it just came out of a camper's knapsack, including Rick, whose tired eyes were holding up tiny little steamer trunks. His jet black hair had a shock of white running through it that made him look like the Bride of Frankenstein.

"You look like shit," I said.

"Thanks. You can buy me lunch."

"Not me. Charge me to some account. Consider this deep background for one of your cases."

"I'll see how magnanimous I'm feeling."

We went inside and Rick flashed his corporate-club card that got us in free. We immediately went downstairs to the restaurant, which, as the guide brochure says, is "one of the few in the neighborhood with a modestly priced menu." Sure. The quality, if I remembered, was modest, too. We sat by the window.

"You paying?" I asked.

"Sure. But let's eat fast, I gotta see the stuff and get out of here."

I ordered the most expensive thing on the menu.

"I noticed you're starting to look thin and tired," said Rick, as he gulped down his Perrier. "A tall guy like you loses his looks real easy, Cliff. Must be all the tension associated with your career."

"Look, if we're going to start knocking professions, let's say *sayonara* right now. I got a lot on my mind. I'm waiting on at least fifteen different things, none of which will happen, but one or two might. For all I know I might be on the next plane to L.A. or someplace. If my agent gets on the stick and makes a few calls." I'd been anxiety-ridden the whole seven months, awaiting the call from my agent—my job pimp, my procurer— that meant employment was once again at hand.

"I still don't understand why you don't just have a lawyer look over your contracts."

"Like you?"

"Or someone of equal estimation."

"Agents are supposed to be part of the cosmic show business chain. They're a necessary species, with dog-eared Rolodexes and contacts under each memo. They're supposed to put packages together in a single bound. Hence, my fate rests with an agent. When I'm big, maybe the calls will come to me directly, but now, I'm dependent. And it's frustrating."

"At least you're your own boss."

"I can always schedule lunches with lawyers at museums without getting permission, true."

"You get up when you want, work when you want. Your day is your own."

"But I'm sick of looking at the same four walls in my apartment. The commute is great. I get out of bed and walk into the next room, boot up and away we go. But I'm never relaxed. I can never sit down and just watch a Jets game without getting a nervous twitch that I should be over by my desk, pumping out another scene in the great American screenplay. Time I don't use to write is time taking money out of my bank account."

"So do something else."

"That's all the advice you can offer?"

"Put me on retainer, you'll get wisdom."

"Wisdom this, Rick."

"Look, I called you up for a quick fix of art. I'm the one with the suit and the tie and career angst. *I* went to law school, for Christ's sake. I did this to myself. I work insane hours for insane people. Half my clients think Judge Wapner is just down the corridor in a nice, clean courtroom, waiting to dish out evenhanded justice. Most of the time I'm writing some damned papers for the senior partners, who I can't fucking stand, or I'm going over standard contracts that haven't been changed since King John signed the Magna Carta. And this morning, it suddenly hit me that I actually paid to do this to myself. I went to law school for three fucking years and borrowed up to my ass to be miserable for the rest of my fucking life. Something can't be right."

"We both need a change," I said.

"Agreed."

"Or a vacation."

"Better still."

"Kuala Lumpur?"

"Too humid."

"Macao?"

"Too Portuguese."

"Two weeks in Barbados?"

"Not bad, but probably boring after the first fuck."

"Hey, this is the eighties, Rick. We don't fuck around anymore."

"Fuck you we don't fuck around anymore. You got that redheaded shicksa back home, wanking your willie. I'm gonna end up like something in a Philip Roth novel."

"She's not home, she works."

"I'll give you she works. Work this."

"So we're not going on any vacations?"

"Cliff, I need to, but I can't. After next week I got to prepare a big lawsuit against some pharmaceutical company accused of selling contaminated infant formula to Third World countries. But as your attorney I advise you to take a trip immediately."

"I'll think about it."

"Can Danette go with you?"

"Probably."

"Don't take her." He swigged down some Perrier.

"Why not? Never mind."

"You need to get away, be on your own. Spread some wings and learn to fly."

"I was only waiting for this moment to arise, right?"

"Right."

"You know me too well. I can't remember when I last used my passport."

"Damn right I know you too well. That's why I know you need a change. All you been doing is bitching how you haven't had any joy in your life, any excitement, any adventure. So, while you're still young and just slightly ugly, take life by the horns and ride it out. Light out for the Andes, go touch Indians, climb Kilimanjaro."

"Bucks, my friend. Swiss Air requires payment in legal tender."

"So I'll lend you what you need till those residuals come through."

"I appreciate the offer, but I make it a personal policy never to accept money from a Shylock."

"Think of it as a humanitarian grant to the arts."

"Finish your lunch, we'll see the paintings."

"Photographs."

"Whatever."

We finished our salads in silence. I looked up and out the window toward the street. The Chinese Communists were gone and I now had a clear view of the roof of the bank across the street. From there, it occurred to me, a sniper could kill someone sitting here in the restaurant and be off before anyone knew what happened. Police would gather at the intersection, TV camera crews would race down the stairs to the courtyard, a few old ladies with blue hair and strands of pearls would stand around in shock, or else quietly go about their business, looking in the nearby galleries for imported rugs. . . .

It's my television training that brings on such thoughts.

Rick paid and we took the elevator up. The Cindy Sherman photographs on the second floor were an odd collection indeed. This Miss Sherman took pictures of one thing: herself. In each photo she wore costumes to look like B-movie actresses or dismembered victims of violent crimes or Lolita-like seductresses. She employed makeup and costumes to alter her appearance: more accurately, to hide her true self.

I could relate to that.

It was like role playing. The information on the wall said Sherman wasn't a photographer per se, but a performance artist. Okay, fine. All I knew was her pictures were depressing.

"She likes to sublimate her own identity with those of pop icons and generic cultural references," said Rick. I looked at him in mock awe.

"Do go on."

"Notice the large, color photograph with the dismembered pieces of human matter."

"I couldn't avoid it."

"Don't you think it's great the way she used those two tiny windup walking dildoes right there in the middle?"

"I'll be outside on earth."

"There's something really disturbing about these pictures."

"Rick, downstairs you sounded like a wombat in heat, up here you sound like Alistair Cooke."

"It's the duality of man, Heathcliff."

"Duality this, pal."

"Come here." We walked over to another huge color photograph that showed a distorted, fish-eye view of the artist as an android. Rick's expression as he looked at it was one of profound interest. I, on the other hand, needed the toilet.

"For an artist, Cliffie, you lack gumption."

I had no idea what he was talking about, but didn't stop to inquire further. When I returned from the facility, Rick had changed back into his lawyer demeanor. I had this image of him suddenly whipping into the appropriate mood like Superman changing in a phone booth.

"I gotta get back to the office, Cliff. I'm running late."

"You be home? I'll call you."

"I don't know."

"Okay."

He started for the exit, stopped, turned and came at me with purpose. "Do yourself a favor, see the rest of the museum. Get in touch with your artistic soul. You need it, man. Make changes in your life at once."

"You sound like a fortune cookie."

"Wise ass."

He turned and left.

On the top floor was a wonderfully colorful exhibit by Red Grooms, who I originally thought was something do to with horses. A "figurative artist," per the brochure, he built these large, elaborate, oversized sculptures that were meant to focus new light on the world around us. His *Woolworth Building* featured a fire-breathing papier-mâché dragon. His *Wall Street* was a narrow collection of alleys and buildings that distorted yet reflected the essence of downtown New York. There was a news vendor who sold mostly pornography, and a rickety bridge leading to the Staten Island Ferry. *Subway* was a large subway car that rattled and rumbled with huge sculptures of seated passengers gazing into oblivion just like real people. I sat down on the bench in the subway car, looked up across at an oversized papier-mâché sculpture of a Hasidic Jew, and felt as though I'd dropped acid. Finally, there was a barnlike room filled with horses, cowboys and rodeo sounds. The floor was covered in stuffed burlap, so as you walked you had to lift your feet to avoid falling. I suppose this was meant to represent either hay or horse shit.

It was a terrific exhibit, filled with life and excitement. It was a major contrast to the photos downstairs, but it did remind me that all art was perspective and execution, so maybe, just maybe, I'd missed something earlier.

I went next to the third floor, which consisted of highlights from the museum's permanent collection. Fewer people were there and it seemed much quieter. There were some standard works of twentieth-century art I remembered seeing the last time I visited, so I walked around and gazed with a nice sense of familiarity.

A short, bearded man in a dark gray business suit suddenly caught my eye. He was ambling through the gallery, not really concentrating on the art, and he kept pivoting his head around like a nervous turtle, evidently looking for someone. In his right hand he carried an old-fashioned black umbrella with an intricately carved wooden handle, though rain wasn't predicted until Friday. His left hand kept darting in and out of his coat pocket, but every now and then he tried stopping this by smoothing down the pocket and resting his stubby, hairy hand at his side. I got the impression he didn't want to appear conspicuous, but the way he carried himself achieved the opposite effect.

He was standing in front of Jasper Johns's famous *Three Flags,* but was gazing so intently at the superimposed images of Old Glory he couldn't possibly have been able to see it.

A tall woman stepped beside him to look at the same work. She had teased, dirty blond hair, was wearing a tight-fitting brown skirt that came down to her calves, a cream-colored blouse with oversized sleeves, and appeared to be seriously studying the brush strokes. From where I stood I couldn't be sure, but she seemed to be whispering something to the bearded man. He flinched but didn't look at her. The woman easily turned and walked into the next room.

I was intrigued. I don't usually make a habit of following strange women in museums, but a chance encounter with a sophisticated adult female in a respectable art establishment was a fantasy I'd entertained once or twice. Not that I'd really do anything, but . . .

I slowly moved past the bearded man, who seemed more tense than I thought. In the next room Dirty Blond was strolling in front of the other works of art, and I got a glimpse of her face for the first time. She had narrow, hazel eyes that seemed to peer rather than look. Her cheekbones were of the high, pronounced variety, and her lips were pencil thin. On someone else the combination might have looked wan and Oriental, but on her it worked. She reminded me of Faye Dunaway before she clowned out in *Mommie Dearest.*

She walked slowly around the gallery, casually admiring the pictures. I moved beside her at one point, looked up at the painting, then casually shifted my gaze to her. Our eyes met, she smiled perfunctorily, then glided past me like I didn't exist. Well, now. I turned to watch her and was surprised to catch her turn her head to give me a second glance. Her smile this time was a bit more sardonic, like she'd sucked a lime, though she kept moving and disappeared behind a large white wall into the adjoining room.

I followed, but she was moving quickly and was already around the next corner and into another part of the gallery before I could see her. I moved fast, but missed her again. The bearded man was standing in front of Edward Hopper's *Early Sunday Morning,* but I paid him no mind as I now felt a manic urgency in trying to find Dirty Blond.

The gallery seemed emptier than before, and the silence was

annoying. I was racing now, trying to find the woman. Where could she have gone? Had she already left?

I was back in the main foyer of the third floor when suddenly the bearded man with the umbrella, standing to wait for the elevator, clutched his chest and crumpled to the floor. There were no guards, no other visitors, so I had no choice: I rushed over to help. The man was clearly having a heart attack. I bent down, loosened his tie. He struggled to sit, to grab my arm for support, but was gasping and weak. He looked at me, a total stranger, with so much hope. What could I do? His left hand was fidgeting in his pocket, but another spasm of pain twitched his body, and he grabbed onto me with both arms. He looked like he wanted to speak, but his lips never moved.

"Aaahhs," he said.

"What?"

"Aaahhs . . ."

The guy was dying. "Guard? Somebody!" I shouted, as two security guards rushed over.

One guard rushed to a hidden telephone and placed a call. A group of visitors had formed a circle to watch, but the other guard was trying to force everyone back. The bearded man suddenly became rigid, his arms dragged down the sides of my body, and I gently placed him to rest on the ground. The crowd murmured its appropriate shock. I looked up to see the frightened face of Dirty Blond peering at me through the crowd. All I could think of was: where had she been? Suddenly she seemed less poised, with real concern on her narrow lips. Quickly she assumed an air of indifference and moved away.

I stood up, pushed my way through the crowd, followed her downstairs. I don't know why, but she seemed to know something about the dead man. Also, if she did know him, wouldn't the right response have been to stay behind and offer help?

She moved out through the front exit before I could reach her, and as I pushed my way onto the pavement, she was closing the door on a taxi, zooming downtown, disappearing with the traffic. I was about to rush for another cab when an ambulance pulled in front and the EMS people raced into the museum. Duty-bound, I reentered the Whitney to report what had happened.

But all I could think about was that woman.

TWO

"Here, put this on."

Oren handed me a dark green bowling shirt with "Cliff" spelled out in red script stitching over the left breast pocket. He had a custom-made bowling shirt for each of his friends, and there were an assortment of bowling balls lined up in a huge closet at one end of the loft. A highly polished, two-lane bowling alley was situated against the wall farthest from the windows. Since this was the ground floor of the building, there were no neighbors downstairs to complain.

"Got any brews?"

"Check the fridge, Cliff. I just went shopping."

Oren Petrowicz was a man after my own heart. He stocked all my favorites, from Taddy Porter to Red Stripe to Foster's in a can. He had a few assorted single bottles of Hacker-Pschorr Weiss Beer, with the heavy yeast still inside, and a collection of Belgian and Austrian monk brands that cost nearly three dollars a pop. Like me, Oren didn't go in for the current trend of Mexican lagers, beers so light and pale they tasted like watered-down piss. There was one particular brand that had been written up in New York magazine and had subsequently become so popular with the yupwardly mobiles it doubled in price and became scarce. Neither of us liked that one anyway,

31

but on principle wouldn't put it to our lips now if it were the last brand on Earth.

"I got some Cool Ranch taco chips if you want," Oren said as he rubbed a tiny yellow grit bag between his fingers. He looked like a member of the pro bowlers' tour, limbering up, getting psyched, knowing full well that he'd beat the pants off me in our usual semimonthly match.

"Popcorn'll be fine." I said. "I'll make some."

"Already done, sport." He reached back over the scorer's table and pulled up a huge bowl of freshly made Orville Redenbacher. "No salt, just like you like."

"Cheers, *compadre.*" We clinked bottles and quaffed away.

Oren Petrowicz was a fabulously wealthy art director who lived an eccentric life-style. A former college philosophy student, he received his M.A. in art history and was currently pursuing a Ph.D. in Ancient European cultures. He worked whenever he wanted, usually on big-budget science fiction movies that required elaborate special effects, or on tiny, specialized art films that challenged his sense of style and taste. He was a dedicated bachelor, though that was probably because the women he dated usually couldn't keep up with him intellectually. Either that, or they thought he was nuts. He lived in a huge loft in Alphabet Land, that area on the Lower East Side of Manhattan whose avenues are designated by letters. The loft was so sparsely furnished it seemed the perfect setting for an anonymous mob hit. What objects d'art that did occupy the thirty-two-hundred-square-foot floor space consisted of a professional kitchen with an enormous six-burner restaurant stove, a few scattered director's chairs, a wall grouping of gymnasium lockers, two rows of genuine airline seats lined up to face each other around a granite coffee table, a wall-sized television screen straight out of *1984* and an authentic two-lane bowling alley with automatic pin reset and ball return. Despite pretensions to sophistication and the avant-garde, Oren loved the popular American pastime.

He also loved drugs, and spoke as though he'd abused more than his fair share in his twenty-nine years. He was on the short side, a bit out of shape, and wore John Lennon granny glasses.

"Where's everybody else?" I asked as I selected my usual black-and-blue speckled bowling ball from his specially designed closet. Each of Oren's friends had to submit to the ritual of being measured for weight and grip so he'd be sure to have the proper ball always available. Oren also had enough bowling shoes to stock a commercial alley somewhere in Pittsburgh.

"Working on a new film I designed. Something about aliens from space taking up residence in the New York subway because it reminded them of home. I came up with this intricate space design for their living quarters. Picture if you will a giant bee's nest with rooms for drones and the Queen sequestered in various corners and catacombs of the IRT." He went up to the alley, measured his shot and bowled a perfect strike with enormous grace. "The whole thing's supposed to be directly under AT and T headquarters, and part of the alien's plan is to take control of America's communications system. Pretty kicky, if you ask me."

"I didn't know they read Machiavelli out there in bug space."

Oren grinned and quaffed some more beer.

I was still a bit drained from my afternoon experience with the local constabulary. After returning to the museum, I gave a description of what happened to the police. They asked me the usual questions: Did I know the deceased (for the chump had clearly expired)? Had I ever seen him before? Why was I near him when he collapsed? Was anyone with him at the time? I gave them a basic outline of the truth—that he'd caught my eye with his offbeat manner and that he did speak with a woman, but it didn't seem like anything more than idle museum chatter.

The investigating dick was a thin Hispanic with a narrow mustache and the air of a man who took obscene delight in being licensed to carry a pistol. "How can you be sure about what they discussed?" he asked. "Did you hear them?" It wouldn't have been out of character if he'd twirled his mustache.

I told him no, I couldn't be sure, I didn't actually hear anything. I gave him a description of Dirty Blond, but neglected to mention that I was following her, nor did I give a good enough description of what she looked like to help him track her down. After all, I didn't want to get any innocent people involved.

Finally, the ambulance came and carted off the corpse, the crowd dispersed and the dick took my address and phone number. He failed to thank me for my help.

"Come on, Cliff, hop to it. Pins are a-wasting."

I walked up and took aim. My release was a bit off, not surprisingly, and the ball went sailing into the gutter.

"Forget it. Practice frame." Oren was, if anything, cheerful about his beloved game and didn't want anyone feeling undue pressure. "Finish the frame and start from scratch."

Things didn't improve, but we both managed to put away a six-pack each of Red Stripe. It was almost eleven, he'd already beaten me in three straight games, so we settled down to munch more popcorn. I turned on the TV. Oren lit up a joint the size of Jamaica, but I was too anxious to see if the dead man at the museum made the news, so Oren enjoyed it alone. Thirty minutes later, when the news was over, I was sorely disappointed.

"Don't worry. Maybe it was on the other channels."

"Don't humor me."

"I'm not humoring you."

"You won't believe me if you don't see it reported."

"I'm not like that, Cliff. Sure you don't want a hit?"

"I'm wacked enough just breathing in here." I took a hit anyway and finished it. "I just don't understand how a story like that can't be reported."

"Lots of people die in this city." He opened a cigar box to reveal a row of reefer each the size of ripened bananas. He selected one, lit up and leaned back. "Part of the natural order. But are they always on the news? Check the *Times* tomorrow, if it'll make you happy."

"It won't make me happy. I'm not happy that some guy died in my arms. I just want to know that his death didn't go unnoticed. People in this city should know what goes on. Attention must be paid."

"Why?"

"Why? Because."

"No." He got up and began waving the joint like Groucho Marx in *You Bet Your Life*. "Something inside you wants to see death verified by the media. Unless the press sees something it doesn't exist, right? Are you after some sort of public validation of what happened? Is that it?"

"Damn it, Oren, I'm serious. A man died today! At the fuckin' Whitney Museum! It has to be on the news!"

"Easy, Cliff. Chill out. Take a hit."

I got up and began pacing alongside the bowling lanes. "You oughta get some real furniture here," I said, kicking the side of the alley. It didn't move—it was too damn well constructed. "It feels like an airplane hanger."

A look of profound understanding suddenly descended over Oren. "I get it. You're having a breakdown."

"I am not."

"You ever see anyone die before?"

"What's that got to do with anything?"

"Just answer the question."

I paused to consider the point. "Have you?"

"Twice. My grandparents, one after the other. He died working a laundry in Brooklyn, had a heart attack and keeled over right into the blue soap. I was there. Then Grandma couldn't take the stress and popped an aneurism the day of his funeral.

It was sad, and I quit philosophy to study art soon after. Death is a very heavy encounter. It affects people in different ways. I needed to get existential."

The fact that my nerves were frayed and I'd been considering taking the final plunge myself was a clear sign death was affecting me in ways not sanctioned by the Bible. Was suicide really painless? "I'm starting to lose it, Oren," I said. "I can feel it. My life can't go on like this."

"Need another brew?"

I started pacing. "I mean the lack of work is getting to me, the people I know are getting to me. This city is getting to me. I'm too young to have a midlife crisis."

"Bullshit." Oren got up and together we paced beside the alleys. "You got lots of pressure. You got money pressure, women pressure, health pressure, pressure pressure. Too much pressure. Abso-fucking-lutely natural. What you need, young man, is a vacation."

"You're the second person today who said that."

"Wisdom runs in threes."

"I'll remember that."

"So where're you going?"

"I'm not going anywhere."

"Yes you are. Sanity demands it. Besides, I need something delivered to a friend and I don't trust it to any of the commercial services."

"Take it yourself."

"I hate flying."

"Don't lie to me. You're a cheap prick and want to take advantage of my good nature."

Oren walked across the loft to the row of gym lockers, opened one and removed a small brown package the size of a shoe box.

"What's in it?"

"Two detailed cornices. Wood thingies, with carved gargoylelike faces on each. Rare antiques, kind of thirteenth-century Gothic, only made in the late nineteenth century down in New Orleans. They sit on top of a chest of drawers, and have little storage compartments inside. They used to use them in the old days to hide precious gems, money, even documents."

"Expensive?"

"You don't want to know."

I took the box, which was wrapped in brown paper and sealed with packing tape. There was no address on the outside. "Where's it going?"

"A designer I know in Paris has been looking for one for months. It's all part of some elaborate project he's working on, and he *insists* photos or facsimiles won't do. He must have the real thing."

"How'd you get it?"

He paused for dramatic effect. "I move in unusual circles. I have access to unusual things." This was characteristically mystical of Oren, who for the two years I'd known him delighted in appearing the inscrutable mandarin.

"And if I go traveling, you'd be my best friend for eternity if I dropped it off, right?"

He smiled widely. He sat down in one of the airline seats, pushed a button and reclined.

"I'll think about it," I said.

Oren sucked in the last of his joint and let the smoke pour through his nose in a slow, stupefied haze. The old iron water pipes of the building gurgled with someone flushing from upstairs, and then all was suddenly silent.

"Go to Europe and live for the moment," he said imperiously. "Be open to new experiences. Commune with strange women. Sample exotic delights. Enjoy thyself."

"You're just a font of wisdom this evening, aren't you?"

"I *am* less expensive than a shrink."

He had a point, but I didn't want to give him the satisfaction of admitting it. I put the package on the granite coffee table, got up and slid open the heavy iron door. "I'll call you," I said, slamming it as I left.

I got home after twelve. Danette was already asleep. I undressed and slid in beside her, trying not to move too suddenly. I turned over, and in the moonlight cast through the blinds, she looked peaceful. Her world was so simple, so ordered. She seemed to know exactly what she wanted to do, what she wanted from life, where she'd be next week, next month, next year.

Christ, I envied her.

In the morning I got up first and went down to pick up the *Times,* the *News,* the *Post,* even *Newsday.* Back upstairs, Danette was already in the shower, so I sat down to rifle through each paper.

And there it was, buried in the *Times* like an afterthought beneath a story about a Korean market on Park Avenue, with the brief headline "Nazi Hunter Dies at Whitney." The article said that Eli Sternberg, seventy years old, was a Nazi hunter who had retired following confirmation of the death of Joseph Mengele. Born in Strasbourg, France, Sternberg fled to Avignon, where he spent much of the war fighting with the Resistance. He later worked with famed Nazi hunter Simon Wiesenthal and was instrumental in bringing many former Nazi criminals to justice. He'd been living in a suburb of Washington, DC, for the past fifteen years, working as a consultant and private businessman. He left behind no survivors.

Well, well, well. At least I could claim to my small piece of history, having witnessed the death of an important man like Sternberg. I'd never heard of him, but somebody somewhere must have, so there. I put down the paper.

But a man died, how could I be so callous? At least there were no media conspiracies covering up the truth, and I could tell my grandchildren (would they also be Danette's?) about this.

But a man died.

"Have a nice day, yesterday?" asked Danette as she sat down at the kitchen table, freshly scrubbed from her shower.

THREE

I sometimes do my best thinking on a bike. In New York bike riding is a war that's been divided into two camps: those that do it because they have to, and those that do it because they want to.

The Have Tos are the bike messengers, a boon to business but a bane to mankind. They zip in and out of traffic with little regard for human life, and aside from their notorious body odor, bike messengers are famous for the renowned battle cry: "Hey, I lost my brakes!"

The other camp, the Want Tos, are either amateur athletes, commuters too disgusted with public transportation or trendy under-forties who enjoy the raw excitement and reverse snobbery that comes with *feeling* like a bike messenger.

Anyway, I was out being a Want To, riding through the park later that week, noodling around the angst of my life. It was after seven and Park Drive was closed to traffic, leaving it filled with bikers, joggers, runners, strollers. Sometimes you could even mistake the place for a small-town common, sans the usual urban paranoia. Sometimes. But as I pedaled and fought my gear derailleur, which had the annoying habit of constantly slipping into a more resistant mode, I wondered how the hell I'd make it to Christmas.

I was having a breakdown, that much was clear. And I'd just

read that between Thanksgiving and New Year's there were more suicides than at any other time because people became more reflective and depressed, which was not, to say the least, a comforting concept.

But how many people did I personally know who were as stressed out as me? I mean I'm educated. I know that all life is a crapshoot and most poor fools don't know what the hell they want. Oren was an art director who wanted to be a mystic, or at least a pro bowler. Rick wanted to be an artist. Danette wanted to be married, or so I suspected. Risa, an ex-girlfriend I've managed to stay friends with even though we drove each other crazy for six manic months, wanted to be a porn star— although in her occupation as nurse at a local hospital she often had the chance to practice her pet craft on recuperating patients anyway. My agent probably wanted to be something else, too, since his efforts on my behalf clearly indicated he had no interest in being an agent.

Me? What did I want?—aside from making a living as a writer, which was a secret only from everyone in my industry. I wanted adventure. Back in college I used to sit around with friends and discuss the halcyon days of a generation we never lived. Hemingway, Fitzgerald, the expatriates living in Paris. Sure they had it rough, hungry and cold and poor half the time. But somehow it seemed idyllic, creative, wildly spontaneous. That's what I wanted.

You could argue New York of the eighties was the same as Paris of the twenties. You could argue that. I wouldn't. Sure this was—is—the hub of civilization as we know it. The art world is here! The the-a-ter! The clubs! The publishing world! The hot editors! The rising literary lions! The restaurants! The social vortex! The psychosexual dynamics all hard at work! New York literally throbbed with synergism.

But it lacked. It lacked something necessary to make it as romantic, as haunting, as bohemian and intellectually vital as Paris between the wars.

Unless of course it didn't, and I was just missing it.

Despite our college degrees and our food processors, our magazine subscriptions and our bran flakes, suppose we were all just drifting, in our jobs, our romances, our lives, without direction, without focus, awaiting inspiration, hoping Fate and Destiny would call up, invite us for drinks and lead us to genuine fulfillment. Suppose we Boomers In The Eighties constituted our own Lost Generation, eager to jump at the chance for spontaneous, unusual adventure.

That's it! Eureka! Watson come here, I want you! I knew what to do. I'd investigate my contemporaries, seek out new adventures, and I'd write it all up.

And I'd call it *A Lost Generation.*

I rushed home, popped Benny Goodman on the CD, scribbled a few notes, and took a nice hot shower. Benny wailed through "Sing, Sing, Sing" just like he did in the old days, and since I had the stereo cranked I could hear it through the shower. Listening to jazz on compact discs had become a very New York magazine/Upper West Side thing to do, but some fashions were stupid to resist. A good clarinet solo was one of them.

I was renewed, refreshed, alive with ideas. I'd go to Europe as soon as I could book a ticket. I'd visit the haunts of my spiritual ancestors and seek diversions. My life up to now had been terrible, miserable, unsatisfying. Now I'd go out and do things a person always regrets never having done. I'd grab life by the balls and *squeeze!* I'd have no regrets, and maybe, just maybe, I'd get a book out of it.

After my shower I bopped around the room, sliding across the floor to the horn riffs of that great 1938 Goodman concert at Carnegie Hall. I called an agency specializing in last-minute bookings, no cancellations please, use it or lose it, and for $180 I could fly one way to Paris. I checked my bankbook and realized I could barely cover my rent, my utilities and the ticket, with less than a few hundred for necessities like food and shelter. Fuck it. I gave the salesperson my Amex number and was told I could pick up my ticket tomorrow.

Fabulous. I whipped out a legal pad and planned my day. I had to get ready and organized for a badly needed sojourn. I'd visit my agent, go to the bank, make a few calls, clean the heads on the answering machine, pick up the shirts I'd kept at the cleaners far too long, have dinner with Danette, dig up my passport and pack a carryon. No use traveling heavy: a man on a mission needed mobility, flexibility. He had to be unencumbered by possessions.

But by this time Saturday I'd be in a café on Boulevard Saint Germain sipping café au lait and sneering at rude waiters.

I couldn't wait!

I'd book my return passage whenever I felt like coming home.

The doorbell rang. Still wrapped in nothing but a towel, my drying hair making me look like Buckwheat, I peered through the peephole—and there on the other side was Dirty Blond. I nearly dropped my towel.

Oh it was Dirty Blond, all right. I couldn't forget that bone structure. She was dressed in a cream-colored business suit, and had large, round, black-framed glasses. I hadn't noticed those before, but maybe she needed them to read my apartment number.

"Be right there," I said, quickly checking the hall mirror to see how I looked. There was nothing to be done—my hair already dried. I licked my palms and tried wetting it back into place. No luck. "Coming," I shouted. There were no clothes around so I figured, fuck it. If I answer the door wearing nothing but a towel, maybe it'd end up like one of those scenarios usually found in the letters column of Penthouse.

(But there were all those diseases out there, and I was, after all, involved with Danette . . .)

So I grabbed a trench coat from the closet, wrapped it over my shoulders and opened the door.

No one was there.

"Hello?" I looked up and down the hall. Silence. I moved to the stairwell. "Anyone there?" A bare echo was all I heard.

Wuh? I didn't take that long answering the door. Where'd she go? I know I've been foggy, but I couldn't have been having visions of nonexistent women. Could I?

I moved to go in, but couldn't. My door was locked. I'd left my keys inside. Damnitfucktohell. Wearing a towel and a trench coat, I trudged down to the super to borrow his passkey. It was damn polite of him not to raise even an eyebrow at how I looked.

Around one I sat down to read my lunchtime *Daily News.* I have a small table set up by the window in the combination living room/office I use so I get a nice view of the street. It's one of those typical, Upper West Side side streets, tree-lined, with redeveloped brownstones painted in various shades of red or brown. Not all the buildings had been converted into luxury co-ops, and those that weren't reflected the neglect of their landlords. Mine was one that showed it, with a particularly badly cracked stoop that was a hazard to climb. The third step, continually in need of repair, was currently missing altogether, so you had to literally leap to the top. But it was an okay place to live, and the view of the street was better than staring at a brick wall.

The sports pages were dull, and the Jets were in trouble, again, so my mind started to wander. I was staring out at the kids playing on the sidewalk, at the cars driving by, at life in all its various mundane forms fighting entropy, when all of a sudden I saw Dirty Blond come out of the building across the street. I smacked my face a few times to make sure I was awake, but there was no mistaking her. Those cheekbones, that stride. Definitely Dirty Blond. Did she live directly across the street? Or was she visiting someone? Why hadn't I noticed her before? Or was this all coincidence?

Unfortunately, she quickly walked off toward Amsterdam Avenue and I lost sight of her. This was getting sick. Maybe she wasn't ever there at all?

It was four when I went to see my agent. Sam Tardibul was a slick Armenian with an office on the seventh floor of a building off Times Square. At street level was an international newsstand and a movie theater that offered peep shows for a quarter. Sam's office was just four rooms. A reception area with month-old copies of the *Hollywood Reporter* and *Kirkus Reviews,* a few movie posters of huge hits Sam had absolutely nothing to do with but figured if he hung them someone might think he did, and a water cooler with no cups in the dispenser. His receptionist was an old crone with a smoky voice named Gerty. The receptionist, not the voice.

"Hi Gerty, what's up?"

"Sam's on the phone, Mr. Dandridge. Have a seat."

"Thanks."

A few minutes later Wendy Considine came to collect me. Perpetually tan, impeccably dressed, always pleasant and polished. As Sam's general factotum, she served him in various ways, which had clearly caused strain in her relations with Gerty. Gerty and Sam had once been lovers, hard to imagine though it may be, but all that had ceased when Wendy came to town. Now Wendy and Sam were lovers.

The other three rooms of Tardibul and Associates consisted of Wendy's office, a conference room with more movie posters and a huge map of the world and "Sam's Palace." Literally. He called it that. Plush sofas, a telephone extension by every seat, and a wonderful view of Broadway. He had a glass Parsons table for a desk covered with manuscripts and screenplays. Behind him, in nine-inch Styrofoam block letters painted a warm beige tone, was the phrase "Sam's Palace." It was left over from a failed Off-Broadway show he once produced on his own, and he told me he kept it there to remind him never to use his own money again for "anything whatsoever" in show business.

"Cliffie, you're looking great," he said, reaching out to grab my hand with both of his. "Sit, sit, sit."

Wendy asked, "Can I get you something to drink?"

"No, thanks."

"I'll call you if I need you," said Sam. Wendy dutifully left. "So?"

"So I made calls all week. I'm still waiting to hear from Disney, Vestron and a couple of small companies in Canada. You know, a lot of production is moving up there. You should think about going."

"Get me a job and I'm there tomorrow."

"I like your attitude. I always have."

"What about that book project."

"What book project . . . oh, the *book project.*" He casually scrambled through his papers, looking for a piece of yellow Post-it notepad. "You sure you want to do it? I mean absolutely sure?"

"The book was okay, but I think I really have a handle on how to make it work." It was this multiperspective story about a religious revolt in some Communist East European country. Lots of action, intrigue, that sort of thing. The producer who optioned it thought I'd be perfect to adapt it.

Sam glanced at the notepaper and began fingering its edges. "Well, don't get your hopes too high. There's trouble."

"There's always trouble."

"This time the guy who bought the book doesn't have a good

relationship with the studio who once had the book but doesn't have it anymore but is still committed to the story and feels it has to make it."

"Huh?"

"It's not too complicated, Cliffie. It's just that it's complicated."

"How much is it complicated?"

"For you to be attached, you'll get a bit over scale."

"Scale? Fuck them, scale. I've been working a decade in this business. I've got more credits than both the producer and the novelist put together. What are they getting?"

"It's a package from one of the bigger agencies. I'm having a tough time fighting to get you in on it as it is. If you want to do it, leave it to me."

"Sam, I have always trusted you."

"I've never steered you wrong."

"But I haven't had a gig in seven months."

"No one's working these days."

"I don't care about no one. There's more production going on in New York since the golden age of television and you're telling me no one's working. Who's writing that stuff? Cab drivers and the homeless? Can't you push a little?"

"I'm pushing on this book deal. And I'm still waiting on Disney and—"

"Please don't give me the runaround. It's me, Sam. We're friends. We've been together ten years. Since I was starting and you set out on your own."

The door opened and Wendy came in with a tray of Perrier. "Just in case," she said, demurely slipping out again.

"Cliffie, I'm doing my best. You're one of my favorite clients. It gives me pleasure to see you work. Just be patient. We're close. You'll either be doing this book thing or I'll have you on a series in six months. I promise."

"Look, I'm thinking of taking a vacation."

"Terrific."

"If I go away, I'll call you every few days to see if anything's happened."

"Fantastic. You need a rest. We all could."

"If anything comes up, I can be back in a day at the most, so don't worry. Just get me work."

"Where are you going?"

"I was thinking of starting in Paris, then do some wandering around Europe, see the sights, meet the people. I haven't been there in years. I may even start writing a novel."

"Now that's what I like to hear. You give me a great story, we'll sell it to the movies, get you writing and co-producing credits, really set you up big."

I got up from the plush sofa, my back hurting from trying to sit straight against the puffy pillows, and shook hands with a beaming Sam.

"By the way," he said, "how's that girl friend, Josette or something?"

"Danette's fine." I saw he was waiting for something else. "But I'm going to Paris by myself."

Sam nodded sagely, then a leering smile spread across his lips. "Does she know about this?"

She will tonight, I thought, closing the door as I left. I just hope she doesn't kill me.

"You bastard, you goddamned sonofabitch bastard. Take me with you."

I would have expected this from Danette, but it was Rick expressing his opinion.

"That's not the point of this exercise," I said.

"Exercise? You on some fucking military maneuver? You're going to Europe to get laid. As your attorney I advise you to take me with you."

"I am not going to get laid."

"You're a lousy liar, Cliff."

"I am going to relax, get in touch with my creative soul, maybe do some research for a new novel."

"Research this, pal. How's Danette feel?"

"I'm telling her tonight. I'm taking her up to this American Indian restaurant I heard of."

"So you can buffalo her over dinner?" Over the phone I could hear Rick break into hysterics. He thought he was funny and enjoyed making himself laugh.

"Wasn't it you who said I needed to get away?"

"I didn't mean literally," he said. "I meant you had to find your own mental space. Besides, did some rich aunt suddenly croak and leave you air fare?"

"Actually, I punched out all I had at Citibank. If that god-damned residual check would show up, I'd be a bit more relaxed."

"Who do I call, Cliff? I'll raise a little hell on your behalf. I'll send 'em a letter on legal stationery. We got forty-eight partners listed in raised black ink. Scares the bejeesus out of people. Makes 'em settle out of court every time."

"Thanks for the concern. But I'll send you a postcard."

"I really wish I could get away, but the people fighting the pharmaceutical company keep complaining their babies are dropping like flies around horseshit, so we gotta settle fast."

"Maybe next trip," I said. What else could I say?

"Wait a second. When are you going? You forget Sunday? We got tickets to the Jets-Dolphins."

"I had to take a last-minute cancellation. I'm outta here tomorrow, Rick."

"But the Jets-Dolphins—?"

"My life is in a state of flux, so even that hallowed rivalry has to be forfeited. Besides, I can always check the score in the *Tribune.*"

Rick paused for dramatic effect. "You really must be down." I could almost picture his brain spinning. "All right, I suppose I can get someone else to go. But you be careful. And if you meet anyone in Amsterdam with a sister, I'm on the next flight east."

"I'm not going to Amsterdam."

"Yeah, but if you do . . ."

I still had time till Danette, so I took another quick spin around the park, picked up my dry cleaning—the woman behind the counter gave me a dirty look because the due ticket said "Rush" and I'd left it for three weeks—and checked my mailbox. Viola! My residual check had arrived! Thank you Jesus! Not counting various and sundry deductions for the president (read Federal Government), the governor (state) and the mayor (city), I'd cleared almost two thousand, four hundred and twenty-eight dollars and seventy-one cents. No king's ransom, but if judiciously apportioned was more than enough to get me through a few weeks of bohemian living.

Coleman Hawkins played as I dressed for dinner. It was going to be a special night—I had to bullshit my way out of a major scene—so I thought, screw it, I'd go preppy. I dug a navy blazer from the back of my closet, a pair of beige slacks, oxblood loafers, a buttoned-down blue shirt, a yellow tie. I felt like an insurance salesman.

The lights were on in all the apartments across the street, except one on the third floor, exactly opposite mine. I stood staring at the dark window, tying my tie in my own reflection, wondering who lived there, wondering if it were a family of Merrill-Lynchers or Colombian drug dealers, when the lights clicked on. The shades were open wide and a tall figure moved to the windows.

Dirty Blond.

Not now. I didn't need this. I was leaving in thirty-six hours. But what's a fellow to do when he's suddenly confronted with the reality of his mystery woman? I mean, did she know the man she talked to in the museum was dead, had died soon after she spoke to him? Did she care? Did she realize she was so beautiful, the object of a serious masturbatory fantasy?

Whoa! Stop right there! You're a simple guy about to go in search of Hemingway's ghosts. You have a beautiful girl friend who's going to put your nuts in a Cuisinart because you're not taking her along. Your professional life is at a standstill. You have absolutely no business staring at beautiful women in open windows, hoping to engage in an inviting wave or suggestive gesture that will lead to other opportunities. . . .

Like hell I don't.

I quickly went downstairs and across the street to Dirty Blond's building. How to figure out which apartment was hers? I checked the buzzers. There were twenty-six apartments in the building. By computing the number of floors and the placement of her window, maybe I could . . . bullshit. This is stupid. I look like a prowler.

"Hello," said an old lady's voice.

I turned to see a sweet old lady I'd occasionally held the door for at Gristede's. She was turning her key in the locked entrance door.

"Hi," I said. She was carrying groceries. The door opened, I reached over to hold it for her, enabling her to pass.

"Thank you," she nodded with a smile.

"Need help carrying those?"

"Not at all. Little old ladies need to stay in shape, you know."

"Good for you," I said, casually following her inside. She turned and walked down the corridor.

Now what? From where I stood I couldn't see the buzzers or the mailboxes anymore, and I couldn't hold the door open and stretch out far enough to see them without getting locked out again. All right, Sherlock, no turning back now. Let's proceed with the investigation.

I walked to the third floor, left the stairwell and looked down the corridor. Five doors. Which way was I facing? North?

South? Let's see . . . there were no lights coming from beneath the two immediately behind me, and since I knew all the lights were already on in front . . . Got it.

I looked at the nameplate on apartment 3D. Mr. and Mrs. Joel Ginsburg. Not here. The name was scratched out on 3E, and 3C had no nameplate at all. All right, wiseguy, let's do it.

I knocked a few times on No Nameplate. There were footsteps. I knocked again. I felt a presence behind the door. The peephole cleared and an eye pressed to look through. The peephole quickly shut.

"Hello?" I was trying to sound as cheerful and unthreatening as possible. "Hello?"

"What do you want?" she was distinctly afraid.

"Ah, I'm your neighbor"—a lie, why lie?—"well, not exactly your neighbor, I live across the—ah, well, what I wanted to say was . . ."

"Go away, please."

"Um, I don't mean to frighten you."

"I will call the police. I promise."

"You don't mean it. I just wanted to talk, to tell you that guy you spoke with at the museum yesterday, well . . . I—do we have to shout through the door?"

I heard the peephole open and close again. I guess she decided I looked harmless enough, so she began unlatching various locks. Finally she opened the door, keeping her body behind it in case she wanted to slam it on my foot. I smiled. She looked frightened as hell.

"Hi, Cliff Dandridge." I reached out my hand like the insurance salesman I looked like. She ignored it. "I live across the street. I noticed you the other day at the Whitney, I think you remember. You smiled at me?" I waited for a response. She gave none. "Right. Well, anyway, I noticed you were talking to some man at the museum, you seemed to know him. Did you know him?"

"I knew him."

"Did you know he died soon after you walked away?"

"Why are you telling me this?"

"Why? Because, well . . . Did you know?"

A beat while she considered her response. "I read it in the newspaper."

"I see."

She squinted her already-narrow eyes. "If this is some kind of warning, you do not have to worry about me."

Huh?

"We are not going to bother you," she said. "You did what you had to. We understand. Just leave me alone."

"Wait a second. What are you talking about?"

"Please, Mr. . . . Dandridge." She didn't seem to believe this name. "Sternberg had many enemies. If not you, it would have been someone else."

"What is it you're trying to tell me?" I asked.

"I do not want any trouble, from you or anyone."

"Look, I don't think you understand. I just thought you should know your friend died. I meant nothing—"

"He was not my friend."

"But you knew him?"

"I knew him." She paused, looking me over. "What did you say your name was?"

That's better, I thought. "Cliff Dandridge. I live—"

"I think you better come inside."

She opened the door and ushered me in. The room was expensively appointed, with a complicated, wraparound sofa built into the floor. There were nice antiques set against ultra-modern tables and chairs. The wood floor was so highly polished it looked like glass.

"Sit down."

"Thanks." I did.

"Look Mr. *Dandridge*—"

"It *is* my real name."

"For your sake I hope so."

"And what's your name?"

"My name . . . is unimportant."

"I see."

"No, I am beginning to realize you do not."

"Run that again, please."

"Let me ask you something directly, Mr. Dandridge."

I detected a slight accent, I couldn't quite place it. Middle European somewhere. "Shoot," I said.

"Why did you kill Eli Sternberg?"

I sat there, my jaw dropped, I thought, *This dame is nuts.* "Did I just enter the Twilight Zone?"

"I am being direct with you, Mr. Dandridge. I hope you will be the same with me."

"You ask me why I killed someone and call that direct? Well, I guess that is kind of dir—"

"Why did you kill him? And why did you come here to tell me?"

"Look. I didn't kill anyone. I take unusual delight in squashing cockroaches, but death of my fellow man is not something I'm easily comfortable with. I'm beginning to think I made a mistake coming here, so if you'll excuse me . . ."

"*Why* did you come here?"

I was momentarily stumped, and couldn't really remember. Then I collected my wits. "Well, to be frank, Miss Unimportant, I thought I'd do a kindly, neighborly gesture. We New Yorkers are often accused of being heartless, soulless and selfish, and I thought since you seemed to know the guy in the museum yesterday, maybe you should be told he died soon after you left. Besides, when I went out to try to talk to you, you had run off in a cab. You piqued my curiosity. We were flirting, if memory serves. But maybe I'm getting too old, too out of practice, or just plain too hopeful. In any event, excuse this outburst, but I see I've made a mistake. If you'll excuse me."

I stood and walked toward the door. Dirty Blond watched as I opened it. I hesitated, hoping maybe she'd say something to make this end up less odd.

"I think your life is very much in danger, Mr. Dandridge," she said finally.

It wasn't what I was hoping to hear.

FOUR

"Won't you sit down again?"

"Thank you, no. I'm not sure I want to stay and hear how my life is in danger."

A friendly, concerned smile crossed her face. "I am sorry for the misunderstanding. But I was not sure how much you were involved. For a moment I thought you had come to kill me. But now I realize you know absolutely nothing."

I knew several unique sexual techniques, but didn't think that's what she meant. I *was* starting to feel like I'd stepped into a movie without seeing the first twenty minutes. I said, "I realize it's a paranoid city, but do I look like a mad killer?"

"To tell you the truth, no. But that is exactly the type that is most dangerous."

"You asked me to sit, so I'm sitting. When are you going to stop speaking in riddles and tell me why you think my life is in danger?"

"The man at the museum, Eli Sternberg, had many friends and many enemies. I was neither, merely a go-between. I was supposed to meet him and get something from him. I did not know it if was an envelope, a book, a password. But at the last moment he seemed to panic. He became greedy and said that since his life was in danger, he'd require more money from my people, as well as safe passage out of the country."

56

Good God. I've landed in the middle of a spy novel.

"Did he give you what you wanted?"

"No. When he died, I thought you had killed him and taken it with you."

"But I didn't."

"I realize that now. But tell me, you were with him at the end?"

"So to speak. I held him in my arms and called for help."

"Did he tell you anything? Give you anything?"

"Nothing except bad dreams about the Grim Reaper."

"I am sure he must have said something."

"Look, all the guy did was gasp and die. I could make something up, but I don't think that'd help."

She pondered this. She went over to the window and looked across the street. "How long have you been living here?" she asked.

"About eight years. I always lived in New York, but I used to have a small studio apartment in the Village. Gave that up when I moved uptown, though I could shoot myself for not hanging on to the lease. I could have sublet for a fortune."

"There's been a terrible mistake, Mr. Dandridge. You must leave New York at once."

"You keep saying that."

"I am serious. You gave a statement to the police, so now everyone has your address."

"Everyone?"

"There is not enough time to explain. You will not have to be gone long. Just until I can straighten things out. I have no intention of involving an innocent bystander."

"Fine. I appreciate that. So if you'll excuse me . . ."

She turned around and sat down beside me. She smelled of fine soap and fresh linen. Her skin was flawless, her eyes deep and intelligent. She looked like someone who had all the answers.

"Mr. Dandridge. Eli Sternberg had some very serious information to pass along to my people, but he was a very twisted man. He could have delivered the message in code. It could have been the number of a postal box, an address, a phone number, a cleaning ticket. It could have been on a matchbook for all we know. But it was valuable information we'd been working months to secure. There were many other people who wanted to see we did not get that information. They will now think you have it."

"But as I said, I don't."

"I know that. But they do not. Word will spread, and you will be caught and tortured until they realize you know nothing. Then, because they are not nice at all, you will have to be destroyed."

"Like a wounded horse?"

"Well put."

"These things come to me."

"So please, take my advice and go away. I will do my best to let it circulate that you are innocent, but unfortunately that may only cast more suspicion on you and jeopardize me as well. But we are not barbarians."

"Mind telling me who's *we*? So I don't have to go out and buy a scorecard?"

"I am with the Organization, that is all I can say. The less you know, the better."

"So they can't torture it out of me, you mean."

"You can catch on quickly."

"I'm a writer, It's my job."

"Then you will understand that no plot is too implausible if it is based on truth. And this is the absolute truth. You must believe me."

"A pretty nifty coincidence, then, your living across the street from me."

She looked back out the window, across the street, studying the front of my building. "Nothing is ever a coincidence, Mr. Dandridge."

I stood up. I was sorry to move away from her delicious smells, but this was getting to be a bit much.

"I wish there was a way to make you believe me," she said.

"Me, too." I opened the door. "I'm late for a buffalo steak, so *auf wiedersehen.* Sorry I disturbed you." I walked out and closed the door behind me.

Danette had used her copy of my house key and was sitting on my sofa. "Where were you?" she asked, idly fingering a lose thread on the couch.

"Across the street visiting a neighbor."

"A neighbor?"

"Ah huh."

She glanced out the window, avoiding my shit-eating grin. Had she seen me coming from Dirty Blond's building? "I assume we don't need reservations at this place," she said with a clear trace of sarcasm. I glanced at the clock and noticed I was late.

"If we do we'll just go elsewhere. Columbus Avenue is a veritable cornucopia of dining establishments. We'll grab whatever we want."

From the look on her face it was clear that a whole bunch of thoughts were trying to get out, but all she finally said was, "The phone rang twice, but whoever it was kept hanging up before waiting for the beep."

"If it was important, they'll call back. Answering machines intimidate some people. Come on," I leaned over and kissed her full on the mouth. She tasted wet and warm and minty-fresh. "Let's saddle up and move out. I'm hungry."

"Then let's forget dinner," she said, suddenly pushing me back onto the floor, slipping her hand down my stomach and inside my pants.

"Come on, Dani," I said. "What's the rush?" I couldn't help but kiss her cheeks, her lips, her eyes. Her long red hair came over her head and poured onto me like a million tiny fingers, tickling my face as she lowered her mouth to mine.

We were fumbling to remove our clothes when she said, "I don't want to lose you."

"I'm there all right. Keep moving your hand south."

"I mean it. I'm serious. I feel something's wrong."

"Give it time, it's called foreplay."

"Heathcliff."

Did this lassie have antennae? I stopped undressing her and sat up. "Look Dani, you're not going to lose me. Come on. Where'd this mood come from?"

"I feel as though we're drifting. I don't know, it's just—I can tell something's the matter."

"We're not drifting. It's me. It's my head. I'm a little fucked these days. I've got a lot on my brain."

"Maybe what you need is a change of scenery?"

"So wisdom *does* come in threes."

"What?"

"Something Oren said. You're the the third person this week to tell me to take a trip. Actually the fourth." I recalled Dirty Blond's advice to disappear immediately. "But the last person didn't count."

"Who was that?"

"My neighbor."

"The one you just came from?" she said with a dubious grin.

I looked out across the street. There was no light on in Dirty Blond's apartment. "Exactly." Danette dove on top of me, and we continued to strip.

Later at the restaurant: "I never told you this before. No reason to. But it suddenly popped into my head. It's not the kind of thing one talks about."

"*One* talks about?" Danette was dipping a piece of lamb into a brown sauce, then resting it on a tiny hibachi burner. This was some kind of native American Pu-Pu platter, but the assorted meats, fish and vegetables all tasted pretty ordinary. "Since when did you start using the term *one?* You sound so stiff."

"Sorry. Anyway, about two summers ago I went back to visit my ol' alma mater. I was walking around the campus, looking at all the old and new buildings, remembering my past glories, you know how people do." Reminiscing wasn't my favorite pastime but it seemed an appropriate way to lead up to other topics. "Sure I fucked up in school, but I did some damn good there, too. I literally lived the shit out of that place. Somebody once told me that college would be the best four years of my life. I didn't believe it then, but looking back, I see their point."

"I enjoyed college, too, Cliff. But life has gotten much more interesting since."

"In some ways. But remember all the dreams you had in college? Everything you wanted out of life? Your goals, your hopes, your ideals? The stuff inside your head that made you anxious to get on with living your life? And there I was, nine years later, walking around the exact same campus with a Walkman on my head listening to some movie soundtrack with all sorts of emotional strings and drums and choral voices, when it occurred to me that I should've been further along in my life. Nine, ten years after college and *this* is where I am? So I sat down on the steps of the campus chapel and looked out across the Common, and you know what I did? I cried like a goddamned baby."

"Poor Heathcliff. You felt sorry for yourself."

"Ab-so-fucking-lutely I felt sorry for myself. And I hate feeling sorry for myself."

"What made you think of that tonight?"

"It's starting again, Danette. The frustration's setting in. I feel it coming on like some twelfth-century plague. But this time I'm not going to let it get me. This time I'm going to take action. This time I'm going to take life by the balls and squeeze."

"If that's what you're into."

"Very funny."

"I'm serious. Take me seriously for a minute, Heathcliff." There was something in her voice, something I hadn't heard before. "Just because I work with bankers and brokers doesn't mean I can't be taken seriously."

"I'm sorry. Mea culpa."

"Forgiven. But somehow I feel this is all leading up to something."

"Astute little vixen, aren't you?"

She smiled. The waitress came, removed the hibachi and brought around our meals. Danette had a dish of rabbit stew, I had buffalo steak. The stew tasted like chicken, "Bugs Chicken" Danette called it. It was served with fresh rolls, assorted vegetables and special sauces. The buffalo tasted like a super-lean piece of sirloin. I ordered it medium, but it was overdone and tasted dry. It came with interesting vegetables, too. Regardless, it occurred to me that native Americans living on remote poverty-stricken reservations probably never ate like this in their lives.

A breeze blew across the back of my neck, and I turned to see the front door closing as two men in dark suits entered. They took up seats at the bar, the only patrons not choosing a table, and ordered something to drink. The rest of the room was filled with typical Yupper West Siders, with a smattering of genuine-looking American Indians. You live in New York and you think there are all kinds of foreigners around, but somehow you don't expect to see American Indians. Yet there they were, a whole bunch of them, families and dating young couples.

It was culturally interesting, if you're into those things.

It also made the two gentlemen in suits at the bar very conspicuous.

That, and the fact that they were staring at me, caused hackles to rise on my neck. Genuine hackles, too. Not the cheap kind.

"What's the matter, Cliff? Don't you like it?"

"It's fine."

"Finish your story, then. You were about to tell me what was on your mind."

I looked at Danette and was about to tell her how I planned on writing a book and was going to do some traveling to research it, when an elderly man sitting directly behind her turned toward me. I smiled, but he just stared. *Stared like he hated me.* Why? How the hell should I know. I just felt it. I swung around to look back at the men at the bar, and they, too, were looking at me. Was Dirty Blond right? Was my life suddenly in danger? In an American Indian restaurant on Columbus Avenue?

"Let's finish, Dani. I gotta get going."

"What are you talking about? We just got here. Cliff, what's the matter? This isn't like you."

Did you ever see *The President's Analyst?* There's this scene in a restaurant where psychiatrist James Coburn, privy to presidential secrets, gets paranoid that the whole world is after him. He turns around and sees that everyone in the restaurant is wearing dark sunglasses and trench coats and staring maliciously at him. That's how I felt just then.

"We gotta leave, Danette. There are people here, who—I mean, let's just eat fast."

"What people?"

"Humor me."

"Cliff, you're frightening me. Are you all right?"

"No, actually, I'm not."

She put her napkin down and assumed her Serious Face. "I know what it is. You're feeling trapped. All men in new relationships feel trapped, especially when they see their girl friends too regularly. I was afraid this would happen. That's why I tried spacing out our times together."

Huh?

"Look Cliff—stop staring at me with your mouth open like that—I value our relationship too much to want to see it spoiled. You guys are like little boys sometimes, you want things but then when you get them you get tired of them. Toys, stereo equipment, even women. Either you get tired of them, or you get afraid we're taking over. Is that what happened with Risa? Well, I'm not taking over, Cliff. I like you too much. I think we can have a solid future, but not if you're going to get all jerky on me. Too many guys have done that in the past. 'Uh-oh, 'scuse me, Dani, but, well, like, man, we're getting too close too fast, you know, and like, well, I don't think we oughta rush things. We oughta just have some fun, don'tcha think?' Well, I don't think, Cliff. So, if you're trying to tell me it's time we slowed things down because you're afraid we're getting too emotionally attached, say it, be honest, but don't fuck around and tell me you're going to take a vacation without me because you want to research a novel. I won't swallow that bullshit, no matter how much sugar you put on it."

I'd never heard Danette speak like that.

I liked it, but I was speechless.

She'd hit on a few indisputable truths, so now I couldn't tell her the truth as I saw it even if I wanted to. She wouldn't believe me.

Therefore: "Danette, my life is in danger and I have to leave the country" is what I said.

She was sipping water when I said this. She spit most of it out when I finished.

"You're crazy, Heathcliff Dandridge."

"You're the only one who knows," I said.

"I saw this coming. Well look. We're two adults and—"

But there suddenly came a loud crashing noise outside the restaurant. My nerves were so jumpy I ran to see what happened. Three cars had piled up like used tissues right in front. At the bar the two men in suits cursed and raced out to look at another parked car that had taken a terrible beating. It must have been theirs because they went rifling through the glove compartment like they owned it. The cops arrived to sort things out, but the two men kept turning to look from the cops to the restaurant and, I felt, to see if I was still there.

"Come on, let's go to your place while there's still time." I grabbed Danette and flipped some bills on the table. Outside, I hailed a cab, but not before I noticed that the smashed car belonging to the two suits had U.S. Government license plates.

We made a kind of frantic love back at Danette's downtown apartment. There was a unique urgency in the way she clawed my back, and my thrusts into her were of the overtly manic variety. We looked more like animals than humans, but then again, can there really ever be any distinction made when two creatures are engaged in The Act?

Afterward, as we sipped wine coolers in bed, we talked. I told her about what had happened at the Whitney, at Dirty Blond's, and though she didn't believe me, she seemed willing to give me the benefit of the doubt. She did think it was the most creative way she'd heard of putting a relationship on hold. I assured her that was not my intent, though I could see how she would feel that it was.

In any event, she agreed not to be too pissed off if I went off in search of adventure in Europe, as long as I wrote regularly, called semiregularly, and came back eager to discuss living together. *Seriously* living together. Not a bad deal, I thought.

"Think of my feelings once in a while," she said.

In the morning, I let myself out before Danette woke up. I took the subway to Seventy-ninth Street, but as I approached my corner I noticed a lot of commotion. I turned and saw a crowd watching firemen finish putting out a blaze in a brownstone.

Holy Shit, my Building! Jesus Fuck! I wasn't home and my house burned down!

But I was wrong. It was the building across the street. Thank God—someone else. The whole structure seemed to be a charred, black mess.

I went to the police barricade and was stopped by a short female cop. I told her I lived down the block and she let me pass. In front of the burnt building I asked a fireman what happened. He said the fire started in an apartment on the third floor. He pointed up to a window and I realized the fire had started in Dirty Blond's apartment.

"What about that lady who lived there?"

"What lady?"

"In 3C. You said that's where the fire started. Was anyone inside at the time?"

"That's where the fire started, Ace, but no lady lived there. Thank God, too. Place must've been an inferno."

"I don't understand. I thought someone lived there."

"Nope, nada. Totally empty." He checked some notes. "According to the landlord, no one's lived in that apartment for a year."

FIVE

"I don't understand."

"What's to understand? Some vandals probably got in and torched the place."

"Any furniture left, any—"

"C'mon. I just said no one's lived there for months. The apartment's totally empty. Landlord musta been warehousing 'case he went co-op. Now the people who live downstairs"—the fireman raised his eyebrows—"well, I just hope they got insurance."

I ran over for a closer look. I couldn't believe it. But the proof was staring at me like Cyclops. Looking up from the street through the gaping hole in the wall it was clear there wasn't even so much as a charred chair still in there. I could probably grill the neighbors, but what good would that do?

I went to my apartment and the phone rang as I entered. "Hey man," it was Oren, "Rick told me you decided to take our advice and do some traveling. Mind dropping off that package?"

"Sure, Oren. I'm a bit swamped. I got a lot to get ready, and there was a fire across the street."

"A fire? Pretty nasty."

"Get it to me by four, otherwise you're out of luck."

"I'll be there by three."

I hung up and the phone rang again. "I'm glad you spent the night," said Danette with a faint purr.

"Why?" I asked without saying hello.

"Because while you're away I'll have your smell right here on my sheets." I could picture her lying in bed just then, stroking the pillow, wearing nothing but a smile.

"I may be gone a while. You'll have to wash them sooner or later."

Silence. Then: "You be careful, Heathcliff. Call me if I can help."

I packed my carryon with as many clothes as would fit. In the outer pouch I stuffed a book of bound blank pages I once got as a gift and vowed to use as a travel journal. In my camera bag—bought at Banana Republic at great expense; it looked great and made me feel like Robert Capa on his way to cover the Spanish Civil War—I checked my assorted lenses, put in some film, found room for a Berlitz European Phrase book, my passport, my traveler's checks and some pens. I grabbed a quick lunch at the corner Greek diner, phoned the airline to confirm my departure and tried relaxing with the sports pages of the *News*.

But again my mind started drifting. What happened to Dirty Blond? How does a person disappear like that? Wasn't I in her apartment only yesterday? Didn't she smell of fresh linen and soap? Didn't she have all that neat furniture?

There was a bit more mystery going on here than I wanted.

Sure, I'm normal like everybody else and have fantasized about getting caught in danger and intrigue, living out James Bond adventures.

But this was a bit too intriguing for my tastes. A man dies in my arms at the Whitney. A beautiful woman thinks I killed him, then tells me since I didn't kill him my life is now in danger. She tells me people think I was given valuable secret information by the deceased, but she doesn't tell me what kind of information, and I have no idea what she's talking about, let alone who she is, who she works for, or why she happens to live across the street from me, which she doesn't, it turns out, when the place is torched by vandals and the firemen tell me the place has been empty for a year. Then two U.S. Government agents follow me to a restaurant, though they may only have been federal employees dining wherever they chose. Given my current mental state, I didn't believe that for a second. Coincidence breeds paranoia breeds fear. You heard it here first.

Carve it in stone.

Ignoring all this would have been the soundest course of action. There was no way I could find Dirty Blond. She was probably already airborne, winging her way to someplace like Tegucigalpa or Damascus. Or she was dead, killed in the fire. The people she worked for could have hushed up her presence in the building, could have carted off her furniture in the dead of night, could have removed any corpses before the fire department got there. Any number of simple explanations could be made to account for her sudden and mysterious disappearance. . . .

So why didn't I know what to believe?

Sure, fine, okay . . . grab hold of yourself. You're taking a trip to Europe until your agent comes through with a job, an assignment, a badly needed gig. You're going to explore your emotional space doing research on a novel about today's generation of Lost Americans, creative souls in search of motivating spirits, in search of neurotic identity. You're going to indulge in hedonistic delights. You're not going to get involved with strange killers, arsonists, Nazi hunters, government agents and dirty blonds.

If I believed that for a second, I'd have been a much happier person.

Oren arrived right on time, dropped off his package and gave me the Parisian address of a friend who lived in the Ninth *arrondissement,* near the Gare du Nord. He promised that the guy would probably take me to dinner.

"Probably or definitely?"

"You cheap all of a sudden?"

"All of a sudden? I'm an unemployed hack scenarist. I eagerly welcome all free comestibles."

"Look, it's a good neighborhood for restaurants. After you get past the tourist traps, it has kind of a Columbus Avenue charm."

I looked at him in horror.

"Oh, well, then get him to take you to this bistro he loves in the Marais district."

"The what?"

"The old Jewish quarter. It's wonderfully atmospheric. Victor Hugo lived there."

Ah. We're back to *Les Miserables.*

"Anyway," he said, "have a nice time. I hope you find what you're looking for."

The traffic to Kennedy was for shit. My cab driver was a Russian émigré who said he loved America but felt Russia wasn't so bad if you knew the right people. He had a degree in engineering from Kiev University, which meant squat in the States, so he was forced to drive a cab and save his greenbacks until he had enough to go back to school and get another degree.

"America," he said as I got out at the airport, "what a country." I guess he heard the expression on TV.

One thing I love about airports is their sense of spontaneity. Anything can happen at airports. You can go anywhere, meet anyone. Comedian George Carlin once said airports were a great place to play spy. You knew there were spies at the airport. "Your job," he said, lowering his voice, *"find them!"*

Yet given the recent events in my life, I preferred that spies kept their distance from me at all costs, thank you very much.

I checked in, then wandered to the combination newsstand/ bookstore/trinket shop. Did I feel any compelling need to buy a last minute "I Love New York" coffee mug? A copper-painted plastic model of the Statue of Liberty? How about a clear plastic paperweight filled with water and "snow" depicting the New York skyline for my loved ones overseas? Sure, why not. I bought that and a copy of a Graham Greene novel I'd wanted to re-read. It was about a guy who'd had enough of the regular world and sought refuge with a tribe of lepers. I could have bought one of the tomes written by the latest hip, downtown literary *wunderkind,* but having already read most of that psuedo-literate tripe, hyped to an unsuspecting public, I wasn't in the mood. Besides, who needed to wade through yet another installment in a genre that was beginning to sound like *Bright Slaves From Rockaway With Zero Attraction?*

I looked out into the corridor of the airport and nearly swallowed my tongue. The two government goons from the American Indian restaurant were quickly approaching the international departure lounge. Their goose step clicked along the cement loudly enough to be heard in Munich. I paid for my book and sprinted in the other direction.

Jesus Fuck. What to do? I had less than fifteen minutes until boarding. I could sneak into the men's room and wait till the last minute, but I had to first see where the Two Goons were if I was going to map out a strategy.

I bought a Jets cap at the souvenir stand, slipped on my shades and walked to the metal detectors. No sign of the goons. I placed my carryon and camera bag on the conveyor belt and walked through the wooden archway.

BIIIIINNNNGGGG!

"Would you mind stepping over here and emptying your pockets?" The short black guard looked bored, and clearly didn't want to be bothered with this diversion. I emptied my pockets and handed a metal money clip to him. I walked through again, this time no beep. Obviously I wasn't a renegade

Iranian or Sikh extremist, so I was allowed to proceed. Had the goons heard me bing?

Apparently not, because I still didn't see them. I quickly moved toward my gate. They were already letting people board, but my row hadn't been called.

I paced around nervously. I gazed out the window toward the runway, trying to focus on the figures in the departure area reflected in the glass. I noticed some sudden movement, but nothing. I turned to board the plane, and saw the Two Goons across the way, casually searching the faces of people in lounges on their way to Vienna and Rome.

I became the obnoxious American tourist, pushing my way past a few old people casually strolling down the ramp toward the plane. I grinned at the stewardess by the door, but she looked at me, decided "geek," and silently took my boarding pass without so much as a twitch.

Luckily my seat was on the aisle, so the goons wouldn't see me through the window. Besides, while I love flying, I hate window seats. I'd rather have some fat slob climb over me than have to climb over them. This way I could move freely, get a better view of the movie, and talk to the stewardesses.

I reached over to glance at the exit diagram, when a female voice interrupted my concentration.

"I believe I am sitting with you."

I turned to see Dirty Blond staring me in the face.

The exits were closed and the stewardesses positioned themselves for takeoff. I blinked, but Dirty Blond was still there.

"Of all the lousy airplanes in the world," I said in my worst Bogart, "you had to pick this one."

"A clever disguise, Mr. Dandridge," she said indicating my Jets hat. "You are the only one with a bright green baseball cap in the entire airport. Fortunately, they"—she nodded toward the departure lounge—"were not expecting Paris." Her legs pressed against mine as she slid into her seat. She still smelled of linen and soap.

"I assume this isn't a coincidence?"

"Do not say another word until we are airborne," she said as she buckled her seat belt in one motion.

The plane taxied away, and I could see the two goons angrily staring out the departure-lounge windows.

PART TWO
Paranoia on $30 a Day

SIX

I gazed at my complimentary copy of the in-flight magazine with disinterest as we waited for takeoff. It occurred to me that the logjam on the runway was a sight purposely obscured from travelers to keep them artificially calm. Unless you work for an airline or drive near a runway during peak departure time, you never see the three dozen jumbo jets lined up like elephants at the circus. All that volatile fuel and red-hot steel waiting impatiently, one in back of the other, for a chance to zoom off at top speed on a simple cue from a strike-breaking air traffic controller? *Be real.* It's obvious the airlines care not a whit for passenger comfort or realistic scheduling, so even if you're seated and buckled, forty minutes could pass before your plane is cleared to fly.

This non-motion was killing me.

"I see you have taken my advice to leave New York," said Dirty Blond.

"I only need a couple thousand frequent-flyer miles for a trip to Honolulu. Figured I'd start now."

"Do you always use sarcasm when you're afraid?"

"It is a skill I developed over the years, yes."

A pause. "There is nothing to be afraid of."

I paused right back. "Then I suppose those goons at the

airport were just looking to give me first prize in the Publisher's Clearinghouse Sweepstakes?"

"No," she said, turning away to suppress a smile.

I was on a roll. "And your being next to me right now is nothing but a coincidence?"

She looked at me with appropriate inscrutability.

"Oh, I remember," I said. "Nothing is a coincidence."

The steward, a well-scrubbed, neatly groomed, blasé young buck, was working the aisle with a huge plastic bag. "Would you like a headset for the movie?"

"No thanks."

"What is it?" asked Dirty Blond.

"Madonna and Griffin Dunne in *Who's That Girl?*"

"Thank you, no."

The steward moved along.

The flight crew demonstrated the use of oxygen masks and life preservers. Last time I flew this presentation was made on the video screen with lifeless performers. I liked the live version better, though no one was paying attention.

I turned to Dirty Blond. "Isn't this nice?"

"Will you be long in Paris, Mr. Dandridge?"

"Will you?"

"I am not sure. Will this be your first time?"

"I was in the airport there eleven years ago making a connection, if that counts. Somehow I never got back."

"Life sometimes slips by too fast."

Oh, if she only knew. I said, "Did anyone ever tell you you have a nifty knack for pithy aphorisms?"

"Yes."

Ahh.

The captain announced we were cleared for takeoff. He had a Texas drawl. Pilots the world over all seem to have a Texas drawl. Like the flight crew in *Dr. Strangelove.* It must be a prerequisite.

The plane moved ahead and soon we were airborne.

I love flying. I hate heights and avoid cable cars at all cost, but flying is different. When I stand near the edge of a cliff, or walk up the side of a steep hill, or look out the window of a tall building, my palms get sweaty and I feel like I'm going to tip over. You'd think that sensation would increase thirty thousand feet up, but the fact that I was in a plane and no longer relying on my own equilibrium made me feel secure. Of course, the engine could suddenly give out, a plane with faulty radar could smack into us, our pilot could fall asleep, a terrorist could commandeer the aircraft, a vicious wind shear could sweep us into the Atlantic. But still, I felt safer.

Go figure.

"So how long are we going to play this game?" I said to my row mate.

"There is no game, Mr. Dandridge." She was cool and poised in a brown leather bomber's jacket over a loose, red blouse. "The danger is real."

"What about you?"

"I'm real too."

I liked that answer, but: "I meant the dangers. Aren't you concerned?"

"I understand what is happening, so I am safe."

"Safer than me?"

"Exactly."

"Even though someone set fire to your house?"

She studied my face a full minute, deciding what to reveal. "An unforeseen development. But no one was hurt."

"So your people don't give a rat's ass about anyone else and don't think twice about setting fire to apartments?"

"It wasn't my people."

"But there was no record of your having lived there. I thought—"

"*That* was my people."

"But—"

"But the opposition found me out. Luckily, we have a mole

who works close to the top of their organization. I was informed in time and had the place cleared of all traces of my having been there."

I knew from reading John Le Carre that a mole was a deep-cover operative who worked within one organization while spying on it for another. I didn't know what organizations we were talking about.

"I am afraid I cannot tell you more than that."

I looked around and lowered my voice. "Well, you're either CIA or FBI or NSA." No reaction. Completely stoic. She could've cleaned me out at poker. "On the other hand, you could be the enemy, KGB or GRU, and not to be trusted. Then again maybe you work for one of the third-rate powers or a Soviet satellite, or you're a contract employee or a terrorist for any number of angst-ridden groups."

"Finished?"

"Or very possibly you're a studio executive."

"Why is that?"

"It would at least explain why you're tormenting me."

She smiled. Her teeth were as polished as the bottom of a freshly buffed surfboard.

"I assure you I do not work in the film business." But she was still smiling. Maybe some ice was breaking.

"You're one of the few people willing to admit it," I said more for my benefit than hers.

"Would you mind putting my jacket in the overhead compartment?"

I stood in the aisle as she removed her jacket. As she handed it over I could see her thin arms move beneath her loose silk blouse. She didn't look all that powerful, certainly not a professional killer. How would she do in hand-to-hand combat? Her jacket smelled of warm leather and soap. Her soap. I was falling in love with the smell of that soap.

"Thanks."

"*De nada.*"

She raised her eyebrows. *"Habla espanol?"*

"Sorry. All I know is what I learned on the subway. I can say I have hemorrhoids or that the train tracks are dangerous or *las cucarachas entran, pero no pueden salir."*

"Somewhere I suppose that is helpful."

Dinner wasn't too bad. Dirty Blond and I remained quiet as we ate. She seemed calm and unbothered by our silence but it was driving me nuts. I had so many questions but didn't want to sound like a putz, since this lady seemed to know her way around and you never know when having a professional from whatever side as a friend would come in handy. So I played it cool. Real cool. I could've snapped my fingers and danced in the street I was so cool.

Finally: "I don't suppose you're ever going to tell me your name?"

"Call me Anne."

"Is that your real name?"

"Of course."

Bullshit. "All right, Anne. And where are you from, Anne?"

"I was born in a small village near the Austrian border."

"Which border?"

"That would be telling."

"And when did you first come to America, Anne?"

"I am afraid, Mr. Dandridge, that would be telling, too."

"Look, I have a feeling we're going to be seeing a lot of each other, whether we want to or not, so please call me Cliff."

"No."

"No?"

"No, we won't be seeing a lot of each other. As soon as we get to Charles De Gaulle Airport, I must ask that you not follow me as I leave."

"But I thought—"

"I do not care what you thought. We cannot be seen together."

"A-ha! A jealous husband."

"Mr. Dandridge . . . Cliff. Please, no more jokes. This is serious. You are best to visit whatever tourist sights you wish in Paris, and continue your holiday, but quickly. Never stay in one place too long. I suspect you will be followed here. Those men do not give up."

"But you said if I left New York—"

"And it was best you did. But the situation is volatile and there are other factors, other players, who will not be satisfied that you are gone, or that I am presumed dead."

Here we go again: huh?

Dirty Blond, Anne, reached into her purse and pulled out a tiny notebook. She quickly scribbled something on it, tore the page out and gave it to me.

"What's this?"

"A telephone number in case you need help. I want you to memorize it, then destroy the paper."

"Oh good Christ—"

"This is not funny, Clifford."

"Heathcliff. Cliff is short for Heathcliff, God rest my mother's soul."

"Just memorize this number."

I took the paper, looked at the number and began to memorize it. It was pretty long, and obviously contained the country and city dialing codes. I'd have to check those out in a phone book. I memorized the number and put the paper in my pocket.

"Please destroy that as soon as possible," said Anne.

"Scouts honor, I promise."

"Good." She patted the back of my hand, sending a spasm of sexual energy rushing up my arm. This lady had sizzle. Her skin was too exciting, her fingers alive and vibrant. I patted her hand right back and felt her bones through strong muscles. What could she do with such strong hands? Was there enough time to become a member of the Mile-High Club and find out?

"Umm, so Anne, I, ah—"

"This is the captain. Please return to your seats and prepare for landing. Thank you."

Anne turned to me. "You were about to say something?"

I looked deep into her clear, narrow eyes, saw nothing, took a whiff of her delicious smell, and shrugged. "Never mind."

By the time we cleared customs, we were still together.

"Remember to memorize the number and destroy that paper," she said.

"I'll swallow it whole."

"Of course you will," she smiled, winked and disappeared through the crowd. I fought off the urge to follow her. And she was gone.

I bused into Paris. The morning weather was bright and sunny, but I was sleepy from the night flight and was still on New York time. It may have been nine in the morning here, but it was only three on the Upper West Side.

The bus was filled with businessmen and backpackers, so I was forced to stand as we traveled through the Parisian suburbs, passing a number of warehouses and corporate offices, until finally we entered the city from the north. We disappeared beneath a building near Porte Maillot, at the northeast corner of the Bois de Bologne, the westernmost of the major Parisian parks. Everyone trundled off.

The terminal, a kind of impersonal hodgepodge of postwar architecture, was dark and concrete and cold. The crowd moved knowingly forward, so I followed, ending up at the end of a line that snaked through a series of glass doors. I waited without moving for a full ten minutes, then gave up. I walked alongside the line, which stretched farther than I realized, up a long, nonworking escalator to a taxi stand in an underground garage. Private limousines were parked and their drivers chatted amongst themselves, occasionally bargaining over fares with anxious businessmen. They were way too expensive, said a woman with white hair and a Flatbush accent, so everyone just stood listlessly waiting for the odd taxi to cruise by. I noticed a ramp toward sunlight and followed that, figuring I'd have more luck out on the street.

The sun was strong, the traffic chaotic. On the wide boulevards of Paris you immediately realize that just like in Manhattan no one pays attention to staying in lane. Especially when there are no lines dividing the road.

I lifted my arm and a shiny taxi sped over. I hopped in, the driver said something which I didn't understand, but as soon as I opened my mouth he stopped and said, *"Ah, Americain"* with such knowing contempt I wanted to punch him, but I wasn't drunk and couldn't use that as an excuse, and it was no way to start a sojourn. I gave him the name of a small pension in the Latin quarter I'd cut out of the New York *Times,* and he raced on.

I leaned back, already feeling my head clear, my body relax. I was in Paris, goddamn it! Famous for its *joie de vivre!* No more beautiful city existed anywhere on earth. The streets were like museum pieces, the people were well dressed and beautiful, and the hum of adventure literally buzzed in the air.

Fuck Anne and her goons, her moles and her enemies! Fuck show business! Fuck New York! Fuck art! Let's dance!

When you first visit a strange city, the sights and sounds are more apparent and you see things with a freshness you lose almost immediately. You are a sponge, soaking up the new, however mundane, and all your impressions are important. If you live in a place all your life you may never notice that store, those billboards, the intricacies of the streetlamps, the way cars are parked along the curb, because your eye and your mind take them for granted.

As I rode in the back of the cab looking out, the cream and beige facades of the Parisian buildings with their wrought-iron balconies, their heavy wooden doors, their row upon row of neatly ordered windows and slanted awnings, all gave the impression of a city in partnership with change. Modernity could force its way in the form of strange white structures at curbside (which I later learned were public toilets), while ancient cobblestone streets passed eighteenth-century apartment buildings and corner bistros, brasseries and cafés.

Fortunately I have a fine sense of direction, which comes in handy since I hate asking directions but always like knowing where I'm going, so I was able to follow our route. We drove past the busy shops along Boulevard du Montparnasse, and soon I could see the famous Observatory Fountain at the southernmost tip of the Jardin du Luxembourg. We made a sharp left and wound slowly through busy traffic up Boulevard Saint Michel toward the neighborhood of the Sorbonne. Traffic was painfully congested, and though we had a green light, we couldn't move. My driver took this with a cabbie's universal resignation, as the meter clicked furiously away. A group of students, dressed loudly in black leather and chains, wove through the stalled cars, banged on hoods, and laughed. A Parisian McDonald's was overflowing with morning eaters, and at a large courtyard filled with outdoor café tables students and tourists rubbed elbows and read newspapers. Beyond the courtyard was a building covered in scaffolding. This must have been the famed Sorbonne, founded in 1253 as a place to study theology (so said my green Guide Michelin). At a corner newsstand a beautiful woman in a white floor-length cloth coat, with round, blue eyes and short, neon yellow hair, looked into my cab and smiled. (Thank you). The traffic suddenly eased and the taxi lurched forward.

After winding through a number of tiny streets, we turned and I could see Notre Dame Cathedral over the treetops. It was glorious. The sky was blue, clouds stretched beyond like flayed cotton, and all I could think was, "I'm here."

"Monsieur, monsieur?"

"Pardon?"

"Your hotel?"

I paid the man in funny money and got out. The hotel was more run down than I expected, and inside was no better, but the clerk spoke English and had a room with a shower available for a five-night minimum at a reasonable rate, breakfast not included. I walked up three flights, and though my room had the dingy odor of mildew and smoke, it was clean and had a wondrous view of the cathedral. A desk was in front of the window, and the ceiling sloped up toward the roof. The bed was too soft, the carpet threadbare, but the toilet worked and the shower was hot. I unpacked, shaved and lay down for a nap.

And for the first time in weeks, I slept the sleep of the dead.

Ah, Paree! I had to get out and smell the people as soon as possible.

I found a café off Place Saint Michel, overlooking a crowd making its way north toward Point Saint Michel and Ile de la Cité. Far enough from the tourists who milled in the narrow streets of the Quarter, the café gave off a nice mix of seedy charm and old-world arrogance. I sat alone just inside the portico and ordered café au lait. The waiter, a tall, austere, balding man with glasses, deposited it with a clink, spilling some onto the table. I looked up to protest but he was gone. In the background the French equivalent of Muzak played havoc with the Beatles, but the café au lait was good and hot, so I sipped and watched the world pass by.

I studied the faces of the other patrons. The tourists were obvious for obvious reasons, but I also noticed that their faces looked conspicuously different. Only the French look French. They have a distinct physical appearance and it's all in the face. They walk and talk with their eyebrows tilted up toward the center of their forehead as if constantly suffering a headache. Also, when they speak, their upper lip is extremely animated, probably a result of all those vowel sounds in their language. Nevertheless, their eyes, their eyebrows and their lips all contribute to an air of contented disdain.

I finished my café au lait and was tempted to order another, but realized this wouldn't endear me to the waiter, so instead I ordered a *pastis,* the licorice-tasting alcoholic beverage of my literary forebears. The waiter suffered my Berlitz-aided request, but rather than being impressed seemed convinced I was yet another fool trying to look ridiculously continental.

The drink was harsh, sweet and delicious. I leaned back to watch as a young couple parked their motorcycle directly in front of the café. My waiter signaled to someone behind the counter, and a large man wearing a poorly tailored business suit came and exchanged words with the hostile young driver of the bike. The exchange became a shouting match, included shoving, but eventually the young couple got back on their bike and left. A murmur of approval filtered through the café, and a few people even applauded.

I caught the eye of my waiter and nodded. He nodded back, pleased that I was equally glad the bikers had left. In perfect English he asked if I liked the *pastis.*

"Delicious," I said.

"You should cut it with a beer chaser," he said.

"Bring whatever you suggest."

He returned with a bottle of Kronenbourg, which tasted different than the same brand I'd sampled back home. The locals must keep all the best bottles for themselves. But he was right: it made a nice chaser. I was feeling woozy, having drank without eating, but I wasn't going to have as my first meal a ham sandwich in a café, so I paid, left an inordinately huge tip (hoping by this he'd remember me when I returned), and went in search of haute cuisine.

I found it, I think, at a tiny run-down café along one of the many side streets in the Quarter. I didn't see a sign outside, nor was there much light inside, but it was crowded, the kitchen smelled good, and if you're not bold in Paris you might as well be dead. I had a wonderful meal of salad, veal au poivre, and left.

Night was falling and the Quarter filled with couples. I suddenly felt lonely for Danette. Should I have brought her along? I thought about it: nah. But it was lunchtime in New York so I didn't want to call and risk finding her not in. Besides, the point of this trip was to have new experiences, new adventures, not to wallow in the romance of the moment. Still, I'd call her later.

I turned a corner and found myself in front of Shakespeare and Company, the famed English-language bookstore. There was one with the same name back on the Upper West Side, but that didn't have the historical sense this one did. I looked at the old building and wondered: Were there people living upstairs who were broke, near starvation? Were great novels, short stories, political manifestos, being written here by the next generation of literary wonders?

Probably not.

I suppose in the old days the place was run by English expatriates, but all I could see now were American girls who looked like NYU drama students. It still seemed a drop-off point for mail—and perhaps other, more sinister things as well.

I was close to my hotel so I went in and called Oren's friend in the Marais district to arrange a rendezvous. I wanted to get rid of Oren's package as soon as possible so I wouldn't have that responsibility hanging over my head.

"Hello? *Parlez-vous anglais?*"

"*Oui,* yes." The voice was deep and strong.

"Is this," I quickly glanced at the slip of paper Oren gave me, "Raphael Arnot?"

"It is."

"I'm Cliff Dandridge, Oren Petrowicz's friend. I have a—"

"Yes yes, I know. When can you meet?"

A bit abrupt. Still: "Well, I'm not too busy, say, anytime anyplace."

"Okay . . . tomorrow afternoon come to me at four. You have the address?"

I read it back to him.

"Tomorrow then."

The phone clicked off. My, my, my. Not friendly at all. Well, what kind of people would Oren know anyway? Others like himself, probably: selfish to a fault.

Back at my café (note the possessive) my waiter greeted me like an old friend. He ushered me to the same seat I'd had earlier, and brought me a café au lait without delay.

"Are you on holiday, monsieur?" he asked.

"More or less."

"Will you be long in Paris?"

"A week or two, at least."

"I am Claude, if you need anything," he said with the barest of smiles. I nodded thanks and he walked behind the counter.

The nighttime crowd was busier than the daytime, providing a voyeur's delight. I sipped slowly and noticed a beautiful brunet seated at a table to my left. She was either alone or waiting for someone, but she ordered from my waiter, who was neither friendly nor cool to her, yet as I heard her speak my heart leapt up: she was authentic, a true French native.

I'll skip the details of our eye contact equivalent of cat and mouse, but eventually we'd flirted enough to break the ice with a few casual words. I invited her to join me at my table, and ordered some cognac to go with the coffee. I was already somewhat buzzed, so what the hell, right?

"Waiting for anyone?" I asked.

"Not particularly."

"Me neither."

"I come here whenever I'm in the Quarter."

"It's nice. You live in Paris?"

"Near the Opera."

"Ah. Are you a singer?"

"You can live there without singing, you know."

"Well, what do you do?"

"What do *you* do?"

"I'm a writer."

She suppressed a giggle, smiled at me with her dark, wide eyes, shook her head and turned away. The next was said without looking at me: "Why is it I always meet writers? You are always so dangerous to get to know, always thinking, always creating."

"I'm not so dangerous," I said, wishing the opposite were true.

She turned around with a devilish grin. "Well *I* am."

I thought: Yipes. Check, please. Get me out of here.

"Oh, I am teasing. Come, let's have another cognac. I'll pay this time, so you don't have to worry."

"I think I've had more than enough, thank you. I only flew in this morning." She had already signaled the waiter. "Well, if you insist . . ."

She turned back to me. "You are from New York."

"Is that a question, or am I that obvious?"

"Only New Yorkers are not bothered by Paris. They know how to handle themselves in foreign cities better than other Americans."

"I suppose that's because New York is a foreign city itself. We're used to it."

"I've always wanted to visit New York."

"Ever been to the States at all?"

"No, unfortunately. Someday I will. I have dreams New York cannot possibly live up to. But I have traveled around Europe. I love meeting new people."

This hung in the silence between us as we drank our cognac.

"You never answered my question," I said. "What do you do?"

"I'm in the fashion business."

She had the look and style of a designer or buyer. Her black hair was thick on top, spiky in all directions, but the sides were razor-cut, though not so short as to look like a military butcher job. Her high cheeks were smooth and sharp, her dark eyes had flecks of gray, and there seemed a permanent smirk on her wide mouth that hinted at unexpected challenges. Or humor. Her clothes were of the multilayered variety, with belts, sashes, a loose shirt and sweater concealing her true physique. I thought of the Soviet Union: "A riddle wrapped in a mystery inside an enigma."

"My name is Emma Bovary," she said finally.

"And I'm Gustave Flaubert."

She laughed. "Well, at least you're educated."

"Huh?"

"Most Americans I've met never heard of either of us."

I laughed too. "Actually, I'm Cliff Dandridge."

"Actually I wanted to *be* Emma Bovary, it was my favorite name as a child. I was going to take that name when I was old enough to have it legally changed, but I grew up and finally read the novel and realized what it was about and changed my mind. So instead I kept the name my parents gave me."

"And that is?"

"Josephine Lavant."

We shook hands in mock refinement. "Now that we've been properly introduced," I began, feeling the cognac warming my brain, seizing control, "maybe you could tell me where a foreigner interested in learning more about Parisian culture could see something interesting?" Did I really say that?

Josephine looked at me as if she wasn't sure what to say. I'd caught her off guard, and she seemed momentarily annoyed at my brashness. Something, though, quickly skirted behind her eyes and across her mind, since all at once she looked amused and ready to reveal one of France's deepest, darkest secrets.

Then she saw something over my shoulder, and waved, and stood up.

Oh no! They'd found me!

But when I turned I saw not the goons, but another beautiful brunet, tall and skinny with a boyish figure. She walked over to Josephine, and they kissed each other, or rather they bussed the air on either side of each other's cheeks in that distinctly phony way girls from Long Island do to simulate warmth when they really feel the opposite. Josephine and her friend quickly discussed something. I saw the boyish brunet look in my direction for a second, but Josephine grabbed her and turned her away. They continued talking, the friend nodded, then turned toward the street to hail a passing black Renault sedan. It slowed to a stop. Nasty-looking men were inside. Two of them. Big, beefy and bearded.

Hmm.

Josephine returned. "If you're still in Paris tomorrow night, meet me here at ten o'clock. I'm afraid my friend needs me now, an important business matter." She paused to see my reaction. What could I say? I simply stared ahead. The nasty-looking men sneered at me.

Josephine reached over and squeezed my hand. "Thanks for the cognacs. It was really nice meeting you, Cliff. Be careful walking home."

"See you tomorrow, then," I said, but she was already in the Renault with her friend and her associates. Edith Piaf had replaced the Muzak and was singing an emotional torch song. I asked my waiter what it was called.

"*Mon Dieu,*" he replied simply, as if that said it all.

I always believed life should have a soundtrack just like the movies, and if music wasn't playing a person should think of appropriate songs whenever the mood struck. I missed my jazz discs back home, and though Piaf was the perfect sound for Paris, Muzak Beatles I could live without. I suddenly felt the urge to go in search of Parisian nightlife, to find a club and hear the current sounds of the city, but after downing a fifth cognac with Kronenbourg and paying the bill at the café, I stood and the world swirled in my head like the amusement park ride called "The Whip." I was overtired, my throat burned, my lips were working toward a serious state of chappedness, my eyes stung from all the goddamned French cigarettes.

And there were too many people in the quarter. They were getting on my nerves. Did they know who I was? Where I came from? What my name was?

Were *they* after me too?

What about that old guy across the street with the hawk's nose in the trench coat, tying his shoelace? The hippie couple singing folksongs for coins? The swarthy Arab with the pencil mustache, cleaning his nails with a pocketknife? Were they all sent to keep tabs on me, too?

And who was this Josephine Lavant, anyway? Since when did I have such luck meeting women as easily as that?

As I walked the narrow, crowded, pedestrian streets, the shouting hawkers trying to get people to eat kabobs and brochettes became a mind-bending roar. My blood raced, sweat beaded on my face. I staggered up the three flights to my room, rushed to the bathroom and Called For York On The Great White Phone with gut-wrenching abandon.

Ooh boy. I managed to wash my face and find the bed before passing out, visions of spy-demons and beer chasers dancing in my head.

SEVEN

I slept twelve hours. When I woke it was too early in New York to call Danette or my agent (though I should have called him at home to get his day off to a lousy start), so I shaved, showered and went out in search of breakfast. Last night's tossing chunder thoroughly cleansed my system, so I felt a mix of nauseousness and starvation. Obviously, I needed food.

The streets were quiet at this time of day. The shopkeepers were out cleaning the sidewalks in front of their stores, using water that poured up from the sewers to wash away the dirt they swept into the gutters, and I had this image of them all quietly humming "La Marseillaise."

Breakfast was a quick café au lait, croissant, bread and jam. The tiny, crusty *petit pan* was delicious, and I noticed that the true native cut it not in slices but lengthwise, buttering and jamming each half. No country had mastered baking and eating bread like France.

The *International Herald Tribune* delighted me with a report that the Jets had beaten the Dolphins in overtime. Knowing Rick, he probably sold the tickets and spent the afternoon bitching in a bar about what a lousy friend I was for making him miss such an exciting game.

There was plenty of time to kill before meeting Raphael Arnot, so I took my camera and journal and rode the metro to the Eiffel Tower. The ride was impressive. The cars were all clean and quiet, and I loved the vinyl-covered seats that moved up and down on hinges to create more standing room. Could you imagine them lasting six minutes in New York? Some drugged-out freak would bang them up and down till they fell off, then use them as first, second and third base in a Central Park pick-up game until the stuffing was ripped out and the exposed steel frame cut a dog.

The Tower was overrun with tourists, but the view from the third *étage* was magnificent. Music from some unknown Disney movie played in my head as I looked out across the rooftops of Paris, feeling a nostalgia I had never even known.

Downstairs I walked to the stone quay alongside the Seine, watching barges and kayaks ride past, and sat down on the steps leading to the water. I took out my journal and slowly began writing about the past few days. If nothing else a journal would provide a valuable record of my thoughts and impressions, and I could probably use it for reference when I got home to write my book.

And of course if I died in some mysterious, horrible tragedy, it might provide clues as to the identity of my assailants.

Later that day I got off the metro at the Bastille station. I'd hoped to see the last vestiges of the famed prison that sparked the French Revolution, but all that remained was a tall monument in the middle of a roundabout and a stone line set around the perimeter that marked off where the walls were that came tumbling down to signal the start of the 1789 uprising.

I went north to a street with a name that sounded like "a place mules used," turned left and followed it until I came to a large square. Guide Michelin said that this, the Place des Vosges, was the oldest square in Paris. Surrounded on four sides by perfectly symmetrical buildings, the central park was filled with old people on benches and young mothers watching their children. I walked round the perimeter on an arcadelike sidewalk beneath the buildings, and *voila*—I found Victor Hugo's house!

It was like a pilgrimage to a sacred site. The door was ordinary, but a plaque outside announced that, yes, indeed, Victor Hugo had lived there. Images of Javert and Valjean flashed through my head. It was less than three weeks since I'd seen the musical *Les Miserables* in New York, and now, here I was, standing in front of the home of that noble French poet. The fact that I'd been haunted by that story, by feelings of artistic inadequacy, by whatever else, made standing there seem profoundly meaningful, though I couldn't exactly say why. There are times when something happens, when a person sees something or does something, that for some strange, inexplicable reason, resonates with importance. It's as if you know something special, something deep, has happened. You can point to that time and place and see it as a landmark, a milestone, a point of reference in the scheme of life. I felt that now, God knew why, and couldn't wait to touch the artifacts inside.

But it was Monday, and Maison Victor Hugo was closed.

So much for profound moments in life.

A few blocks later and I was deeply lost somewhere in the Marais. At one time a swamp, this area had gone from being one of the most envied in all Paris to being the site of a huge, Byzantine, mazelike Jewish ghetto. Though filled with interesting museums and old, restored palatial residences, the ethnic influences were still evident, and old synagogues and new kosher restaurants competed with reconverted buildings that attested to a recent renaissance. Gentrification had found its way to Paris, and what was once run down and abandoned, was quickly becoming chic and expensive, the Parisian version of the Yupper West Side.

I turned off Rue de Turenne onto a side street shrouded in shadows. It was daylight, but the street was so narrow that even the short buildings were tall enough to obscure the sun.

A khaki green van was parked half on the curb and half on the street, with a surfboard strapped to its roof. I was looking for number fourteen, but the numbers went from thirteen to fifteen. A wooden door cut into the middle of the block of buildings, so I pushed it aside and walked into a dark, garbage-filled alley. Rusted iron pieces, a wooden pushcart, a collection of milk bottles, lined its walls. I stepped over them: the silence was tomblike. A cat jumped off a ledge overhead and scared the shit out of me. The clicking sound of a door unlocking drew my attention to the end of the alley, and a male face greeted me from the shadows.

"Monsieur Dandridge?"

"Raphael?"

"Come inside please." I moved ahead, saw the number fourteen painted in faded letters on the door, and entered.

The man who had opened the door was walking quickly down the hallway into an adjoining room. In contrast to the congestion of the alley and the hall, it was huge, clearly an artist's studio. But rather than empty and cavernous like Oren's downtown loft, it was cluttered top to bottom with every conceivable piece of junk. Or rather art, since I knew that Raphael Arnot, per Oren, was a designer of enormous repute.

There were canvases strewn haphazardly on the floor, on bookcases brimming with paperbacks, on pieces of furniture totally obscured by drop cloths. There were literally hundreds of what people where I come from call *chatchkes,* brightly colored ornaments, gadgets and gizmos, windup toys and hand-painted figurines. There was a Victorian quality to the clutter, which appeared to have no sense of order at all, but which, if Arnot was any kind of artist, would be in some precise, arcane system known only to him. There were death masks and complete Medieval costumes. There were American cigarette advertisement posters, there was a huge still-working lava lamp. The tinny squawk of an old transistor radio blared from some unseen speaker.

"Did you bring the package?" asked the man I assumed to be Arnot.

"You are Raphael Arnot?"

"Of course I am! Now, if you please?"

I gave Arnot the package, and as I walked closer I could see what he looked like. He was tall, over six feet, with the build of a football player. He was Bozo-bald, with a tightly cropped band of brown hair horseshoeing his skull. He had a closely trimmed salt-and-pepper beard, and as he tore the paper off the package I could see he had enormous, powerful hands, with thick, hairy fingers.

He did not look like a sensitive designer to me.

Arnot's manner changed as soon as he held up one of the cornices. His face became reverential. He handled the objects as if they were long lost friends. And from a distance I caught my first glimpse of what I'd smuggled to Europe. The cornices were entirely black. They appeared carved out of solid wood, and aside from the frou-frou details that cluttered up the design, there was a central cherub's face at the peak of each piece. Nice but no big deal. Still, artists were entitled to want what they wanted, right? Who was I to complain?

"I am very much thankful to you and Oren."

"You are very much welcome."

"I have been most anxious to receive this."

"Well, there you are." Shut up, fuckhead, I thought. But I was standing like a monkey at a wedding, waiting for a drink or a chair, so I guess I should be forgiven.

"Forgive me," said Arnot, suddenly coming out of whatever trance he was in. "My manners. Please, sit. I will put this away and be right back." He disappeared with the cornices behind a curtain and came back empty-handed.

"It is indeed nice to meet you, Monsieur Dandridge," said Arnot, pumping my hand with his strong, beefy grip. "It was kind of you to go out of your way and bring me the two cornices."

"Well, Oren's a good friend, I was coming to Paris anyway, so you know . . ."

"May I offer you something?"

"A beer would be fine."

"I have other things available . . ."

I glanced at my watch: still early. I wanted to stay up late, to meet Josephine at the café, so I really didn't want to get shitfaced just yet.

But: "Sure," I said. "What've you got?"

Arnot offered me an assortment of powders and pills, all of which I was tempted to try, but ultimately passed on. You never know what evil lurks in the hearts of men, and taking advanced substances from total strangers didn't strike me as the key to a healthy future.

Arnot had a veritable pharmacy hidden beneath a huge Dali print, and he took pleasure in describing to me the various functions of each elixir and chemical. It was clear why he was Oren's *ami.*

I settled for a beer. Arnot did a few lines of what he called "serious powder" and became eminently more friendly. His energy also shot up to the level of a Saturn Five booster rocket.

He shouted as he spoke. "Oren told me you would like to eat some good food! I, too, would like to eat some good food! Someone will be here in . . ." He looked at his watch, made an effort to read it, but turned it toward me. "What time is it?"

"Four-thirty-three."

"Someone will be here in, in . . . soon. Then we can go to one of my favorite restaurants."

"Fine." Under normal circumstances I would have left. This guy was loony-tunes and a friend of his was coming over. But I was looking for adventure, right? So . . .

"Do you like my collection?" he asked suddenly, still shouting.

I wasn't sure whether he meant the art or the drugs. "Sure," I said to be safe.

"It has taken me a lifetime to collect. Everything you see before you is authentic. I use them to make copies for the movies I work on. I sell the copies to art dealers, but I keep the authentic ones for myself. Every man must have enthusiasms, and collecting intricate pieces of art is mine. What are your enthusiasms?"

"Traveling, seeing the sights, watching football. Having fun, basically. Or at least trying to."

"Then you should at least try this," he said, reaching into his pharmacy again and removing a glass container that held a huge, hairy-looking gray sphere.

"Another time," I said as friendly as possible. Maybe it was time to leave. . . .

But my host was insistent. He toured around his cluttered studio, showing with pride the various gadgets and gizmos he'd amassed, until at five exactly I heard a knock at the door. Arnot went to look through the peephole, knocked twice in response, but did not open it. He then disappeared into the curtained room. I heard drawers being opened and closed, and something fell loudly to the floor. Arnot shouted what must have been a string of French profanity, I heard something smash against a wooden table, and he finally came out holding a white plastic bag wrapped in tape. He exchanged the bag with whomever was outside, and returned to the curtained room with a fist full of francs (a new Sergio Leone *Croissant Western?*). He didn't close the curtain completely this time, so I saw him counting a huge pile of money.

I also saw that one of the cornices was lying in a smashed-up heap, its cherub's face smiling up at me in conspiracy. Was it drugs, government secrets, stolen gems? Suddenly I felt the long arm of the law clamp tightly around my chest . . .

And I passed out.

I came to and saw Arnot's concerned face hovering over me. "What happened?"

"You fainted."

"I felt like I was having a heart attack."

"J'ai eu une attaque, is how you say it. But do not worry. I put something in your beer, everyone reacts differently. I am sorry. Come, I will take you to dinner."

"What time is it?"

He showed me his watch again. Couldn't this drug fiend tell time? Anyway, I was shocked to see I'd been out almost three hours.

Whatever Arnot had given me made me hungry, so despite little alarm bells clanging wildly in my head, I went off with him to eat Hungarian goulash at Goldenberg's. This kosher deli in the heart of the Marais was more popular with tourists and terrorists than with local French Jews. In fact, ever since it was the scene of an Arab bomb in the early 1980s, American Jews seeking a taste of danger but not bold enough to visit the Holy Land dropped by to see if they could find any signs of a huge hole that had been blown in the wall. No such luck, since reconstruction was complete. Still, wasn't it daring to visit such a place?

After passing through a series of rooms reminiscent in style if not quality of the Carnegie Deli back home, we were seated in a lower level complete with Formica tabletops, Middle Eastern art and wooden chairs. Kosher kitsch. All I noticed was that the rye bread had a crust unlike any I'd ever tasted.

Arnot apologized again for slipping me whatever he slipped me and launched into a zestful description of the schlock films he'd been forced to work on in order to pay for his habit of collecting "memorabilia" (his word). He'd had to engage in illegal smuggling, "don't you know," to get some of the more precious pieces, but working on international films and television productions made smuggling much easier.

Did I believe that was all he smuggled? Well, no. But if I didn't, then I'd have to assume I was guilty of violating various international laws myself. Visions of Turkish prisons and huge sweaty guards pounded through my head.

"Are you all right, Cliff?"

I was on the verge of panic. I didn't want to go to jail. I didn't know what was really in those cornices. I gulped down the seltzer. It was thin and tasted like Perrier. Was every food or drink in this goddamned country subtle? I was in desperate need of a Seventy-second Street hot dog . . . "I'm fine," I said.

I had to get a grip on myself. Nothing had happened, no one was after me . . . well, that wasn't completely true, if Anne was to be believed. There were two goons who'd chased me to the airport. Was Arnot somehow involved?

Don't be ridiculous . . .

Yet I *was* disappointed with the restaurant. Not because the food wasn't fine. It was. And the goulash was truly memorable. But I'd hoped to see some trashy new hotspot instead. Maybe they didn't have any in Paris? Still, I didn't want to seem too much the tourist, and figured it would be best if I left Arnot as quickly as possible.

To be polite, I reached for my wallet. Arnot grabbed my arm, a bit too tightly, and said, "No. Please. This is my pleasure. We must get together again while you're here, then you can pay."

I didn't resist. I didn't plan on seeing Raphael Arnot again.

It was a bit after ten when I took a table at my café. Claude was still on duty, busily clearing tables, but we nodded acknowledgment.

"Hello."

I turned to see Josephine Lavant dressed to kill. A stark black leather outfit she couldn't possibly have sat down in wrapped her nonstop body. Thighs for days disappeared beneath a skirt a shade too high for polite society. Her breasts were waging a war with the material of her blouse, and the material was losing. The neckline was obscene and the backline nonexistent. If I was back in high school I would have had to walk to my next class with a notebook covering my crotch.

"You came," I said.

"Not yet," she said. Oh please.

"I didn't think you'd show up."

"But you hoped," she said with confidence.

"You piqued my curiosity."

"That's a funny word."

"Curiosity?"

"Piqued."

Yes, well. Ahem.

"Mind if I sit down?"

We drank our standard cognacs, staring suggestively into each other's eyes. This was ridiculous, absurd, I couldn't believe it was happening. I mean she was wearing black lipstick, for God's sake.

"Last night you said you wanted to see something unusual. If you like, I think I can still arrange that."

At that precise moment I was ready to turn back. The door to adventure was being opened: Did I want to go through? Were all the days, months, years of talk back home with Rick and Oren and Risa and Danette going to slip away out of fear? Or was I willing to grab my destiny and ride it out? Was I going to follow the rainbow to the pot of gold, or discover I was all hype and chickenshit?

"Let's go," I said.

I opened my wallet to pay for our cognacs, and my heart stopped. It was empty. My credit cards, my driver's license, my Citicard, my traveler's checks. Everything. The Pierre Cardin leather was laughably thin without the detritus of my life.

"Is anything wrong?" asked Josephine.

I didn't want to blow it, but what could I do. "I think I've been robbed."

Her face fell. Claude must have overheard because he came and lingered a bit too close. Bond or no bond, if I was broke, he'd turn on me in a second.

"I, I, I . . ." I said.

Josephine reached into her purse (where she kept it I couldn't say) and paid the bill. Claude took his money and left.

"That wasn't really necessary."

"This way you can worry about your money later. Besides, you paid last night, remember?"

"Arnot!"

"What?"

"I think I know where my money went."

"Really, Cliff, don't worry. You can pay me later. We really must be go—"

"Come on. If we catch a cab maybe we can get him while he's in."

Josephine must have thought I was nuts, but she seemed as game for a good time as anyone, so she hailed a taxi and translated my directions for the driver. We sped over the Pont Saint Michel and the dark Ile de la Cité, over the Pont au Change, around and behind the Hotel de Ville and over toward the Marais. The taxi eventually stopped outside the alley and Josephine waited while I went to knock on the door. I knocked repeatedly for what seemed like hours, but nothing.

"Come, Cliff. Forget it till tomorrow."

I was sure that bastard Arnot lifted my wallet after he drugged me. No wonder he didn't let me reach for it at dinner. I banged on the door some more, trying to calm down. I was steamed and Josephine saw it. I stopped banging and leaned against the wall, emotionally spent and temporarily broke. Then Josephine leaned over and gave me a soul kiss I can still taste. We came up for air, I saw she had mischief in her eyes, so we kissed again.

Back in the cab Josephine gave the driver new directions and sat back to talk. I noticed she was wearing a killer perfume, and her stocking-clad legs rubbed mine.

"You're a very nice tourist, Cliff."

"I'm not a tourist, I'm a traveler."

"I see," she said with a laugh.

"No, really. There's a difference. A tourist wants everything the way it is back home. He adheres strictly to his favorite guidebook and is totally uncomfortable with foreign culture. I have none of those faults."

"I am glad to hear that." Her eyes were smiling, so I could tell she was buying what I was selling.

"Look, Cliff, we are strangers, but I like you. You're cute, and funny, and not without a certain sex appeal."

Backhanded compliment if ever there was one.

"I know some unique Parisian places," she continued. "I think you would like them. But first, I must know what you don't like."

I wasn't sure how to respond, but was spared further difficulty when the taxi stopped at a street near the Pigalle metro. The neon signs of the shadowy clubs and dance halls reflected brightly on the pavement as we got out.

Josephine took my arm and lead me through a variety of twisting back streets. I knew I wasn't going to be robbed because Josephine knew I was broke, so for whatever reason, I trusted her. I guess she had a kind face. Actually to be honest I wanted to get under her skirt, so I suppose that's *really* why I went along.

Besides, if this was a setup and she was involved with the conspiracy against me (Listen to me!), there was very little I could do about it now.

We walked up to a tiny door beneath a poorly lit marquee. There were words on the marquee, and beside the ticket booth were pictures from what appeared to be a movie. As we slid into the theater, I noticed that the people in the photos were naked.

Ooh boy.

Josephine led us to a seat in the back. The place wasn't crowded, but the movie was already in progress. The action was fairly specific, but also fairly mundane. I mean if this was a French porno film, I wanted Manhattan Cable and *The Robyn Bird Show.*

The setting was a convent school, but all the students looked way older than twenty. A sexy Mother Superior proceeded to pair off each of her initiates with various farmers from the local village, when suddenly the film did a jump cut to a completely different young couple banging away like rabbits. This went on for some time, with the appropriate moaning and groping, until the film returned to the narrative of the convent girls. Cut back to the sex scene, and once again to the convent. You get the idea. A few old-timers in the front were groaning, but I noticed that the rest of the audience seemed silently intent. Poor bastards.

Outside, Josephine asked what I thought. I tried being polite and said it was okay, but dull. She nodded.

"I thought in France the sex would be more adventurous."

"It can be," she said.

"Do you live near here?"

She squeezed my hand and pecked my cheek. "Not yet. The night is just starting."

We took a taxi down Rue Blanche toward Boulevard Haussmann, to a neighborhood behind the Opera. The great Parisian department stores were closed for the night, but in the adjacent streets eager men were still doing their shopping, cruising by in their cars, windows down, checking out the females for sale. Josephine said something to our driver and he slowed down. I looked out to see a few bored girls lighting their cigarettes end to end at the corner of a tiny park, their platinum hair shiny in the streetlamp light. A black Mercedes limousine pulled over, a window slid down, words were exchanged. As our taxi turned a corner, I could see two of the girls lifting their blouses to reveal their breasts to whomever was in the Mercedes. Whether that was it, or they drove off with the passenger, I never found out.

Josephine was watching me as I was watching the action, gauging my responses, judging my reactions.

We finally stopped in front of a huge mansion set back off the street. There were iron gates along the sidewalk, and a lit walkway that led to heavy oak doors. It looked like the haunted mansion at Disneyland. Josephine paid the driver and led me out. My heart beat faster, and I suddenly grew nervous.

Maybe this wasn't such a good idea. . . .

"Come on. If there is anything you don't like, tell me and we'll leave."

We were greeted by a butler, who led us into a high-tech reception room. I was expecting Victorian reds and woods, but instead found the place to be decorated in blacks, whites and grays with splashes of bold colors used as highlights here and there. Lots of marble, steel and leather. Dim lighting. We walked up to a bar and the bartender nodded to Josephine, who smiled and ordered us drinks.

"It's a rather special nightclub. You have to be a member to get in."

"So I'm your guest tonight?"

"I do not usually bring guests. It is more fun to come alone and see what happens. But tonight is a special night, and you seemed particularly curious, so I thought you would be the perfect friend to have along."

"I'm honored. What do we do now?"

"There are many things. If you like, we can just walk around and see what is happening. There are special rooms where people do what they want. No one makes value judgments, every form of self-expression is permitted."

"A socially liberal environment."

"If you like. You can watch, or participate."

I was expecting Sodom and Gomorrah, and I wasn't far from mistaken. In one room set up as a tiny theater five rows of seats faced a small stage, where a live sex act was taking place. Two burly men, oiled and hairless, held a tiny Oriental girl fixed in a position with her legs wrapped behind her head. They kept lifting her up and down on the rigid erection of a large black man strapped to a table. The musclebound men moved the girl with increasing speed, like pistons on an engine. The black man was squirming, teeth gnashing in pain, but the Oriental girl remained passive, probably drug induced, and showed no signs of reaching orgasm. This went on for some time, until the girl began scratching the chest of the black man with her nails, causing him to writhe even more. The audience sat stoic.

In another room that held what resembled a boxing ring, there must have been two dozen naked bodies squirming around like slithering snakes in various oral and anal acts of sex. Three women were lazily humping a fleshy three-headed dildo—I'd never seen anything like it before—while sucking the dicks of three guys sitting tensely on the boxing ring rope. Another girl was sandwiched between two men and was taking both of them at the same time, one phallus in each lower orifice. Thwack-thwack, thwack-thwack, as genitals pushed and pulled, was the predominating sound we heard. Two women were locked in erotic embrace, with a bunch of guys watching, cheering and stroking.

In yet another room, actually a nightclub with a stage, an S and M act was unfolding for a small but attentive crowd. An attractive young male and female couple were chained to a cold brick wall as a tall, white woman in black leather hip boots and an excruciatingly tight red corset whipped them senseless with a frayed wet rope. The guy's face was covered in a zippered leather mask, while the girl was choking on a ball gag stuffed into her mouth and tied around her head with nylon stockings. A few people in the audience were furiously masturbating. I recognized the woman doing the beating as Josephine's boyish-looking friend from the previous night.

"That's Olga," said Josephine. "She thinks of herself as an accomplished hedonist."

Right. Absolutely.

I also noticed the big, beefy, bearded nasty-looking men from the Renault awaiting their turn in harness and nipple clips.

"Come on, I want to show you something," said Josephine like an excited schoolgirl. We went through a door marked *"Attention au chien,"* which Josephine translated as "Beware of the dog," and inside I saw a very high-tech security system with a row of television monitors. It looked like the control center for the Super Bowl. Or Super Ball, which it was.

A bulldog with a spiked collar gave us a cursory look and went back to sleep.

"Raymond, this is my friend Cliff." Josephine was talking to a handsome, stocky businessman who would have looked quite at home in a Wall Street boardroom. No sign of kink about him at all.

"Welcome to my club," said Raymond, shaking my hand. His grip was dry and firm. "You are indeed lucky to have Josephine as a friend."

"Raymond and I know each other a long time. He helped me get started in the fashion business."

"I know what you are thinking, Cliff," said Raymond, holding up a hand in protest, "but Josephine's business was always legitimate."

"That is true," said Josephine, nudging my arm.

Raymond offered us comfortable leather seats in front of the wall of television monitors, and pointed to a tray of bottled water and assorted drinks.

"Raymond must protect the integrity and reputation of his *cercle* by ensuring that its members are always safe," said Josephine. "By installing remote cameras in each of the private rooms, he knows when things are getting out of hand, and can send in a security team to help."

"Violence, to a point, is acceptable," said Raymond with sincerity, "but running a successful sex club means knowing when the fun has become too dangerous. Take this room, for instance." He pointed to one of the monitors, and on it I saw that a nervous young man was being wrapped in what looked like white linen.

"A bolt of the finest painter's canvas I could find. The gentleman is being wrapped in it dry, then it will be made wet and will cling to his body. When the canvas dries, it will become tighter, restricting the blood flow and causing a tremendous rush. A tiny hole has been cut so his penis can stick through, and someone with rubber gloves will come and jerk him off."

I coughed.

"Help yourself to a drink," said Raymond.

"I'll pour you a cognac," said Josephine. I nodded my thanks.

"Anyway," continued Raymond, "we have to be careful to cut him out of the canvas before he suffocates."

I was about to ask whether they ran hoses on the guy to wet the canvas, when I saw six naked women line up on either side of the young man. They climbed onto the table and hovered over him, and each began pissing on the canvas. The young man on the screen writhed and squirmed.

"You can hear his screams if you like," said Raymond, reaching for a dial by the monitor.

"No, thanks," I said as quickly as possible.

Josephine leaned over and whispered, "It makes me sick too, but you have to humor Raymond, sometimes."

"There'll be no whispering, you two." Raymond was indignant. "No secrets. Otherwise I won't let you stay for tonight's special event."

"And what is that?" I asked weakly, wishing I had at least enough cab fare in my pocket to go home.

"Have you ever been to Pamplona, Cliff?" asked Raymond. Huh?

"We have a unique version of their annual running of the bulls," he continued. "I promise it's a sight you will not forget."

Raymond and Josephine giggled.

I'm sure Hemingway and Fitzgerald never saw anything like it. The alley behind Raymond's club ran directly behind a variety of other similar buildings. Josephine said the entire block was nothing but sex clubs, and they all shared in preparing this semiannual ritual. In Pamplona an alley is closed off and a truckload of fresh bulls ready for a fight is brought to one end. The bulls are released, left to run wildly down the alley toward a bull ring. But running in their way are hundreds of drunk, brave fools who feel they can out distance the dangerous horns of the stampeding herd.

Well, the unique angle here in the sex quarter of Paris was that the "bulls" were naked men and women, in masks and capes, with plastic horns on their heads, or huge leather dildoes strapped around their waists. The brave fools who ran ahead of them were each given a bottle of whiskey to drink, were blindfolded, then stripped naked. There was but one direction they could run, and along the way various helpers pushed things forward. There was much cheering and drinking from curious onlookers, as the drunk and blindfolded victims ran before the stampeding "bulls." Of course if a bull caught a runner, well, any form of impalement was permitted.

Music played loudly from speakers set up along the route. It was a wonder the police didn't come and close the whole place down, but Raymond assured me there were some policemen involved, "in one fashion or another."

"Yeder mentsh hot zeineh aigeneh meshugahssen," he added slyly. "That's Yiddish."

The drunk "runners" were gathered at the head of the alley, and though the night was chilly, the booze warmed their spirits. Josephine and I had seats on the balcony just outside Raymond's office and could see the tail end of the course, which this year finished inside Raymond's own club. That meant every one of the runners and bulls would be stampeding through the door directly beneath our feet.

Ooh boy.

Raymond was correct: this "Running Of The Bulls" was unlike anything I'd ever seen. The runners staggered down the alley, bumping into each other, clawing with their wet, greased hands at the naked and blindfolded bodies surrounding them. The bulls were "released" from their truck and began stampeding down the alley, screaming and laughing, reaching out to grab the bodies in front. When the bulls had the runners, regardless of gender, they "speared" their victims with their phalluses, both real or plastic. People were lined up and down along the wooden alley getting it in every hole, and I was reminded of starving dogs in heat.

It wasn't pretty. The smell of human sweat and excrement and booze filled the air, and the howling of the onlookers who leaned out of windows along the route turned the bacchanal into a vision of hell on earth. The sex was violent, graphic, constant. No one was moving toward the entrance to Raymond's club, since no one seemed in a hurry to end things. I could see how this might go on all night. Josephine saw me glance at my watch.

"It's not for everybody, Cliff," she said. "But once you see it, you're own appetites are never the same."

I endured the sight until five in the morning, when the last of the bulls stampeded into the club.

Dawn was breaking, the alley was strewn with filth, and Josephine said it was time to go.

We walked a few blocks to her place, which was a quiet one-bedroom apartment on the second floor of a tiny building. I flopped onto her bed and she kissed me, rubbing my chest, but there was no way I was going to rise to any occasions just then.

I made some alcohol-riddled excuses, and we both fell asleep in our clothes.

I woke to find I was in bed with five other people. Thankfully everyone was fully clothed, or at least I thought so, but some people *were* under the blanket so I couldn't be sure.

"*Bonjour,* Cliff," said Josephine, who was standing near the bathroom wrapped in a red terrycloth bathrobe. She had just taken a shower, and steam filled the bedroom.

"Relatives of yours?" I asked, referring to the bodies on the bed.

"Oh, just a few good friends who stopped by after we fell asleep. They needed a place to stay, I didn't want to turn them out so late at night."

"I see."

"Come. They will sleep all day, we will go out for breakfast."

The roof of my mouth felt like Brillo. My eyes were dry and sore, my neck felt like I must have slept wrong. I threw some cold water on my face, put some toothpaste on my index finger and brushed my teeth, and wet my hair to keep from looking like Alfalfa on *The Little Rascals.*

Over café au lait I thanked Josephine for a swell time but said I had to stop living like this if I wanted to live at all. She laughed and actually used the phrase "silly boy" on me.

"Do you have plans today, Cliff?"

"I have to try Arnot again, then visit the American Express office."

"I mean later."

"What do you suggest?"

"I have a shoot today. A fashion layout. Maybe you would like to stop by and watch."

"I don't know. . . ."

"It's for a legitimate magazine, I promise."

She wrote down the address and I agreed to meet her later in the afternoon.

EIGHT

"I'm sorry, no one is available to take your call right now, so leave a message after the beep, and I'll get back to you soon. Please wait for the—BEEP!"

"Danette, it's Cliff. We got a great connection. Anyway, sorry I haven't called but I've been busy. The weather's terrific, I've seen some sights, I also met some really nice people and have been drinking way too much. Gotta watch that. Anyway I'll—"

BEEP.

"Hi Gerty, Sam in?"

"Gerty's sick. Who's this?"

"Cliff Dandridge, calling from Paris."

"Cliff Harris?"

"Cliff Dandridge, I'm in Paris. Paris, France. This is expensive. Is he in?"

Whoever it was put me on hold, and at two bucks a minute I was forced to listen to Muzak across the transatlantic satellite.

"Cliffie-boy, *bonjour mon capitain!* How's it shaking?"

"Fine Sam. Any work?"

"Slow down, Cliffie. How's Paris? Get any yet?"

"I can't afford it, Sam. Unless you got me work. Did that book come through?"

"I'm working on it still, Cliff. I got a call in to the right people, they haven't gotten back to me. Patience is a virtue."

"I'm not interested in virtue, Sam."

"That's why I want to know if you got any yet."

"What about that series in L.A.?"

"Nothing yet, but don't worry. I'm still on it."

"Let me give you a number where I can be reached in case anything comes through."

"Wait . . . what's that Cliff? Can't hear you. Something's suddenly wrong with the line."

"Listen you cheap bastard, take down this number and call me—"

"Cliff, I can't hear you anymore. Call me again tomorrow. Someone's just coming in."

"Sam you fuckhead—"

"Cliff, great hearing from you, buddy. I'll wait for your call."

Click.

The whole world sucks.

The concierge, friendly just days ago, looked at me like I was some sort of pariah, this despite my fresh shave and favorite sportsjacket. He inquired if everything was fine. I said everything was fine, but he didn't seem to believe me.

Well fuck him.

With the last of the cash Josephine loaned me I took the metro to the American Express office. The ground floor was busy and run by cheerful customer-service representatives eager to plan holiday excursions, but downstairs in the corporate version of a dungeon I found a long line of customers cashing checks or reporting stolen ones. Young backpackers rubbed elbows with garish white-shoes-and-floral-print middle-aged couples, and though all were American by birth, the stylistic differences were astounding.

I emerged three hours later re-equipped with a new credit card and more checks. I could do without my Citicard, but a driver's license would be handy, so the office sold me a gray and useless international one until I could get to the Embassy to apply for a replacement. The hell with that. I wasn't planning on driving in Europe anyway. At least I could be thankful my passport was safe in my luggage.

"Anyone home, for Christ's sake!"

I was back outside Arnot's, banging on his door. The alley cat gave me a French sneer and snootily bounced away.

I checked my Berlitz to find something appropriate and came up with *"Au feu, au feu!"* but shouting "Fire!" in a dark alley wasn't genuinely bright, and some old woman suddenly opened her third-story window and began screaming at me in colorful foreign words. I smiled like a schmuck and waved an apology, but she continued blathering until she lost interest and slammed her window back down.

From a phone booth I dialed the number for the overseas version of AT & T and made a collect call to Oren.

"You dumb fuck, what kind of friend do you send me to?"

"Easy, Cliff. I take it by your tone that you and Raphael didn't hit it off."

"The man's scum. He slips me something that knocks me out and then lifts my money. Now I can't find him."

"Mmm."

"That all you can fucking say? Mmm?"

"Take it easy, Cliff. Relax."

"It's your nickel."

"We'll see about that."

"Eat shit and die."

"Look, give Raphael the benefit of the doubt. He's into so many different things he's probably running an errand or two."

"The man hasn't been home for two days, Oren."

"You sure? Have you been there all the time watching?"

"His mail is still there from yesterday."

"A regular Sherlock Holmes, aren't you?"

"And another thing, Mr. Oren. What illegal trafficking have you gotten me involved in?"

"Oh." Pause. "I see." Pause, pause. "Well at least the delivery was made." He sounded relieved. "You must have seen the inside of the package."

"I saw the inside all right. Well, not exactly the inside. But I didn't even know there *was* an inside, you dillweed. Why didn't you tell me?"

"Cliff, this isn't a secure line, but I guarantee you did nothing wrong. Believe me. It's best you didn't see what was inside. I'm not even sure what was there."

"Oren, this is seriously straining our friendship."

"Look, I'll make some calls from my end, see if I can track down Arnot. Call me again tomorrow if you like, I'll see what I can find. *Kapische?*"

"What choice do I have?"

"That's what I like to hear. You know, man, you should go around and check on him again. Leaving his mail untouched like that . . . well, he's usually a bit more cautious."

"Great. You got me involved with a real piece of cake here, pal o' mine."

"Catch you later, Cliff. I'm late for a meeting."

Click.

Everybody was suddenly in a hurry to get away from me. And all I did was go on vacation.

So I went to the museum.

In the Louvre I found the *Mona Lisa* displayed in a glass case hung high enough to be visible over a sea of heads. The mass of humanity milling about the large gallery made me think of Ellis Island and what it must have been like during the great waves of immigration. Certainly everyone here was either tired, poor, sick or huddled. A sign in many languages proclaimed that flash photography was strictly prohibited, yet there they were, the usual assholes for whom the rules weren't written, flashing mindlessly away, only to be confounded by a nifty little device that made the glass-enclosed painting disappear in the dark with each "pop." A neat little tweak on the nose from the French. I wondered how many of the gawkers really cared about the painting, or for that matter how many even knew what it was. I longed to hear Nat King Cole.

Lunch was a snack from a vendor in the Tuileries. The cold weather had broken to create a nice warm autumn day, so the park was full of people. Americans, mostly, which was getting depressing. Were there no French in France? Everywhere I went Americans of every make and model shouted, grabbed, rushed, cut off, moved arrogantly or claimed blind ignorance, caring not for local custom. And it wasn't only in the park, it was everywhere I'd been, aside from the sex club, which most Americans wouldn't understand anyway. The English, perhaps, but certainly not the Americans.

I was getting worried. I mean, how could one study life among foreigners if one couldn't find any?

At any rate, here in the park I did find a few Americans remotely respectful of the customary peace and serenity. They were college students traveling alone, more interested in reading a travel guide or classic novel than yelling, "Come on, Bertha, for Christ's sake. I gotta take a *pissoir.*" Conversely, the "safety in numbers" theory made groups of tour-package Yanks boorish by comparison, and I felt like a leper just to look like them.

There was a tiny, cement pond around which I noticed a number of children sailing wooden boats across the glasslike water. Some foreigners with cameras took their pictures. What the hell, I did too. I mean, it looked like the kind of thing that'd make a great enlargement when I got back home. . . .

Then it crossed my mind: Is this what's happened to the contemporary American traveler? Have we been reduced to reading books, seeing the land through viewfinders, getting our foreign experiences second hand? Have we become voyeurs, unable to create, enjoy, experience directly for ourselves? Is there something in our collective cultural psyche that's altered our ability to really live? To act? To do? I couldn't finger it, but there was something about being in that park on that particular afternoon, with the air smelling of garlic and cigarettes, with its manicured lawns, the sun warming my hair, the muffled sounds of children at play on the dusty plazas, that made me reaffirm my desire to boldly go where no man had gone before.

There was, of course, last night's sex club. But I doubted I could spend my days and nights in satyric bliss. Sure, I was titillated—who could help it?—but the effect wore off as the kink got questionable. The quest to reaffirm life and find excitement and adventure didn't mean just sex, did it?

Did it?

Ahem. So there I was, confused, alone, cut off from friends back home. I gulped down the last of a canned Orangina and looked forward to the day's events. I knew I had to go with the flow for a while . . . even if I did hate that expression.

"I'm here to see Josephine Lavant. She's expecting me."

"Sorry monsieur, no visitors."

"But—"

"No buts. This is a closed shoot."

"If you just tell—"

"She's busy, in conference, getting ready to shoot."

"I'll just wait over—"

"You can't. The whole area is closed."

"Then what am I supposed to—"

The burly guard looked me over and decided he didn't like what he saw. "If Mademoiselle Lavant wishes to see you, she will get in touch."

"But she doesn't know how to contact me."

This must have confirmed whatever suspicions the guard held. "Of course, monsieur. Now please leave before I am forced to call the police."

I scribbled my name and address on a piece of paper and handed it to the guard. He pocketed it without reading it. He was about to close the door when behind him in a large, airy, predominantly white studio I saw a group of people swarm toward an area surrounded by stage lights. At the eye of the swarm was Josephine. I shouted her name, but the swarm was buzzing loudly about whatever was keeping them employed, so she didn't hear. The guard shut the door, and everything became silent.

Back at my hotel the concierge was nowhere to be found, so I reached over the counter at the front desk to take my room key from the row of hooks. Up three flights I opened my door and was surprised to see two cheerless men quietly going through my things. One who wore a gendarme's uniform was fingering beneath the furniture, while the other, more officious-looking individual in a trench coat (naturally) sat idly leafing the pages of my journal.

"*Bonjour,* Monsieur Dandridge. Pardon our little search, but we thought you would not mind."

In New York I would have asked these gentlemen to get the fuck out before I screamed. In New York they would have then beaten the shit out of me. I had no idea how these things went in Paris.

"Find what you were looking for?" I finally asked.

"We are not looking for anything in particular."

"I see."

"Just some things that would help solve a mystery."

"If your friend in the monkey suit keeps looking under that desk, I'm afraid all he's going to find is yesterday's gum and some week-old snot I put there for safekeeping." The gendarme in blue immediately removed his hand. So at least he understood English.

"Allow me to introduce myself. I am Inspector Lonsdale of the Paris police. My associate is Swaim."

"Lonsdale and Swaim of the Paris police," I said to myself. It sounded like a cough syrup.

Lonsdale removed a manila envelope from beneath a hidden pouch inside his trench coat and pulled out a few black-and-white photographs.

"Would you mind?" he said, handing me one.

In the first photo I saw a man. Actually, two sides of a man, with a serial number below each view. The man was Raphael Arnot.

"Recognize him?"

I played cute. "Should I?"

Lonsdale handed me another photo. In this one I could see the alley and front door to Arnot's apartment. I could also see myself.

"I guess I should."

"What business do you have with Raphael Arnot?"

"Am I in trouble or under suspicion or anything insidious like that?"

"What do you think?"

"I think I should probably talk to the American Embassy. I'm not sure of my rights."

"Monsieur Dandridge, you are a guest in our country. You have all the rights and privileges of anyone. Now, if you feel however that you have done something to merit the displeasure of the French Government, well, that is most certainly another story. Your hesitancy to cooperate with simple routine questions, I must admit, does lead me to suspect you have something to hide, which causes me enormous displeasure. After all, here I was, looking forward to an intelligent exchange of views and observations with a distinguished American writer."

"How do you know I'm a writer?" He held up my journal. "Ah," I said, sitting down.

"Now, do you recognize the man in the photograph?"

"Yeah, it's me."

"That's correct, but I mean the other one."

"I met him once."

"Raphael Arnot is his name, am I correct?"

"You must know better than me if that's his name."

Lonsdale's eyes lit up. "I see. Is there some reason you have for suspecting that is not his name?"

"Look, I'm really uncomfortable talking without a lawyer. I mean, yeah, I met the guy, but if that's going to get me in trouble, I should have some legal help here."

"You disappoint me, Monsieur Dandridge. But, as I see from your passport"—he snapped his fingers and Swaim produced my passport—"you are a native New Yorker. I suppose you are naturally suspicious and paranoid."

"It's in our water."

"I shall remember that."

Lonsdale handed me another picture, this one of a tall black man with dreadlocks, standing in front of Arnot's door. In his hand was a tiny white plastic bag wrapped in tape. This must have been the guy Arnot gave whatever was inside one of the cornices.

"Recognize this man?" asked Lonsdale, pulling out a pack of Gitanes.

"Sorry."

"Sorry you don't recognize him, or sorry you won't tell me?"

"Sorry, but you can't smoke in my room."

Lonsdale looked at me with daggers. He gently tapped out a cigarette, stuck it in his mouth, produced a disposable lighter and clicked. Nothing happened. "You would not happen to have a match, would you?" he asked.

I tapped my various pockets in mock helplessness, and was surprised to see that I did, in fact, have a pack of matches in my tweed pocket. How'd that get there? Must have collected it from some restaurant God knew when.

I removed the matchbook and held it.

Lonsdale looked at me, his Gitane sticking limply out of his mouth. "We here in France are not as neurotic as you Americans about smoking. Here it is still popular."

"That must explain something," I said, "but I'm not sure what." I looked at the matchbook. It was from a restaurant in New York I'd never heard of, certainly never been to. The Augsburg House. I opened the cover to light the match and inside saw some handwritten words: "The man in the sand with the plan is at hand."

Huh?

I closed the cover, struck the match, lit Lonsdale's cigarette and quickly stuffed the matchbook in my pocket.

The inspector took a deep drag on his cigarette and puffed out enough smoke to clog Los Angeles for a year. If nothing else my room at least now smelled more authentic.

"Where were we?" said Lonsdale.

"You were showing me your picture collection."

"Ah yes," he said, handing me a fourth photo. This one was also of Raphael Arnot, only this time Arnot was lying face down on a concrete pavement, a dark liquid puddled beside his head. My background in television led me immediately to suspect that Arnot was history.

"When did this happen?"

"Are you certain you wish to know?"

I looked at Lonsdale in silence. He puffed and said, "We found his body this morning behind a kiosk in the Bois de Boulogne."

"And you think I know about this?"

Lonsdale flipped open a small notebook. I mean he really did the *Columbo* routine well, whether he knew it or not. "We know Arnot had many friends and many enemies. A few days ago you suddenly show up at his flat, another man comes and picks up a package. You and Arnot leave for dinner, then Arnot disappears. Aside from the mailman, you are the only one who keeps coming back looking for him." He hands me a few other photos. In each one it's either the mailman dropping off envelopes, or me banging on his door. There's also a picture of Josephine kissing me, but the lighting is poor, and it's impossible to make out Josephine's face. "Why did you keep going back?"

Jesus H. Christ. Or Jesus F. Christ, if you prefer. What did I get myself into? "I went back to see if he'd stolen money from my wallet."

"And what makes you think he would have done that?"

"Because money from my wallet was stolen."

"And why did you not report that to the police?"

"Because I was sure he had taken it."

"Why?"

"Because I . . ." Was I going to tell this cop Arnot drugged me? No thank you. "I fell asleep on his sofa for a few hours, and later that night, after not having been with anyone else, found my wallet was empty."

That seemed to satisfy Lonsdale. He quickly jotted down some notes in his pad.

The telephone rang. Lonsdale nodded his permission for me to get it. "Hello?"

"Do not say anything, just listen." It was Anne. "Be casual. Pretend I am your girl friend."

I suddenly found it difficult to breathe. "Hey Danette, how are you?" I hoped I didn't sound phony. I always hate when bad actors overemphasize their lies and think the person they're lying in front of doesn't see through it. It's usually the sign of poor screenwriting, poor direction or poor acting.

"Listen to me, Cliff. I am still in Paris, but so are our friends."

"That's great," I said, smiling into the phone. "I've got some friends here, now, too."

"I know. Cooperate fully with the police, but tell them nothing about me."

"Of course I will, you know that. But listen honey, I think I found what you were looking for."

"Can you be more specific?"

"Remember what you wanted to get for *Uncle Eli* . . . Well, I found it right here in Paris!"

A pause. "I understand. That is truly wonderful. We must meet as soon as possible."

"That would be nice. We could—"

"Do not say a thing. I will find you."

Click.

"Good-bye my sweet," I said into the dead phone, "I miss you, too."

"Your girl friend from home?" asked Lonsdale, stubbing out his cigarette. He let out a deep, guttural cough, and spit into a tissue.

"Yes."

"What about? . . ." Still holding the spit-filled tissue, he casually tapped with his knuckles the picture of Josephine kissing me in the shadows. I wanted to say to Lonsdale "We're both men of the world, right?" but thankfully resisted the urge.

"Just a friend," I said finally.

Lonsdale tossed the tissue in the garbage, stood up and collected his photos. "Thank you for your time and cooperation, Monsieur Dandridge. You have been most generous considering we surprised you." He and Swaim moved to the door. "I suggest you do not leave Paris until we meet again."

"I'll count the minutes."

"See that you do," he said, closing the door.

"Rick, I think I need a lawyer."

"What'd you do, get arrested in a raid on a whorehouse?"

That Rick, what a kidder.

"I met someone and that someone is now dead."

"I've known you fifteen years and I'm still alive, I promise they haven't got a case."

"One of Oren's friends. Remember he asked me to drop something off in Paris? Well, I think what I dropped off might get me in trouble."

Rick suddenly got serious. "Where you calling from?"

"A payphone near the Luxembourg Gardens. I was afraid the police already tapped my phone."

"Good thinking."

"Sometimes it pays to be paranoid. Especially when people are after you."

"You writing all this down, Cliff."

"Come on Rick, what about a lawyer?"

"I'll look into it as soon as we get off. When I find out anything, I'll call and leave a message, then you call me back from a safe phone."

"I appreciate it."

"I'll also try and find Oren. Maybe he can tell me more about this friend of his, and the package."

"That'd be great."

"Damn straight that'd be great. There's a Cartier-Bresson photo exhibit opening at the Met today I wanted to go see."

"I'm deeply touched."

"I know. By the way, you missed a great game."

"You went?"

"Yeah, the weather was terrific and the Jets won."

"So you got a desperate woman to consent to go with you?"

"Sure as shit did. A real desperate woman. What? . . . Oh great, great! Get that asshole in here now."

"Rick, you're talking to yourself again."

"What? Oh, sorry Cliff. Something's screwed here. Some junior nobody just fucked the pharmaceutical case I've been working on. Gotta go. I'll call you ASAP."

"That's a funny thing to call a person," I said, but all I heard was: CLICK.

Things sure were taking an odd turn. I didn't feel like killing time in my room, and if Anne wanted me, well, she'd have to scour Paris. I turned into the Gardens and took a seat on a sandy terrace overlooking a fountain facing the Luxembourg

Palace, a gorgeous seventeenth-century structure my Guide
Michelin informed me was the seat of the French Senate. I took
out my Graham Greene and began reading, but I kept looking
at the pages and the words kept blurring. After the forth scan
I realized I hadn't retained an iota of what I read.

Back at my café off Place Saint Michel I employed a little
local arrogance and, leaning back in my seat, arm over a
chair, another waiter, not "mine," came over and took my
order. I remembered to say *"s'il vous plait"* with enough of an
attitude to make me seem, if not less foreign, at least more
worldly.

Unfortunately, a huge bus pulled over and unloaded a gaggle
of tour-package Americans, their plastic-covered name tags
displayed chest-high with pride. I quickly finished, paid and
left.

I entered my hotel lobby and noticed that the concierge was
looking at me with renewed respect. Or was it fear? After all,
I'd been paid a visit only this morning by members of the local
constabulary. Come to think of it, maybe the concierge was
wishing I'd vacate posthaste?

But he was too polite to say so and merely handed me my
key.

Paranoia had now become my standard operating mode, so
I slowly opened the door. Silence. The tiny room yawned at me.
I closed the door and went to the window, but there was a
familiar scent in the air, and I wasn't the least surprised when
the bathroom door creaked open and dirty-blond Anne walked
out.

"Bonjour," she said.

"We've got to stop meeting like this." I sat on the bed. "You
know, I've been waiting all my life for a situation to say that."

"Where is it?"

"Hold the phone. No hello, how are you, nice to see you,
Cliff? Don't they teach manners at spy school?"

"You are still convinced I am spy?"

"You leave me no choice, hiding in bathrooms, making cryptic phone calls."

"I see." She looked around the room and decided to sit on the desk chair, which she pulled closer to the bed. "Cliff, we have no time to play games. I can plainly see you are fine."

"But what about the emotional scars. I mean, you left me there all alone at the airport . . ."

She was in no mood for games. "I am in no mood for games. People's lives are at stake. Whole political systems are threatened. Now where is that message?"

I produced the matchbook and gave it to her. She looked at me, confused. I took it back and opened it so she could read the inscription.

She read aloud: " 'The man in the sand with the plan is at hand.' " She looked up. "I do not understand."

"Huh?"

"It makes no sense."

"But it *is* authentic?" I asked, hoping it was. I mean I was involved here, people were chasing me—for one reason or another, actually I lost count who and why—and the notion that I might not really have the correct information and therefore not merit genuine involvement made me feel empty. I didn't want that—I wanted to be involved.

"It *looks* authentic. The Augsburg is a restaurant popular with those people. And the handwriting looks familiar, though we will have to have it analyzed."

"There you go with the *we* again. Don't I deserve a little biscuit, I mean, since I gave you what you were after?"

"Where did you find this?" She wasn't going to be pushed.

I explained how I had found it in my sportsjacket, the same jacket I'd worn that day at the museum, and that Eli Sternberg must have slipped it into my pocket with his last dying gasps. I remembered that he said, "Aaahhs," and dragged both his hands down my side right before he gave up the ghost. Since my travel plans unfolded so unexpectedly, I didn't have time to send it to the cleaners, and that's why it still was there.

"Remarkable. We are remarkably lucky." She reached over and touched my hand. That skin. And that scent. I'd have to get the name of that soap. I thought: here we are, alone in my room. Night was falling. It was Paris. She looked gorgeous. I hadn't had relations since arriving. . . .

She looked at me: I hope I wore the right gaze. She smiled, touched the side of my face. "It was very noble of you to tell me you found this. You did not have to. You could have thrown it out and be done with us."

"Then I wouldn't have seen you again," I said with all the sincerity my quickening pulse rate could muster.

She leaned over and gave me a "How kind you are, thank you" kiss. Her lips were full and wet, my nose pressed into her skin as our mouths pushed together. I parted my lips but was met with a row of clenched incisors. Hmm? I reached to hug her, to bring her close, when I felt her back muscles tense and pull away.

"Don't."

"Why?"

But I never found out because the door to my room opened and there was Josephine, a bemused look on her face, one hand on her hip, the other holding a shopping bag full of packages.

"*Pardon,* monsieur," she said as she turned and closed the door.

"Josephine," I shouted. All at once Anne was standing, smoothing her clothes. Her face was flushed. Did I see disappointment? Should I have been more forceful?

"I am sorry," she said finally.

I felt like an ass. I didn't know who I wanted more. Yes I did, I think, but . . .

"Do not leave Paris until we meet again, Cliff. I had no idea you were expecting someone. I thought . . . I suppose I must have misread . . . never mind." She gathered her purse, said, "But thank you," and left. I watched from my window as she briskly left the hotel and disappeared around a corner.

Josephine was waiting for me at the café on Place Saint Michel. The busload of Americans had left, and Claude was now on duty. I must have seemed preoccupied, because he chose to avoid my eyes.

"I am so sorry, Cliff. I was rude." Josephine didn't seemed bothered, it was more a case of her feeling embarrassed for intruding.

"Josephine, that was—"

"Really, there is no need. It's none of my business. I never asked if you had a girl friend."

"I do."

"Well, she was very pretty."

"That wasn't my girl friend."

"Oh. Well, good for you. I am glad to see you taking advantage of French culture."

"She's not French. At least I don't think so. Actually we only met back in New York a few days ago, then she happened to be on the same plane I took coming over, and, well, you know." This was really uncomfortable.

But Josephine was now laughing.

"Now what?" I said, trying not to join in.

"Cliff, really, do not explain. I have many friends, too." I assumed she meant more than canasta partners. "Men, women, what does it matter? My philosophy has always been to enjoy life. So really, there is no need to say a thing further. I like you. I am attracted to you. I hope we can have a good time together for as long as you are here."

"That's very French of you" was all I could come up with. Obviously it was enough because she rubbed the tip of her nose against mine, smiled widely with her eyes, and gave me a big, sloppy wet one. The playfulness was back, and the night looked promising.

She took me to a cramped apartment over an art gallery nearby. We climbed a rickety wooden staircase that hugged alongside the outer wall of an old, ramshackle three-story building. At the top of the stairs a narrow balcony led toward a party, which I knew was a party by the fact so many people were leaning over the balustrade smoking and drinking and kissing and puking.

Everyone knew Josephine. Her tall boyish-looking brunet friend, Olga the hedonist, was smoking dope with three other equally attractive hermaphrodites. We climbed our way through a crowded entrance into a smoky room, humid and close and stinking of beer. The walls were covered with enormous old tapestries, but I couldn't make out any furniture since people were sitting on everything—tables, chairs, bookshelves. The music, mostly loud, mostly American, was hard to hear because someone had cranked it to distortion. Overall the party felt collegiate, though there were people older than both Josephine and myself and the attitude was bohemian: very avant-garde, very drunk. Someone put on "Shout" from the *Animal House* soundtrack and everyone started dancing, rocking the wooden floor to the point where the building felt like it was going to collapse. When "Otis" got to the part where he sang "a little bit softer now, a little bit softer now," everyone got smaller and smaller until they were all crawling on the floor and each other. The song got louder and everyone jumped up, arms flailing. Though they probably didn't understand the words, everyone felt the energy of the music and bopped along accordingly, shouting at the top of their lungs. And I thought: I must cry now, or die. Because at last I had found my way to a real French party and all they could do was play American music from the sixties.

I ended up around a lace-covered oak table, watching as a group of Parisian Yuppies sat numbly drinking from a single vodka bottle. By now it was probably more spit than vodka, but the social thing would not have been to pass it without sipping. Josephine, however, immediately produced a fresh bottle from her shopping bag and offered me first taste. How kind. She introduced me as a famous American stockbroker, said we were engaged to be married at dawn, that I spoke not a word of French. This seemed fine with everyone, and I marveled at how they suddenly struggled with English for my benefit. Some things came out sounding like, "I really distinguish your American helicopter shoes," but it was the effort that counted. We passed the vodka and drank some more. I wondered: Didn't anyone in France drink wine? Or was that left to Miou-Miou and Gerard Depardieu in films exported to the States? There were some beers I recognized from back home, so I avoided those. A Quaalude or two appeared out of thin air.

The vodka in my system made me ask, "Has anyone ever really seen Catherine Deneuve, or is she a science fiction special effect?"

Ooh boy.

There followed a long, detailed discussion of the French film industry, and I was suddenly disgusted to realize most people here were in show business. In fact, they were so sick of show business themselves they were glad to know I was a stockbroker. Whoopee! They all wished they were doing something else. The talk became theoretical, I don't remember exactly why, with words like "festival" and "verite" and "Spielberg" tossed around, then someone shouted "Jerry Lewis" and the whole party, on cue, stopped and made a collective fart. It was as close to poetry as life gets. I found it far funnier than it actually was, and laughed myself silly. Everyone joined in, until one waiflike girl with a pageboy haircut who'd been smoking Marlboros started crying. I asked her why, and she responded in French.

Josephine translated. "She says she doesn't think we have the right to laugh when there is so much hate in the world." Heavy. Deep. Spiritual, too. I asked Josephine to apologize for me.

The party was thinning, as were the watered-down remnants of whatever alcohol could be found. Josephine and I were entwined on the sofa like a game of Twister, which I mentioned but gave up trying to explain. A few older people were sitting on the carpet at our feet, and Josephine began discussing an old friend named Zelda. Zelda, it seems, had gone off to a Swiss sanitarium to recuperate from great emotional instability. This, explained Josephine, following a failed suicide attempt brought on by immense career frustration. She'd been struggling without success for quite some time and was continually upset at her own inability to break through. She had seen her friends get that initial lucky break and was happy for them, but bitterness filled her soul, she'd lost *perspective*—Josephine verbally underlined that word—and slit her wrists. Luckily she, Josephine, found her in time and rushed her to the hospital. Josephine was surprised to see that the on-call doctor recognized Zelda. It seemed she had tried to kill herself several times before, a fact Josephine never even knew. Now Zelda was going to be recuperating for a long, long time.

"What kind of career was she struggling at?" I asked.

"She was trying to be a writer," said Josephine.

The party soon got boring.

"I paid for my room so we might as well go there."

"You are just afraid there will be more people at my place."

"I *would* like to be alone with you for a while."

"I think that would be nice." She was holding a champagne bottle—the last package in her shopping bag—and I had carefully stolen two plastic glasses from the party. It was the first truly illegal thing I'd consciously done this trip. Perhaps I was finally on the road to degradation. . . .

The streets of the quarter were empty and quiet and wet from a torrential downpour that must have erupted while we were all farting over Jerry Lewis. I took Josephine's hand and swung it back and forth, like Gene Kelly would have done. I started singing an old show tune. Josephine looked at me, so I stopped.

"No, please, continue."

"You like the way I sing?"

"You have a terrible voice, like a frog. But you look so happy."

"I am happy. Grrribbittt." I kissed her.

Upstairs, we undressed each other slowly, savoring each new glimpse of various body parts. Arms, thighs, chests, etcetera. I saw she had terrific muscle tone, as she moved around the room with catlike precision. We stood up against each other's nude bodies, pressing close together from top to bottom as if forcing ourselves to merge, to be one. Her skin felt firm against mine. I kissed her neck, her breasts, licking my way all over her deliciously smooth body. I grabbed her rear and suddenly dug my fingers in the round, warm flesh, pulling her still closer as I moved lower and lower, my tongue doing a wild dance on her most sensitive area. This unleashed in her some pent-up power, and soon we were thrashing all over.

And I thought: am I happy?

I wasn't sure.

I knew I was enjoying myself. I was certainly sweating like a madman. We were working each other over and over, slow and sensual one minute, rough and erotic the next—and once again my mind started drifting.

Goddamnit, no! Can't I have a simple, pleasurable sexual experience without thinking of something else?

But the answer was a resounding negatory, for as the moment of penetration approached, images of New York magazine were back swirling through my head: "AIDS—Absolutely Everything You Should Know," "A Guide to Monogamy on the Yupper West Side," "Sexual Diseases and Work-Related Stress." AIIEEE!!!

"AIIEEE," shrieked Josephine.

"What?"

"AIIEEE!"

I thought I'd only thought that, but I guess I must've shrieked out loud. At any rate, Josephine was sure game for anything.

"I think we'll have to stop," I said.

"Don't worry." She leaned over and fumbled through the clothes on the floor to find her purse. She opened it and removed a brand-new pack of poppa stoppers, opened one with far more skill than I'd ever been able to, and proceeded to make it part of the sex act, as she worked to put it on me.

Oh, those French women, skilled in every aspect of lovemaking. It's enough to make a New Yorker give up lox and bagels on Sunday.

In the morning Josephine playfully refused to let me leave (was she going to imprison me as her sex slave?) as she went out to get ingredients for breakfast. I stood at her balcony window to watch her disappear up the boulevard, and almost choked on my tongue when I saw the two goons who'd chased me onto the plane at Kennedy stalking across the way.

I slunk back to the side, wondering what to do. Could they have tracked me down? Could Josephine have set me up? Could she be involved in whatever was going on?

I slid back over and peeked through the curtains . . .

And whoever I thought was there, was gone.

NINE

Over the next two weeks Josephine and I got to know each other better, though while we could talk endlessly for hours, we never really revealed any deep dark truths. True, I was mentally preoccupied with Anne, the matchbook, the special phrase, Arnot, the Paris Police, kinky sex clubs and the two goons I knew were still out there after me, but I nevertheless tried to appear carefree.

Sure . . .

Anyway, re: Josephine—I suppose if I'd had on my junior spy thinking cap I could have figured out what was on her mind or in her background simply by studying what remained unsaid, but that would have been sick and would have destroyed the time we spent walking in parks, listening to street minstrels and indulging our appetites. We even celebrated American Thanksgiving in a Vietnamese Restaurant.

I did learn she was legitimately involved in the fashion business as an art director for a freelance photographer. She dressed sets, selected backgrounds, even worked with clothing manufacturers and retail outlets designing ads. When she spoke of her work, which she did only reluctantly, it was with enormous pride and the air of the utterly confident. Success breeds confidence, and Josephine Lavant had both in full.

"But do you ever dream of doing anything else?" I asked one

foggy afternoon while we were sitting on stools on the Ile de la Grande Jatte. I hadn't given up researching my themes for *A Lost Generation,* even if I no longer thought there was one.

"Of course. But I don't dwell on them. What's the point? I live them. I want to have fun, meet new people, spend nights as an adventuress, I simply do."

I digested this. "It's not always simple, doing exactly what you want."

"No. But you must never stop trying. Otherwise you die."

Like I said, confidence.

"Danette, I miss you."

"You do?"

"Uh huh." We kissed transatlantically.

"You getting enough work done?"

"Journal's filling nicely."

"That's good."

"But there's too many Americans here, too much American influence. There's a McDonald's on the Champs Elysee, Michael Jackson and Bruce Springsteen posters on the metro, and everyone drinks Coke."

"I'm sorry."

"Me, too."

There was a long pause.

"See any famous sights?"

Is this all we had to discuss?

"The Louvre, the Eiffel Tower, I saw Napoleon's tomb, too, which was pretty incredible."

"That's good."

"Yeah."

"So . . . meet any nice people?"

"Not too many. Some folks in the film business. They're all sick of their jobs, too. I also discovered that not all French like Jerry Lewis."

"That's nice."

"Yeah." That the strain was obvious and mutual here was the only thing alleviating my guilt. There was no point mentioning Josephine.

"So, how's life in New York?"

"It's fine, okay. Busy at work. Wall Street's usual mood swings. Last weekend I—Cliff, I miss you. I can't help saying it."

"It's okay, I miss you too."

"But I want you to enjoy yourself." Like she was reading off cue cards. "Think about what we discussed and where our future might go, but don't feel pressured."

Yeah, right.

"Look," I said, "we'll talk again soon. I'll call you over the weekend, when the rates go down."

"That'll be great," she said, hesitating. "I may not be home till late Saturday, though, and Sunday, if it's nice, I—"

"We'll talk, don't worry."

"Okay. Cliff, I . . ."

"Yes?"

"Never mind. Are you sure you miss me?"

"Ah huh."

"Then say it."

"I miss you."

Silence.

"Well . . . bye," I said.

"Bye," said Danette.

Click.

I called Sam Tardibul three times because I knew he never returned his messages. Gerdy was back, sounding weak with a sour note in her voice, as if answering the phone was doing the world a big favor.

Sam said he was thinking of running off with Wendy but wasn't sure if she felt likewise. He said things were looking up on the book deal, and other gigs were still stewing. The series in LA was getting better all the time. In fact, he thought I may have to cut my trip short and head west on a moment's notice.

"I'll worry about it," I said. He knew I wouldn't.

"Oh, 'fore I forget"—I could see him panning through clutter looking for yellow stick-'em notes—"this editor named Brisketsomething or Fisketsomething, I don't know . . . anyway, he's got a hot new book by one of those kid novelists from Swarthmore or Yale or Dewitt Clinton and thinks you'd be perfect to adapt it."

"What's it about?"

"I haven't read the reader's report yet."

"Right."

"Call me tomorrow, Cliffie, tomorrow the latest. I think we're close."

Autumn in Paris was waning as I spent more time on the phone. Oren said he hadn't been able to reach Arnot, so I broke the news to him that I'd seen a picture of Arnot quite dead. Stunned, Oren said I should henceforth avoid being seen in the Marais. Arnot's death was not a good sign. This information wasn't comforting, and the joys of the past few days quickly vanished from my mind. Fortunately the goons hadn't resurfaced and Inspector Lonsdale hadn't come a-calling. Rick was still finding me a lawyer, "just in case," so I consoled myself with Josephine.

She returned with me to Maison Victor Hugo on a day it was open. She said the only time she ever saw any of Paris's famous sights was when she went with out-of-towners.

Hugo's house was a letdown. There's not much thrill seeing the desk of a dead person. There were assorted clippings in glass cases and a collection of international editions of *Les Misérables* and *The Hunchback of Notre Dame,* along with some sketches made by the author himself.

Would anyone ever care what doodles I made? Did anyone really care what doodles Hugo made?

We stopped for lunch at a bistro along Rue Saint Antoine and watched the bustling power-ties-and-pearls crowd fight for space along the inner counter. I thought: just like home. Over cold beers and a shared plate of coldcuts, Josephine asked me about Danette.

"Do you love her?"

"Do you really want to discuss this?"

"I did ask."

"I think so."

"But you are not sure?"

"Is anyone really ever sure 'bout that?"

"Oh yes, I think. Though being in love and loving someone are completely different."

"Are all French women so philosophical?"

"This is the country of Flaubert, Rousseau and Sartre, monsieur. It is part of our national identity." She smiled. She enjoyed messing with my head. "But I am curious. You will marry her?"

"Look, I don't know. Do we really have to talk about—"

"A difficult subject for you, I see."

"No, it's not. Yes, I guess it is."

"So you came to Europe to think it through?"

"I feel like I'm talking to a shrink."

"A what?"

"A therapist, a psychiatrist, a head-doctor."

"I see. I'm just good enough to fuck but not talk to, is that it?" She was pissed.

"No, not at all." I took her hand. It was wet and cold from the beer glass. "It's just I'm confused enough on my own, why should we waste our time together discussing it?"

"Talking is a waste?"

"I didn't mean—"

"Cliff, I want to know you better. I like you very much, but I am under no illusions. You will go home, you will go on with your life, I will go on with mine, and that will be that. No emotional commitments. Yet there is no reason we cannot care about each other here and now."

I finished my beer and ordered another. Ah beer, the Fuel of Life. "That's true," I said. "But you make it sound so one-sided, like I'm just another tourist taking advantage of yet another foreign romance."

"You think that? You think it is so one-sided? Have you not given thought that maybe I am taking advantage of you? That maybe I never meet anyone nice from your country and that being with you is something I want to do, on my own, for my own selfish reasons?"

She was right, of course. My attitude toward this kind of thing had been formed years ago, from books, movies, not personal experience. For me this was altogether new, but the mutuality of this affair was illuminating. "I'm sorry," I said at last.

"After all, there is something exotic about sex with an American." I had a feeling she didn't mean it to sound so coarse.

"I'm sorry."

"I just think I will be sad to see you go."

"Me, too."

She shivered, cut a slice of ham and forked it. "I don't want to talk about this anymore."

"You brought it up."

She swallowed the ham and drank more beer. For a moment she turned away, ostensibly to look at the crowd, but I was sure she was trying to hide. When she turned back the moment had passed and she smiled again, but the feeling, the unsaid emotion, remained, and I knew it would pervade everything between us.

I paid and we left. Then at the precise moment that I was wondering whether I should have taken Oren's advice and not set foot in the Marais, there was a commotion ahead in the sidewalk traffic. The crowd heading back to work parted, and down the street, perhaps thirty feet away, two men were moving toward us. These were not ordinary men, no siree. These were the same U.S. Government agents I'd seen at the American Indian restaurant and Kennedy Airport and outside Josephine's building. So they *had* found me—this time I was sure. (Of course, by constantly returning to the same neighborhood and having a run-in with the local police, even an amateur flatfoot would have enough clues.)

"Come on." I yanked Josephine's arm and we raced through the crowd, dodging like skiers. The Two Goons struggled behind, pushing people out of their way.

"Cliff, what is wrong?"

"You didn't set this up?" I barked.

"What are you talking about?"

"I'll explain, just come on!"

At a pedestrian crossing *L'homme rouge* flashed and we stopped to let the cars flow past. The goons were getting close, so I pulled Josephine and we zigzagged through traffic, horns honking and brakes skidding as we made it across. I didn't turn back as we kept running, looking for an alley to escape down or a building to get lost in. Unfortunately all the buildings in this neighborhood were low, squat and decidedly unwelcoming. There was no choice but to go into the metro.

Downstairs we quickly bought our tickets and ran toward the platforms. But which way to go? There were three different lines converging there.

Josephine saw my confusion. "This way." I followed as we ran to the number Five, which ran north and south.

"Now what?"

She chose south. We didn't have to linger on the platform since the ever-prompt metro pulled right in. I just hoped the Two Goons didn't see which way we went.

We huddled together at one end of the empty car.

Josephine whispered, "What the hell is going on?"

"Do you trust me?"

"What?"

"Do you trust me?"

Her expression could best be described as insane confusion.

"Never mind. Listen, those men are either U.S. agents who think I know something about the death of a former Nazi hunter, or they're men who think I'm connected with a secret spy organization, or they're men who think I've smuggled something illegal into France, or they're men who want to kill me for fun."

The insane look got worse.

"You don't believe me. I even saw them two weeks ago outside your flat."

This caught her off guard, but she recovered. "Cliff, I believe you. Even if I don't understand. But don't worry. I am on your side. We will lose them."

At the next station I stuck my head out to look up and down the platform to see if the goons were on board, and saw nothing. Big deal. The train pulled out and whisked off toward Gare d'Austerlitz. There, Josephine took control and led us beneath the depot that catered to travelers heading to and from Spain, the Cote d'Azur, Switzerland and Italy. We snaked our way through the maze of interconnecting tunnels and changed to the Regional Express Network. A number C7 heading toward Saint Quentin-En-Yvelines pulled in and we ran to the front. Just as we boarded I looked back to see the Two Goons emerging from the tunnel. Damn! Even as the doors were closing I could see them hop aboard the car all the way in the back.

There was no way to move from car to car during the ride without incurring the wrath of the RER authorities or damaging the train, so we were temporarily safe.

I didn't want Josephine caught up in this any further and said so. Amazingly, she was neither afraid nor exhausted. In fact, she seemed invigorated by the whole experience.

At Saint Michel a huge crowd (Americans, Germans, Italians, South Africans) swelled aboard. I turned out to see the goons moving forward, struggling through the platform traffic.

I spoke quickly. "I want you to get out and meet me at the café. If I'm not there by eleven, I'll call you at home tomorrow. Now don't argue, just go."

She wanted to speak, but before she could I kissed her and forcibly pushed her onto the platform. The doors closed and she disappeared from view as the train pulled away.

Two more stops passed quickly, and at each I resisted the urge to look out and see if the goons were moving closer. It occurred to me how ridiculous this was, that I was being chased across two continents by U.S. Government agents.

Were they, in fact, government agents? Maybe yes, maybe no. I had no real way of knowing. Suppose yes, what did they want from me? Maybe they weren't hostile? Had they ever actually shot at me? Maybe they were trying to warn me? In fact, maybe they were trying to warn me against Anne?

The only way to find out would be to stop and confront them. All right smart guy, you're on a crowded train, no one's going to shoot you in front of hundreds of commuters. Let's Be Bold.

The train stopped at Invalides. I got out and boldly walked back along the platform to where I suspected the goons to be. They were gone. Had I missed them? I turned and saw that somehow we'd passed in the crowd and now they were up front looking for me. They'd obviously noticed I was gone, too, as they turned and saw me standing at the back.

I waved like a schmuck, their faces grew angry, they started to run. Those angry expressions alerted me to the fact they were probably *not* my friends, so I darted back into the car just as the doors slid shut.

I was behind them now, they knew where to get me. At the next stop I ran off and through the crowd, pushing my way through old-age pensioners and panhandling musicians, leaping up three and four steps at a time to the accompanying accordion music.

On the street I noticed a staircase across the way leading down to the quay, so I ran there, hoping they wouldn't see me.

There was a long line of tourists waiting to visit something, so I joined it, and using skills I'd honed as a moviegoer in Manhattan, edged closer to the front, disrupting as many people as I could. I smiled, feigned ignorance, but made it to the beginning. I looked to see where I was.

Well, well, well. If life were a movie, which I'm sure it is anyway, I could have been nowhere else: I was standing at the public entrance to *les egouts,* the Parisian sewers.

Ah Javert! Ah Valjean! You point the way again.

For six chapters in *Les Miserables* Victor Hugo gives a history lesson of this city beneath the city. At one crucial point in the narrative Valjean escapes the authorities, carrying the wounded Marius Pontmercy through the dark, wet, ancient system. Though all I carried was fear, this looked as fine a place as any to escape my pursuers, whom I noticed back across the Quay sniffing around for my scent.

Inside *les egouts* the stench of urban sewage reminded me Paris was not all cigarettes and garlic! A small museum documented the evolution of the vast network of tunnels and pumping stations, and streetsigns along the sewer canal walls at various intersections referred to thoroughfares above. Our tour group, prevented from taking any of the moored boats for a ride along this subterranean Venice, gathered instead to view the huge steel cables sweating from steam and the rushing waterfalls dumping treated water into enormous spillways for circulation around the city.

Security was lax so I snuck away from the tour. I stepped over a low-hanging wire and clung to the concrete wall, edging my way along a narrow pier toward a dock apparently used by sewer employees. I snuck onto a tiny rowboat, untied a rope and gently edged my way slowly down a canal, the sound of my single oar dipping into the water muffled by the thunderous echo of the sewage treatment machinery. By the time I could no longer see the dock, I felt safe from the goons.

Or was I? I mean, what did I know about the Paris sewers?

I oared more swiftly, and the sound of the treatment plant grew distant. All was silent, except for the annoying sound of water dripping down the dark stone walls, making high-pitched pings as it hit the "river." Streaks of light filtered in through overhead drainage grates, illuminating the way. Soon I was at yet another intersection, but thanks again to my rudimentary map skills I could figure out where I was. I headed along a route beneath Quai D'Orsay, hoping to find an exit. The windbreaker I had on wasn't warm enough in the damp coolness, but the effort it took to paddle—as well as my hyperventilating nervous system—worked up enough of a sweat to generate inner heat.

After rowing twenty minutes, I heard loud sounds ahead. Another treatment plant? Soon the water became rough and the current increased. My boat picked up speed so I dipped an oar to keep me from bumping into the walls. No luck. The boat smacked its side against the concrete, knocking me on my ass. There was a steep incline now, and the boat rushed forward toward the increasingly deafening roar. Bright lights suddenly blinded me, and the boat smacked rapidly back and forth between the narrowing tunnel.

Perhaps I had chosen an incorrect route?

The boat slammed back and forth until pieces of its rotting wood fell off. The noise was unbearable: I could no longer even hear the boat banging against the walls. The tunnel made a sharp turn, and I saw the boat heading directly toward a decidedly menacing device. My feet were drenched; I looked down to see I was sinking. Not *officially* captain of this vessel, I sure as shit wasn't going down with her, so with the sewage machine getting ominously closer, well—what the hell?

KER-SPLASH!

I dove into the putrid-smelling thick ooze and watched as my boat edged closer to the machine. Just as it sunk from view the mouth of the treatment device belched loudly and made a harsh grinding sound, pulling my tiny boat up out of the water on a treadmill and forcing it through sinister steel blades that mashed the wood to pulp. I watched, mesmerized, as it became nothingness. It occurred to me I could have met the same fate.

I swam to a narrow ramp and pulled myself up. No one was around so I followed red signs toward *sortie* and climbed up a rusted steel ladder toward an opening on the street.

Outside it took a few seconds for my eyes to adjust to the light. When they did I realized I was standing in front of the French Ministry of Defense. Yes, well. A few people passed by, made a few comments I assumed referred to my appearance and odor, and walked on. I looked like one of the pathetic urban homeless. In New York my appearance wouldn't have earned me a quarter.

I was dripping wet and shivering from cold, but at least I knew where I was. I turned and slowly headed east, confident at least that no one would bother me, or get too close.

TEN

There was an envelope in my mailbox, but the concierge was nowhere. I rang the front buzzer and eventually he appeared, sniffing the air and sneering.

I braved Berlitz with a grin. *"Y a-t-il des messages pour moi?"*

He snatched the envelope from the row of cubbyholes and handed it over. I nodded thanks and started off, but he stopped me, disappeared in a back room, and returned with more towels.

"Merci beaucoup," I said.

He just scooted away.

My room was a shambles. Everything was turned over. My clothes were still there, but my camera bag was gone, as were most of its contents. Even my Jets hat and the snowy New York paperweight had vanished. This could only have happened with the concierge's knowledge and approval, so Inspector Lonsdale and Officer Swaim must have been around with warrants. Christ!

I opened the envelope. "I came for you but the police had just left. Wait for my call. Anne."

Okay, Anne. I shall wait.

I took a shower, washed the ooze out of my clothes, and attempted to straighten up the room. I noticed my suitcase had also been taken. My, my, my, the French *were* thorough.

The phone rang.

"Hello?"

"Cliffie, it's Rick. Greetings and felicitations."

"Rick, great. Find any lawyers yet? I think I may need one soon."

"Glad to hear it."

"Fuck you, too. Look—hey, why do you sound so?—"

"I'm in Paris, Cliff! I bit the bullet and flew the fucking Concorde. I nearly busted a vessel watching the stewardesses, God love those cute little behinds."

"When'd you get in?"

"Few hours ago. I'm staying at some hotel near the Opera house, I can't read the name on the stationery. Real swanky place, bellboys, marble floors, hookers in the lobby. The firm's travel agent booked my whole trip yesterday, spur of the moment. I figured it'd be easier finding you a lawyer from here. Besides, I wanted to see that new art museum. I read they closed the Jeu de Paume and put the Impressionists in a train station. Can you believe?—"

"So?"

"So what? Did I find you a lawyer?"

"Did you find me a lawyer?"

"Glad you asked. Cliff, I realized I could not express the true dimension of your difficulties over transatlantic telexes with total strangers, and considering the delicate nature of all the complications and so on, not to mention the involvement of two of my friends—"

"Screw Oren."

"You're point is well taken. In any event, all things considered, to answer your question, yes, I have found you a lawyer."

"Who?"

"Me."

"No really. Who?"

"Me. Mister Excitement. Rick Partridge."

"Rick, what if they charge me with a serious crime? What do you know about French law?"

"Leave it in my hands. There's a guy at the U.S. Embassy I think I went to law school with. I'll call him and—"

"RICK YOU DUMB FUCK. THE POLICE HAVE RAN-SACKED MY HOTEL ROOM AND THE UNITED STATES HAS SENT TWO AGENTS HERE TO CHASE ME."

"Calm down, buddy boy, everything is under control. Let's meet for dinner and swap war stories. I think my dry spell is over. There's this girl at the information counter downstairs who I think likes me."

"I hope your dick turns to stone and herniates you. My life may be in danger!"

"Well if you keep shouting like that, the whole of Europe will come knocking on your door."

Grab hold of yourself, Heathcliff Dandridge. Rick is full of himself, this is no way to deal with him.

"Fine, all right, you win. Welcome to Gay Paree. Let's dine at seven. Meet me at my hotel and we'll do the Quarter."

"Fab-ola, Cliff. Just fab-ola."

Jesus.

I went out in search of a badly needed drink. I turned the corner in front of Shakespeare and Company when an arm suddenly sprung out from an alley and pulled me aside.

"Cliff, you are all right?" It was Anne.

"My heart just stopped, but I'll be fine. And you? Lovely as ever?"

"There is no time to joke. Cliff, take this and use it."

She handed me an envelope.

"You want me to write you a letter?"

"Open it."

Inside were a set of travel documents: rail ticket, air ticket, hotel voucher.

"Where am I going now?"

"Budapest."

"Thank you, I think I'll pass if it's all the same to you."

"You want to know the whole story, someone will tell you when you get there."

"Behind the Iron Curtain."

"Really, Cliff, you are not that reactionary?"

"Reactionary is my middle name, after coward and patriotic heterosexual."

"Coward you are not, that I have seen."

I didn't want to question this. It made me feel good for some odd reason. "Are you coming with me?"

"Later on I will join you. But you must please use these tickets. You will be greeted in Budapest, you can get a visa at the airport as long as you say you are on holiday."

"Am I *going* on holiday?"

"Not completely."

I pushed the documents back into her hand. "Give them to someone more needy."

"Cliff, it is too late for you to not be involved. The only way we can help you is if you go to Budapest and learn the truth."

"The truth, the whole truth and nothing but the truth?"

"You will not only be saving your life, you will also be doing the world a great service."

"Will the world know that, or is it just going to be our little secret?"

"Why are you being so difficult? All along I thought you wanted to know what is going on, who is involved, why you are being chased. Or is it that you have fallen for that woman?"

I took a deep breath. What was I to do? Josephine and I had no future together, I knew that. And here was Anne finally offering me the keys to the kingdom, information I needed, the true final dimension of my adventure. Did I keep what I'd already won, or trade it all for what was behind door number three?

"When would I leave?"

"Tonight. You take a train to Zurich and change to a flight for Budapest."

"Tonight?" Butterflies swarmed around my stomach: maybe this wasn't such a bright idea.

"There is no time to delay," she said urgently. "I assure you, this is the best course of action."

"Why the train?"

"The airports will be covered with people thinking you are going back to the States."

Sounded wrong to me, but she was the pro and was trained to know better.

"When will you arrive?" I asked.

"As soon as I can."

It dawned on me: this trip was getting expensive. I reached behind and opened my wallet. Anne grabbed my wrist.

"You are right. How foolish. You will need money. Meet me in exactly three hours at the Jardin des Plantes, in front of the monkey cage. There is a huge oak tree near the entrance on Place Valhubert. Enter the park only if you see a short yellow chalk mark on that tree. It will be my sign to you that all is okay. If you do not see the chalk, go directly to the depot and leave Paris at once."

We stood there in silence, looking at each other, she wondering if I was going to accept, me wondering whether I should. A metal boccie ball suddenly came rolling down the alley and a young boy chased in after it. He picked it up, bowed slightly to apologize for intruding, then ran off to rejoin his game.

"Well?" asked Anne.

I reached over and took the envelope.

Josephine!

I was supposed to meet her at eleven! Now there wouldn't be time. I'd have to call her tomorrow from Zurich. Shit, this was no way to leave a woman who was so kind, so generous, so much fun to be with. She'd have every right to think I was an authentic human scumbucket.

But there was nothing I could do.

Or was there?

I called her apartment, but no answer. I went to the café off Place Saint Michel and saw Claude. Now was as good a time as any to see if we'd established any kind of bond over the past—what was it?—almost three weeks I'd been in Paris.

I quickly scribbled a note, apologizing, promising that I'd return to Paris as soon as possible, definitely before I went back to New York. I folded the note and Claude kindly found for me an envelope from the back room. I gave him fifty francs and said I'd be back with more in two weeks if I learned the message was received.

"No problem, monsieur. I remember the lady and will make sure she receives the envelope. And I look forward to seeing you again."

I'll bet. Well, at least this was better than nothing. And I'm sure my waiter had been used as a middleman messenger many times before.

As I handed him the envelope, an image of Josephine flashed through my mind. Her startled face, confused, concerned, genuinely caring, as the train doors closed and she was left standing on the RER platform, watching me disappear down the tunnel.

Outside my hotel stood Inspector Lonsdale, three gendarmes, and Rick.

"*Bonjour,* Monsieur Dandridge. We have been expecting you."

There was no use resisting, so I got into the back of their Citroen and enjoyed the ride to police headquarters. Rick was dressed to seduce women, not policemen, wearing a startling black leather jacket and handknit Arran sweater, but he tried his best to appear solemn and professional and said only one sentence as we drove through the Parisian streets: "Let me do all the talking and you're in the clear."

Ooh boy.

"It seems, Monsieur Dandridge, that we have traced the contents of whatever the late Monsieur Arnot received from you and passed along, to a certain Marcel Coloute," said Lonsdale, pronouncing the name "Coh-loo-*tay.*"

"Who's he?" asked Rick, who was seated beside me at a steel table in an interrogation room deep inside police headquarters.

"Let's ask Monsieur Dandridge."

"Let's not and say we did," replied Rick. Clarence Darrow he wasn't.

"Very well. Marcel Coloute is a known criminal who came to France only recently. Originally born in Haiti, he was a member of their esteemed former secret police, the Tonton Macoute. It seems when the Duvaliers were forced to flee— unfortunately to France, but that is another matter—so too did Monsieur Coloute. He came to France with a large cache of money, stolen no doubt from the Haitian peasants, and set up operations here, dealing mostly in drugs and weapons." Lonsdale walked over to a side table and picked up two wooden objects I immediately recognized as the cornices Oren duped me into delivering to Arnot. "Recognize these, monsieur?"

I looked to Rick for counsel. He nodded it was okay to speak. "Sure."

"Mind telling us about them?"

Rick nodded his assent, so I proceeded.

"A friend of mine back home is a successful art director, working on movies and plays and television shows. He seemed to have found these rare wooden cornices one of his fellow artists wanted, and figured since I was going to Paris anyway I might as well drop them off."

"And?"

"And I assure you I had no knowledge that anything was inside."

Lonsdale pinched the bridge of his nose as if in pain, then removed his hand, wiping on a more concerned expression. "Then how did you know anything was inside?"

Yeeesh. "When I arrived at Arnot's he offered me something to drink. It must have been drugged, because I fell right asleep. When I awoke I noticed that one of the cornices was lying on the floor in a side room and that it'd been cracked open. Presumably it was hollow, and presumably he gave whatever was inside to whomever came to the door. He also stole money from my wallet."

But the latter point was of no concern to Lonsdale. "You had no previous knowledge that you were carrying anything other than wood carvings from your friend?"

Rick interrupted, "I believe my client has already stated as much."

"Would he care to state so again?"

I caught Rick before he defended me some more. "Yes, that is exactly what I said. I had no knowledge that I was doing anything wrong."

Lonsdale picked up the pieces of the broken cornice and weighed them back and forth in the palms of his two hands, emulating the Scales of Justice. "What was the name of this friend of yours?"

"Which one?"

"The art director back home."

"I don't see where that's relevant," said Rick.

"Monsieur Partridge, whoever it is is an American citizen safely home in America. I have no jurisdiction there. It is just that he may be a useful link, we may be able to connect his name to others, see a pattern, that sort of thing. Surely you understand."

"Still," said Rick, "I don't think my client need reveal anything that might incriminate himself or anyone else."

Lonsdale put the cornices down on the table in front of me. "Our two great democracies share many things, but French laws are much different than yours. If I wanted to, monsieur attorney, I assure you I could compel your client to recite me the entire New York phone book. But"—he slid the cornice pieces closer to me—"I am a forgiving man with a trusting disposition. It seems I believe you, Monsieur Dandridge, that you were merely the dupe of others scheming to take advantage of your naive nature."

Rick saw me tensing and put his hand on my arm.

Lonsdale continued. "Do you know what was inside these cornices?"

"As I said—"

"I know what you said, so I will tell you. There was pure cocaine. Our lab experts found traces inside the hollow center. Faint traces, but legitimate nonetheless. Since you have already admitted to bringing these into the country, I could charge you here and now with violating one of our most serious laws."

Officer Swaim silently pushed a glass of water over to me. I drank it in one gulp.

Lonsdale asked, "Have you ever seen the motion picture *Midnight Express?*"

My groan was audible, but Rick rose to the occasion. "Inspector, how sure are you that cocaine was transported inside those cornices? You said faint traces. How faint?"

"Monsieur Arnot was a notorious *toxicomane,* but to be perfectly honest, all we found was a mere dusting, which, to be even more honest, *could* have been added after the cornices were opened by Arnot. Had we gone to court you would have seen our lab reports and determined as much for yourself. I just thought it would be illuminating to mention the possibility." He paused, staring directly at me. "Mostly we found traces of plastic, the pliable, heavy-duty kind used to manufacture large trash bags."

"Ah-hah! I'm sure you can't arrest my client for importing trash bags."

I began wondering if the French still owned Devil's Island.

"*Oui,*" said Lonsdale. "But the question still remains, what was in those bags?"

"Are you charging my client with any crimes?"

"Not yet."

"Then may we leave until you do?"

Lonsdale collected the cornice pieces and handed them to Swaim, who deposited them in a large, clear-plastic evidence bag, which was sealed and whisked away. Then Lonsdale moved his top-heavy bulk to the table where Rick and I sat, and leaned on it, looking down at me from on high like God Almighty. "Before I let you go, monsieurs, I wish to explain the facts of life. Marcel Coloute is a very dangerous man who kills people as casually as others eat breakfast. He is rich and he is ruthless, which, in my experience, usually go hand in hand. The fact that he ultimately received delivery of whatever you unwittingly brought to my country leads me to suspect that your life is in danger. Coloute does not generally leave loose threads, and in his mind you are the annoying equivalent of a dangling ball of yarn. If you lead anyone to him, such as *me* for instance, no matter how accidental that occurrence, you would be responsible in his eyes for bringing down a growing criminal empire. He will not like that and will use his vast network of conspirators to cause you harm. Tremendous, violent harm. Now tell me . . . how does that make you feel?"

"Like a leper at a very fancy party."

Lonsdale digested this. "Yes, I can see you must be a writer. In any event, I need your help. Marcel Coloute and his associates are growing more powerful each day. They are conspirators of evil. They traffic not only in drugs and weapons, but information. They know things the French government would like to know. It is important, therefore, monsieur, that in order to protect your safety you work not against us, but with us." He handed me a phone number. "I want you to call me the minute you suspect anything suspicious. The minute anyone contacts you, follows you, or merely gives you an uneasy feeling. If someone asks you for the time of day, *I want to know about it.*"

"So you're willing to let me slide out of here in the hope I become bait?"

Lonsdale looked at me evenly. "You must indeed be a very astute writer."

"I wrote a crime show once, what can I say? May I consult with my attorney in private?"

Lonsdale nodded, got up and left. Swaim followed. I hoped the windowless room wasn't bugged.

"All right, Cliff. What's up? As your attorney I advise you to tell me everything."

I explained to Rick about being chased by the Two Goons, and about Anne, how we met at the museum, about Eli Sternberg, how Anne seemed to live across the street from me until she was burned out, about our conversation on the flight to Paris, our clandestine meetings, the message I found in the matchbook in my coat pocket, her suggestion I leave Paris. I didn't mention the destination, since I didn't want Rick getting any heroic notions and following me to Budapest.

"My oh my oh my," he said, doing his worst David Letterman. "What will they think of next?"

I was on the verge of a total emotional collapse. "What do I do, Rick? What do I tell Lonsdale? Since he didn't mention the goons, maybe they're not with the United States Government? I mean, I thought they found out where I was by asking the police, but maybe not. Maybe they've got their own spies out after me? Maybe the whole goddamned world has spies out after me?"

"Cliff, you're hysterical."

"But—"

"And clinically paranoid."

"But—"

"But I can see it's all founded on legitimate fear." He thought in silence for a few minutes. "Okay, here's the play. We take our lesson from pro football. Teams always lose when they play conservatively, right? So we open up our passing attack and bomb the hell out of the opposition."

"What the fuck are you talking about?"

"You're the one who lives football, I thought I'd use terms you knew."

"I'm in France, Rick. Forget football and speak words to me."

"Just tell Lonsdale everything. Either he won't believe you, or you'll confuse him with so much new information you'll ruin his dinner. He can't call you a liar until he checks everything out, by which time you'll be gone, evaporated, which leads to my final bit of advice and that is to take Anne's offer and travel. It's what you came to Europe for in the first place."

"I came to Europe because my professional and emotional well-being were shot to shit and I needed rest and artistic rejuvenation. I didn't need to be racing for my life through the sewers of Paris."

I was miserable, but all Rick did was crack his knuckles.

Lonsdale returned with his fellow officers and I told him the truth as I knew it. He listened attentively, jotting down notes of his own even though a legal stenographer was there, taking everything down verbatim. We went over my story a number of times, I suppose since he was checking to see if there were any discrepancies. At one point he sent Swaim off to verify that a boat had indeed been stolen in the sewers. When Swaim returned with verification, Lonsdale looked at me in a new light, as if he suddenly had reason to believe everything I'd been saying all along.

"I want you to know that while I appreciate your cooperation, monsieur, I really should put you in jail. However, I
believe you will be more useful to me loose on the streets.
Coloute will try finding you, and when he does, I will be a mere
phone call away."

"Why don't you just put a tail on me?"

"You have been reading too many novels. We are only the
police. Even with the assistance of the SDECE we lack the
money and manpower to follow such an intrepid traveler as
yourself." He and Swaim shared a smirk at my expense. "As
to the two men who have been following you since the States,
I will make certain careful inquiries. I can assure you no one
from your embassy has contacted my office about you. But the
paperwork on my desk has backed up, so you never know. In
any case those two gentlemen may or may not be connected
with Marcel Coloute. For now we shall treat them as if they are,
and proceed accordingly." He stood and walked to the door.
"By the way, your luggage will be returned to you in the morning. Here's your journal." He tossed it to me. "It needs work."

Rick and I left police headquarters around nine-thirty. Rick
was all excited and wanted desperately to begin an evening filled
with wine, women and song. He seemed totally able to forget
the conversation in the police station in the pursuit of sexual
gratification. Who said man was little more than a zombie led
mindlessly by his dick?

I had less than two hours to meet Anne in the park to get
money and leave. I knew I had no choice. I didn't fancy myself
a worm on Lonsdale's hook, and felt it best to skip Paris ASAP.
I did want to confront Anne about Marcel Coloute, see if she
knew anything about him. I doubted it, but you never know.
I was beginning to wonder if what she'd said when we first met
was true, that nothing was coincidence. Maybe everything was
connected, maybe I'd stepped into some bizarre maelstrom of
shit I could never hope to fathom.

I knew I didn't want Rick getting hurt. Sure, he probably wouldn't give a shit if the tables were turned, he was, after all, a lawyer. But I didn't want his accidental death on my conscience. If I was going to chase any demons to the bitter end, I couldn't very well let selfishness take the place of compassion for a friend.

So . . .

We settled into an Afghan restaurant on Boulevard Haussmann and ordered a complicated *cous-cous prix fixe* menu. I excused myself to pay the water rates, leaving Rick to flirt with a pouty-lipped waitress. But instead of finding the WC I scooted out the front door quiet casually, hailed a cab and returned to the Quarter. I stopped at a rip-off tourist emporium that sold luggage around the clock and bought an expandable vinyl bag, returned to my hotel and quickly packed what possessions I had left. Luckily, I still had my passport. I put more than enough to cover my bill in an envelope marked "concierge" and silently crept downstairs into the night.

The entrance to the Jardin des Plantes was dark and quiet and closed. Anne obviously hadn't checked her Guide Michelin. Still, I saw the yellow chalk mark on the tree, tossed my bag over the fence and climbed up and over. Signs pointed me toward the monkey cage.

Take my advice and never visit a zoo after dark. The silence is too creepy. Treetops hovered overhead, obscuring the moonlight, casting jagged shadows across my path. My heart pounded. I started humming, "In The Hall Of The Mountain King," from *Peer Gynt,* but gave that up when I forgot the second part.

I finally found the monkey cage, but no Anne. The monkeys sat silently on the limbs of fake trees, sleeping or staring at the night, too bored or too jaded to be bothered by my intrusion. I looked at the monkeys there in the dark and wondered why certain souls end up in monkeys behind bars while others ended up in people like Oren Petrowicz or Sam Tardibul or Inspector Lonsdale. A bizarre joke of the cosmos?

Rapid footsteps broke my reverie. I leaned back against the cage and peeked around to see who was coming. Out of the shadows a figure suddenly appeared, and in the sparse light cast by the moon I saw it was Anne. Only when I ran closer did I notice she was favoring her left side, limping, and her left arm was bleeding.

"What happened?"

She pressed a wad of money into my hand, then guided it to my pocket.

"Anne, tell me."

"I am fine. A little accident . . ." She faltered. "Now put that away."

"We've got to get you to a doctor. You're bleeding—"

"There is no time. Cliff, you must leave Paris and get to Budapest. I promise everything will be okay."

She pushed me forward, but stumbled and fell to the ground. I picked her up and sat her on a nearby bench.

"Cliff, please."

"Just tell me what happened."

"They were following me. All along they were. I should have been more careful."

"Who was following you?"

"I am not sure. Perhaps the opposition and their friends. Perhaps not. Whoever it was shot at me, but I was too quick." She tried smiling, but grimaced in pain.

Blood was spreading over her expensive clothes. She was clearly losing a great deal, so I lifted her right arm and slung it over my shoulder, carrying my suitcase in my other hand as I helped her walk toward the exit.

Gunshots!

Not movie magic either, but the real thing. They sure as shit got me moving, as a hail of bullets rained out from the darkness all around us. Anne pulled herself from my arm and led the way, running into the shadows of the zoo.

We swung past a series of old metal cages containing all kinds of animals, but the gunshots kept on, scaring the incarcerated beasts, whipping them into a noise-making frenzy. The birds, the jackals, the monkeys, the bears, all chirped and screamed and howled and growled as Anne and I ran down a long paved terrace. We swung off into a forest of plants and trees, pausing to catch our breath, no longer able to hear the cries of the animals.

"You okay?"

She nodded yes, but her blouse was now completely covered in red. She struggled to stand up.

"Give me your gun."

"What?"

"Your gun, give it to me. You must have a gun, and you're in no condition to use it."

"Cliff, what do you know about—"

I was in no mood for games now myself, what with my life in danger and all. It was time to take action. I reached under Anne's arms, looking for a shoulder holster, but she removed a tiny pistol from her purse. Jeez, it was puny. Didn't look like it had much stopping power.

Footsteps clicked rapidly along nearby pavement, then stopped. I heard three separate, distinct voices argue, then the footsteps resumed, each set going off in different directions. It was only a matter of time till the fun would begin.

I dragged Anne through the forest toward a tiny wooden supply shed, situated near a cage.

"We're together," I whispered, sounding more confident that I felt. "We'll show these jokers they can't mess with—"

A shot splintered the wood above my head. I pushed Anne down behind the shed and fired her pistol in the general direction of the attack. My bullet flew off into embarrassing oblivion.

"What kind of spy has a toy gun like this?"

"CLIFF!"

I turned to see a huge black man with dreadlocks and a metal crowbar, jumping off the roof of the storage bin in my direction. I dove aside as he swung his crowbar like a Samurai. I rolled over once more, this time smacking my hand against a steel plow, knocking my gun loose. The black man swung the crowbar, I ducked, he smacked the wall and ricocheted back. I stretched for the gun, but no luck, so I kicked it to Anne, who scooped it up and ran for cover. The black man swung back and forth, slicing wind but missing me, so I bravely—or foolishly, take your pick—grabbed the bar in midmotion and held it. BOING! The man's momentum carried him forward and onto his face. I had the bar—now what? Emulating Rambo, I banged the hell out of the guy's upper torso with the crowbar until he stopped moving. He also stopped breathing. *What the fuck had I done?*

More shots. Anne was firing at what I recognized despite the darkness as one of the goons who'd been chasing me. Killers? Government agents? What'd I do now? Did I shoot at agents of my own country? Could the president have me arrested? Did I care?

Fuck it. I ran around some trees as Anne kept the goon's attention with her gun until I came up behind the guy and repeatedly smashed his head with the crowbar. He fell with a guttural grunt, blood spilled from his open mouth, but he wasn't going anywhere.

"This way," whispered Anne, pointing me toward a narrow alley between buildings.

"There's one more asshole out there," I said. I was steamed, I was vexed, I was ready for battle. I was out of my fucking mind.

"We'll sneak this way, maybe he will not find us."

"When he sees what we did to his *companeros*, he'll have incentive."

"Come on!"

There was a rusty old bicycle with a front basket leaning against the fence surrounding the bear pit. Down in the pit the huge creatures were snoozing, totally oblivious as I untied the bike and stood it up. I threw my leg over the crossbar and motioned for Anne to take the seat. She clung to my waist as I pushed on the pedals, forcing the gearless ancient wonder into motion. It was like pushing into mud. A rhythmic scraping of the rear wheel against the back fender got faster and louder as we picked up speed, until we were moving fast enough that it dissipated altogether.

My leg muscles burned under the strain, as the bike rocked side to side with every movement. But there was no turning back. I hadn't done much exercise recently and was suffering accordingly. But the old bike did the trick and eventually we were able to zip across the park.

"Over there." Anne pointed to a narrow walkway, so I stopped the bike and gently helped her dismount.

"Thanks for saving my life," she said as we crept around a group of parked trucks.

"De nada," I said.

"D'accord," she said.

We managed to find the opening in the fence Anne had used to sneak into the park. There was still no sign of the other goon, so maybe he'd decided we were too tough.

Yeah, right.

Well, at least we'd outbiked him.

Anyway: we took a bench outside the wall and Anne sat down. I reached over to look at her wound, but she took hold of my hand and held it.

"Do not worry, Cliff. I will be fine. I have friends here who will help. But you must leave Paris at once, before you are caught."

"Didn't we have this conversation before?"

"Now it is even more important. They have not given up. You saw—"

"Let's get you to a hospital first."

"Just go," she said, releasing my hand. "Gare d'Austerlitz is across the road."

"There's a hospital right beside it."

"I cannot go there. Please, do not worry. As soon as you are gone I will be picked up and taken care of."

"I'll wait to make sure."

"I am a big girl, Cliff, this is a dangerous world, we all must take care of ourselves! You saved my life now, but you must go. I hope we will meet again in Hungary. But I promise—you will be taken care of and everything will be explained. Then you can decide what you wish. But at least wait until then. Will you promise me?"

What could I say? I think I'd just killed a fellow human being or two and hadn't puked my guts out. Wasn't a person supposed to feel remorse? At the very least I'd have thought being so close to death would produce some emotional epiphany. But there was no time to linger: Anne was weakening by the second. She desperately needed a hospital, otherwise she'd possibly die from loss of blood.

A car pulled up along the curb a few hundred feet down the street. It blinked its taillights in a distinct two-one-two pattern.

"My friends," said Anne weakly. "I must go."

"I'll help you—"

"*No!*" She yelled for the first time since we'd met. "Are you so foolish as to worry about one person when there are so many other things at stake? What does it matter what happens to me if we do not defeat our enemies. The world, Cliff. Think of the world. If you have ever trusted me before, trust me now and go!"

I paused. "I never trust anyone who says trust me."

"You!" Exasperated, she grabbed my head with her hands and pulled my face close. It was as if she had so much to say she couldn't decide where to start. Yet her eyes spoke volumes. I was helpless to protest anymore. She turned and headed toward the car.

I reached down to pick up my suitcase, and when I looked up, Anne and the car were gone.

I ran as fast as I could to the train station.

ELEVEN

The narrow corridor of the train was congested with travelers and luggage. I forced my way through, looking in each compartment to find solitude, but instead found only the usual mix of elderly couples, backpackers, migrant factory workers, and soldiers on leave. It was approaching one A.M., so at least there weren't any commuters.

Nor were there any pretty girls sitting alone. I had no choice but to select an empty compartment in a *defense de fumer* car and put my bag on the seat beside me—hopefully it would stay there and the seat thus unoccupied for the duration. I slid the door shut and drew the curtains: maybe others would think I was asleep.

Parked on the platform outside my window was a sandwich cart, and from the thin Arab with bad skin who ran it I purchased a ham sandwich, a bag of cookies and a liter of bottled water. I collected the comestibles through my window, but as I sat down I turned to see I had a visitor.

Standing opposite me in the corner near the door and struggling with a huge snot green canvas duffle bag was a tall guy with thinning hair, huge forehead and thick glasses. He wore a blue windbreaker, a buffalo-plaid flannel shirt, faded Levis and Timberland workboots. He swung his duffle up into the overhead compartment and sat down in his corner, nodded acknowledgment, and began reading a crumpled copy of the *International Herald Tribune.*

"Do you speak English?" I asked, indicating the newspaper.

"Oh, yeah, guess I do," he said. "But my teachers, you know, they'd disagree."

"Where you from?"

"Toronto."

"A *Canadian,*" I said, as if it were a miracle.

"Sure. But you can't know how many folks here think I'm American."

"Aren't you? Isn't Canada America?"

"Technically. But we, you know, kind of like the differences. How many terrorists you ever meet go around bombing Canuck buildings? Not too many, eh? No sir. So, like, there is a major difference."

Right. Sure. Terrific. Sorry I asked.

"Name's Tim," said the Canadian.

"Cliff," I said.

"Long in Europe?"

"Couple of weeks. You?"

" 'Bout nine months. Stationed with NATO, see. Information analyst, but I can't talk 'bout it. Right now, eh, I'm on a few days leave, you know, going to visit this girl I met in Geneva."

"Where'd you say you were stationed?"

"That's classified."

"Oh, sorry."

"No harm. But'cha never know when you're going to meet someone who wants to find out secrets like that, eh?"

Tell me about it.

"Real secrets," he continued. "I mean, like, that's why I joined up. You know, I like secrets, like keeping 'em. Ask anyone knows me, they'll say, sure, Tim Spencer's got the tightest lips in all Toronto. Yuh, yuh, yuh. Well, not really. Actually, I'm from Sturgeon Falls, few hundred miles north of

Toronto. Beautiful little place, really. Right on the north shore of Lake Nipissing."

"That right?"

"So you heard of it? Well, that's not so odd. I mean, lot of folks have. You go into a store in Ottowa, say, which is actually closer to Sturgeon Falls than Toronto, but I hate it so I never say I'm from there, right, instead I say I'm from Toronto. Anyway, you go into one of those stores there, like I did this one time, and let me tell you, like you know, they had this sign like in a souvenir shop? It said, get this, 'No Pissing in Lake Nipissing.' "

I chuckled.

"What's so funny? I mean, sure, yeah, it's funny. Not if you live there. Anyway, what kind of a name is Ottawa anyway? I mean it's an ugly-for-shit city, the government's all screwed up, my friends from school all moved there when they graduated, that is, the one's that moved. Most of 'em were too stupid and stayed behind to fish and fight and fuck." Tim was laughing, "yuh, yuh, yuh," all sweaty and wound up. "They made me sick, eh? With their new shiny cars and fancy girl friends who put out only for guys they *think* they like, not for guys that are better for 'em. Know what I mean?"

"Yeah, right." This Tim was crisp.

"Let me show you something." He reached into a tiny vinyl carryon bag that said "Gold's Gym" and began rifling through, looking for something. "Goddamn it, where the fu—Anyway, there was this girl back in school, Katy Louise MacBride was her name. She was called Katy the Studentbody because she was everybody's favorite subject, and most of the guys did their homework on her. Yuh, yuh, yuh. Well, I got back from a hunting trip I made by myself, spent two weeks up in the hills with a tent and some tins of that Eskimo pemmican shit and my rifles and some magazines, and I asked her out. I was in need of a girl, you know, to unblock the semen building up in unhealthy doses, and wacking off'll make you go blind, like this friend I used to have but who hung himself with his mom's fresh sheets one night when she was out turning tricks to make money for the rent. Good guy Tiny was, too. Yuh, yuh, yuh. Only a little messed up in the head on account of being blind like. Well, he wasn't really blind, just needed glasses like me. Hell, his glasses weren't half as thick as these ol' Coke bottles, but he felt self-conscious and all. Thinking the whole world knew he wanked off because Katy the Studentbody bit his dick instead of sucking him like she promised. Yuh, yuh, yuh."

I thought: I must leave this car at once.

I stood to move but Canadian Tim was blocking the door. I felt that uneasy feeling that was all too familiar lately. Was *he* involved with the goons and the conspiracy against me? Or was he just an obnoxious slime, mentally unstable, and not to be toyed with?

"Excuse me," I said, trying not to provoke him.

"Why? Didja fart? Like, well I did, too!"

Yes, well . . .

I grabbed my bag and moved quickly into the corridor. There was less congestion now, as the train was pulling out of the station. I walked down a few cars until I found a compartment that looked empty. I opened the door quietly and sat down on the seat, and I wasn't the least bit surprised to discover I was not alone.

Reclining on the opposite bench was a thin brunet with long, straight hair, wearing a Walkman. Her clothes were in a neat pile beside her, leaving her adorned in just a tight-fitting black leotard. She was swaying to music I could only make out as static, but her precise movements were those of an accomplished dancer.

Ooh boy.

The static stopped on her headphones, yet she kept moving her arms in wide, arclike circles over her head. Finally, with enormous poise and control, she let her arms descend like swans, gently resting them together in her lap. She opened her eyes, totally at peace, and screamed.

"What? What? What?" I asked.

She smiled, totally calm. "I'm sorry. It's part of my routine. You didn't scare me. I knew you were here, I felt you watching me."

"I wasn't watching you. Yes, I was."

"That's okay. That's what I'm trained for. To be pleasing to the eye when I go through my routine."

"Don't tell me you're a dancer."

"God, no. I just use that routine to relax and unwind. My yogi taught it to me."

Here we go again.

"You're looking at me funny," she said. "What's wrong?"

"We haven't even been introduced, and already I know you have a yogi."

"I don't, really. I just took this class once at UCLA and this really old short guy who looked like Ben Kingsley in Richard Attenborough's *Gandhi* came in and taught a group of about fifty of us how to relax."

The brunet stood up and began slipping her clothes on over the leotard.

"Don't quit on my account," I said. She just looked at me.

"Want to do a number?"

"Huh?"

She finished dressing, reached into a huge drawstring handbag and pulled out a clear plastic bag with a substance I immediately recognized.

"Is that yours," I asked, "or did somebody along the way give it to you?" Given the recent past, I had to be careful what I imbibed.

"My boyfriend brought it over from LA when he came to visit. It's terrific. Organically grown. He fertilizes it himself."

She rolled two neurotically tight joints and passed one to me. What the fuck. I'm never going to become a Supreme Court Justice anyway.

"I'm Cliff."

"I'm Ellen."

"Glad to know you Ellen."

"Likewise, Cliff."

Why do these things keep happening to me?

I took a few hits and Ellen started telling me about her life. She'd been a foreign-exchange student the past semester in London and was now on holiday, traveling around the Continent. She was in a program at USC, studying to become a "hotshot film producer." She'd already had an internship as a reader for an independent production company, which she hoped would turn into a full-time development job "real soon," but from which she said she learned almost nothing, except that producers seldom read the books they buy the rights to. Talking about show business was, as you can guess, the last thing I wanted to do, but life is funny that way. . . .

"There was this story I heard," she began, leaning back in her seat, stretching her legs across the cabin to rest her feet beside me, "about a famous producer who bought the rights to this fabulous novel." She spoke with her hands, which had long fingers and highly glossed nails. "It was this incredible tear-jerker with wonderful Oscar-caliber characters. Loads of substance, grit, high conflict, etcetera. You know. Anyway, the writer came to meet the producer and talk about his book. Well, it was pretty clear the producer hadn't a clue as to what was really in the text, and the writer, still an artist, still a virgin, since this was his first Hollywood sale, got all indignant and said, 'You haven't even read my book. Why did you buy it?' And the producer, all glib and excited and wired on coke, said, 'Well, I'll tell you. I cried all through the reader's report, so I bought it.' And that, Cliff, is my lesson of Hollywood. Tell me, what do you do?"

I really wasn't in the mood. "I'm a spy," I said. "On a secret mission."

The train stopped in the middle of nowhere and the engines groaned to a halt. The lights flickered off and on, then the train lurched forward, which this time was actually in the direction we'd just come from. It suddenly occurred to me, or maybe it was the pot, that Canadian Tim and Ellen of LA could be working together, two unique subspecies of humanity sent to seduce me into carelessness and lead me into the hands of my enemies. Otherwise what were the chances of meeting two North Americans on this train, at this time, in this way?

I panicked. I opened the window and cold air rushed into the congested compartment, but it cleared the cannabis and woke us both right up.

"Relax. We just dropped off some cars at some nowhere station and are now moving ahead on a different track." Ellen said this without moving her lips. I swear.

I leaned back in and closed the window, trying to mask my drug-induced anxiety. "Are you sure?"

"I've traveled a lot, Cliff. This is how trains work in France." She grinned. "What kind of spy wouldn't know that?"

What kind indeed? "A very stoned spy," I said. "That stuff was very good."

"It's the organic process. Rex, he's my boyfriend, is an artist."

"He paints pictures?"

"He's an artist at growing shit. He's also an artist at cutting cocaine, and lately he's been experimenting with designer things, like—"

"Forget I asked. You don't really do all that?"

"Getting provincial on me, Cliff?"

"It's just that I saw the best minds of my generation destroyed by madness, starving hysterical naked, dragging themselves through the Negro streets at dawn, looking for an angry

fix, angelheaded hipsters burning for the ancient heavenly connection to the starry dynamo in the machinery of night."
Whew. Did I really remember all that?

"Where'd *that* come from?"

"I made it up."

"Really? Wow. That's cool."

She believed me. This lack of literary knowledge was depressing. "How old are you?" I asked.

"Ladies don't usually reveal that information."

"Excuse me."

"I'm twenty."

Let's see, that means the girl sitting with her legs stretched
and her feet against my thigh was one year old when *Abbey
Road* was released. Christ, I felt old.

"Tell me, what was the music you were listening to?"

She grabbed her Walkman and popped out the cassette. "The
Smiths, *Louder Than Bombs.* They're great. Totally depressing.
There's this one song, 'Heaven Knows I'm Miserable Now'? It
speaks to the mass angst of my soul."

"You don't strike me as having much angst."

"Thanks. It's all a facade. My analyst told me how to appear
in public so as not to depress people."

"You have an analyst?"

"Since I was twelve. Everyone in the Valley has shrinks. My
parents thought it would be good for me to learn to express
myself and search deep within my subconscious at an early age,
so I wouldn't be all fucked when I grew up."

"And now that you're grown up?"

She began rifling through her handbag, extracting various
cassettes, trying to decide which one to listen to. "Now that I'm
grown up I've got life in perspective. I know what I want, I
know how to get it, I know what will make me happy." She
opened her mouth and quickly licked her lips.

I coughed, then said, "I used to think that way when I was
younger."

"Come on, you're not so much older."

"Older than you think."

"Twenty-eight, twenty-nine?"

"I'm two years into middle-agehood."

She seemed genuinely impressed. "Wow. You were already into puberty before I was even born, and here we are sharing drugs together on a train in Europe."

"Life's funny that way."

She paused and squinted her eyes. "You know, Cliff, I've never done it with an older man before."

Oh, no, not now.

"Don't get all red and embarrassed." She popped Bruce Springsteen's *Tunnel of Love* into the Walkman and produced a second set of earphones from her bag. She smiled. "Come on, let's listen to some music together."

She turned off the compartment light and opened the curtains on the passing landscape. I opened the cellophane bag that contained my ham sandwich and offered her half. We ate in silence, listening to the Boss, watching as the telephone poles and evergreen trees raced alongside the train in the moonlight. We finished the sandwich and shared my cookies. I offered her a drink from my bottled water, but Ellen smiled her devilish grin and found a tiny flask of Courvosier buried in her bag beneath cassettes and nail polish. For some reason it seemed a more appropriate beverage, so we sipped it slowly away. Then she came and sat beside me on the bench, leaning her head on my shoulder, pulling my arm around her for warmth. All thoughts of sex, however, were numbed by the collection of substances we'd ingested, and soon we fell asleep with the music still playing.

"Votre passeport, s'il vous plait."

I opened my eyes and saw that a tall, menacing customs agent had slid our door open and was staring at us, one hand open and expectant.

"Votre passeport, s'il vous plait. Ihren Pass, bitte. Il passaporto, per favore. Your passport, please."

The train had come to a complete stop and light from the border station filled our compartment. Ellen woke slowly, stretching against my body. We both removed our headphones.

"Good morning," she said as she stretched.

"We have company."

We handed over our tickets and passports and everything seemed in order, which satisfied the officer, who bowed, left, and slid the door shut. The train chugged ahead a few hundred yards and we crossed into Switzerland.

"God, I'm hungry," whined Ellen as she curled her arm under mine.

The snack car was crowded with hungry travelers, so I had to wait fifteen minutes on line for strong coffee and dry croissants. Canadian Tim was there and he smiled at me from further down the line. Thankfully the car was too crowded for him to get closer. I smiled and waved and rushed off with my purchases. Back in the compartment Ellen was once again in her leotard, going through some bizarre ritual, so I put the coffee down on the tiny collapsible table near the window and settled in to watch.

"Join me." With her hands on her hips she was stretching her back like a cat, and for the first time I noticed she wasn't wearing a bra.

"We'll be in Geneva soon," I reminded her. "Isn't that where you're getting off?"

"I changed my mind. You're going to Zurich, right?"

"Only to get a connection."

"I'll go with you. This way we can spend the rest of the day together."

Lucky me.

"Won't that ruin your plans?"

"What plans?" She affected an English accent and flounced playfully around. "I'm on holiday, having an adventure. I've got to be open to new experiences, be spontaneous. Why not go with you? Besides, I have a Eurail Pass and can go where I like. I can always call home to see if a job came through, and Daddy'll let me charge my ticket home from anywhere if I have to get back. Now, come down on the floor next to me and I'll show you how to relax."

The whole thing was a silly flirtation, and was getting on my nerves. Sure she was cute. She was even sexy, but the way she moved around the car, stretching, groaning, prattling on and on about how confident she was about her career and her future, combined to create the impression in my mind that she had much growing up to do.

She was old enough, technically, for other things, but if we fooled around it would have felt like child rape.

We had to change trains in Geneva, so with an hour to kill I went to the post office at the depot and placed a call to Danette. I needed a dose of reality and was beginning to feel guilty being away from her so long. But I was also learning, despite diversions to the contrary, that I cared about her very much.

That was a dangerous revelation.

"Hi Danette, it's me."

She sounded alarmed. "Cliff, are you all right? Where are you?"

"I'm fine, I'm fine. What's wrong?"

"Rick called and said you disappeared from a restaurant last night right after you got out of the police station. Cliff, what's happening? Are you being held hostage or something?"

"Danette, I'm okay, really. I just had to leave and didn't want Rick following me. I didn't want him getting in trouble."

"Then you are in trouble?"

"No."

"Well Rick is."

"What?"

"After you disappeared he went to the police and saw some inspector or detective—"

"Lonsdale?"

"That's it. When Lonsdale heard you were gone he threw Rick in jail for helping a fugitive escape. Cliff, are you a fugitive now?"

"No, Danette. How'd you hear about this?"

"Rick called."

"You?"

"He figured you might have called me if you were able to. He was really worried you were kidnapped or beaten or, or—"

"Danette, I assure you I haven't been kidnapped or beaten, and since I'm talking to you I must be very much alive."

"But you're in trouble."

"I'm not in trouble."

"Then where are you?"

"In a phone booth in a train station."

"Where?"

"Look Danette, believe me, I can't tell you. It's better you don't know."

"Why? So when some goon who's been looking for you comes to get me instead and tries beating the information out of me I won't have anything to tell him and when he realizes that he'll have to kill me?"

"What have you been reading since I left?"

"That's really selfish of you, Heathcliff."

"Sorry."

"Cliff, how much longer is this literary sojourn of yours going to last? I mean, how much sojourning are you doing?"

And I was just thinking how much I missed her.

Ellen came by and tapped my shoulder. "I'm going to get us some food," she said, dancing off.

"Who was that?" asked Danette.

"You heard that?"

"All right, Cliff. And I was worried about you. I can see you're doing fine on your own."

"Dani, you're jumping to all sorts of incorrect conclusions."

"Am I? You abandon your friend who flies to Paris to help you, and then you can't tell me where you are but I hear you're with some woman who's getting 'us' some food? What am I supposed to think?"

I wasn't going to win this no matter what. "Look, how's Rick?"

"He was fine when we spoke. He called this friend of his at the U.S. Embassy to get him out of jail, but he was worried about you."

"When he calls, tell him I'm fine."

"I'm sure you are."

It was impossible to salvage this. "Danette, I've got to catch my train. If everything goes the way it should, I'll be home in less than a week and I promise I'll explain everything."

"Good-bye, Cliff." She hung up, pissed as hell.

"Have a nice trip?" It was Canadian Tim, standing outside the post office, licking stamps, smacking them onto postcards.

"Not bad."

"You left without saying good-bye."

"Sorry."

"Where'd you say you were going?"

"I didn't."

His smile dropped. "You're not being very sociable or friendly."

"Forgive me," I said. "Tell me something."

"Maybe." He sounded hurt.

"Aw c'mon, Tim. I'll be straight with you if you'll be straight with me."

"Hey, you think I'm not straight? You think I'm one of them queer-boys?"

"No, Tim. Sorry."

He was unstoppable. " 'Cause if you do, I'm not. I'm not one of them bathroom slugs with key rings and hankies in my back pocket."

Methinks the man doth protest too much, yet I kept this to myself.

"I just want to know," I said, "if you're from the Opposition and if you're following me. Because I *hate* being followed, I hate it, and I've been known to severely *hurt*"—I pounced on that word—"people who get me mad!" I then bared my teeth and growled.

Tim looked at me like the kook I must've seemed. He collected his postcards, turned and walked quickly away.

"What was all that about?" It was Ellen. "What did you say to that guy?"

"I told him I'd kill him if he didn't stop following me."

She nodded knowingly. "The spy thing again, huh?"

"Exactly," I said.

We found an empty compartment aboard our next train, settled our bags into the overhead racks and busied ourselves with reading. I finished the Graham Greene, while she read this book about the *Heaven's Gate* motion-picture fiasco.

"It's amazing," she said, looking up from her text. "Hollywood types are so easily seduced by hype."

I was surprised that this child could come up with anything so astute.

The next morning, after we'd woken up from a fitful—if virginal—sleep, Ellen turned to me. "You're not really a spy, Cliff, are you?"

"Not really."

"What are you?"

"A writer."

"Really?" She literally bounced up and down. "That's great! What've you written I might've heard of?"

I told her about *The Underground Force* and the Saturday-morning kids' show, and she seemed genuinely impressed.

"I take back what I said about hype."

"Forget it."

"A real writer. Wow. Are you here in Europe doing research?"

"I thought I was. I thought I came here to recharge my literary batteries. New York was getting to me, and things seemed on hold for so long I felt my career was becoming the human equivalent of a corporate telephone. Now, I don't know. I haven't been keeping my journal like I promised myself so—"

"But I'm sure you've met some interesting people and had some interesting experiences."

"I guess I'm still having one."

She almost blushed. "Thank you."

"What?"

She smiled and squeezed my hand. I didn't have the heart to say I wasn't referring to her.

"You know, maybe it's fate." She said this as if it were a profound thought. "Maybe you're a writer, I'm going to be a producer, maybe we were supposed to meet like this now so we could end up working together someday."

"Maybe." I remembered when I was a kid and used to have those kind of fantasies, thinking I'd end up working only with people I knew and liked. Then I grew up and discovered life didn't work out that way. Life was the same kind of bullshit as high school, and you were often forced to work with the same ridiculous, arrogant, talentless stooges you hated working with at sixteen, only now the stakes were higher, since money was on the line. I had lived long enough to know that kids never grow up, they just get paid more.

Ellen handed me a business card. "My dad has these printed up so don't laugh. Anyone with a card's a producer, right? Anyway, here's my number in LA. I want you to *promise* you'll call me next time you're there. I know some people who're always looking for good writers."

"I promise."

Yeah, right.

"Good. Who knows, Cliff? Maybe one day we'll look back at this and tell the LA *Times* Calendar section how we met."

She leaned over and chastely kissed me, and by the time we parted at Zurich, I was happy to see her go.

It occurred to me as I crossed the *Bahnhof* that women were becoming increasingly detrimental to my emotional and mental health, and if I wanted to reach a ripe old age with my body and psyche intact, I'd have to swear them off at once like cholesterol.

TWELVE

I checked in at the Zurich Airport, bought a copy of the *International Herald Tribune* and sat in the Tax Free Shopping area to catch up on the National Football League. I then boarded a shuttle bus, which took us from the new terminal onto the concrete runway to meet our white-and-blue Malev Hungarian Airline. I was the last one aboard and climbed up a steel gangway through the tail of a small antique plane.

But it wasn't crowded, so I took an aisle seat. A very antisocial brunet who read German- and English-language newspapers sat by the window and reluctantly let me borrow her Hungarian *Daily News,* which was written in stilted English, but offered little of genuine interest to read.

A surly, oafish male flight attendant who reminded me of the kids in school who got picked last to play on sports teams, carried our lunch plates under his arm and passed them out like exam papers. I avoided the lettuce and cheese, opting instead for an oddly-spiced salami and pressed ham loaf.

Six seats across and every bit a rickety deathtrap, the plane swung up and down with the wind and clouds until landing at one-thirty P.M.

I went quickly through customs and the money exchange. A group of taxi drivers with name cards, looking for certain passengers, hovered by the exit, but a short, prematurely balding young man in a ski jacket appeared from nowhere, took my arm and led me to a car marked *fortaxi*. As he eased into traffic, he smiled and popped a cassette into a portable deck. "Good Vibrations" by the Beach Boys was the first song I heard behind the Iron Curtain, followed by the soundtrack from *Flashdance*. What a feeling!

At a traffic circle near the city center another older man, with a veiny nose, ruddy complexion and rheumy eyes, got in and welcomed me to Budapest. He kept smiling at me as we drove through the various streets crowded with workers.

He did not tell me his name.

He said I should rest at my hotel and I'd be contacted at midnight.

The hotel was huge, clean, right along the Danube. I was ushered through a revolving door into an immaculate lobby filled with business types, and a bellboy insisted on taking my only bag. On the way to the elevator I saw a strong-looking, gray-haired gentleman in an expensive blue suit and white turtleneck leading a monstrous white animal the size of a small cow. A helpful bellboy said the animal was a komondor, the native Hungarian sheepdog. It looked like a sheep, too, with thick clumps of straggly white hair like yarn, drooping down over its entire body. As I passed it, I smelled its meat-soaked breath. The owner, with imperial, pashalike grandeur, collected his entourage and glided out of the lobby into a waiting limousine. The dog, too.

I over-tipped the bellboy. There was an English-language teletype on TV giving approved, detail-less news. It was thirty-seven degrees outside.

Later, I walked around the streets and discovered that much of the city near the hotels appeared designed exclusively for tourists. The hotels themselves were big and Western, but there were some old shops stuck in narrow side streets, and the wheels of trade and commerce spun with ancient regularity.

Many buildings still displayed pockmarked holes, a memorial to the events of the Revolution of '56.

I saw many of the city's squares. Engels *ter* is a big square with a playground for children and a bus depot. Vorosmarty *ter* is paved for pedestrians, and the huge pastry shop at the northern end with its two brown steel-and-glass outdoor gazebos, serves as a reminder of the long-lost splendors of Empire, of low-echelon royalty and patronized artists sipping coffee and munching strudel. Now it was filled with tourists.

I then walked down crowded Vaci *utca.* It was a shopping boulevard that could have been anywhere in the world, with people rustling packages, tourists gawking at windows. I was surprised to see private merchants offering to sell their wares. Was capitalism afoot? Yet there were few billboards advertising products. Snow started falling; I bundled my jacket closer and walked quickly to my hotel. I opened my journal and wrote all this down, so at least I could say I did *some* work on my book. Then I quickly fell asleep.

By the time I awoke I was starving. My own money was running low, but Anne had given me a healthy wad of bills, which I hoped would last for the few days I was going to be in Hungary.

The concierge at the front desk suggested a few restaurants, and when I told him I was in the mood for something authentic, something delicious, something the ordinary tourist wouldn't visit, he nodded knowingly and snapped his fingers. He consulted a special list and immediately placed a call to reserve me a table.

He covered the phone and asked, "How many for dinner, sir?"

"Unfortunately I'm alone."

This didn't faze him. He said a few more phrases into the phone, hung up, wrote down the address and wished me something in Hungarian.

"Ah, is there a place I can get a phrase book?"

He pointed me around the corner to the gift shop.

A *fortaxi* deposited me on a dark, narrow, snow-covered side street behind a trail of sleek limousines. (I suddenly wondered whether the concierge wanted me here for a purpose. He did, after all, know *exactly* where to send me for dinner.) I walked tentatively toward a dimly lit door and saw the name *Margitkirt* painted in simple letters on a wooden sign. The name means Margaret Garden in a language I understand, and evidence of same was provided as I passed through a Spanish-style garden, though it was currently covered with black tarpaulins for the winter. I passed through an outer courtyard into the dining room, where three waiters in imitation tuxedos were expecting me because I had a reservation for one.

They sat me at a table by the door, a table for four.

A young woman in a raincoat was also sitting there, ostensibly waiting for a group of friends, or so I was told, but by the time I ordered my wine, appetizer, mineral water and pheasant entree—all at the suggestion of an unctuous waiter—no one had arrived to meet her. She was wet from having walked through the snow, so she said, and spit curls of tawny hair drooped in lazy circles on her freckled forehead.

My wine came and I offered her some. Her name was Agnes, she was a native Hungarian, and soon I learned she'd been raised in Africa by her father, a career diplomat. She spoke excellent English, but since she was waiting for friends she seemed reluctant to let me break any ice. I wiped on my most charming smile and assured her I was just interested in conversation, that I was a writer on holiday and simply enjoyed meeting people. Her friends were over an hour late and it didn't look like they'd be showing up anytime soon, so she relented and joined me in some wine. It was thick and too sweet, but I was too self-conscious to send it back. I didn't want to seem the ugly American this early in our conversation.

Agnes said she worked in a clothing store along Vaci *utca* and that she'd met her friends there. She seemed to trust them

when they said they'd show up. (Why this insistent reference
to friends?)

My meal came and it was enormous, so I offered to share.
She was very appreciative, since this was supposedly a fancy
restaurant where "limousines only" parked outside with rich
tourists or visiting dignitaries, and she never thought she'd
ever be able to afford to come on her own. The "friends" had
offered to pay.

It's amazing what a little food will do to get the conversation
flowing. Soon Agnes and I were talking about movies we'd seen,
books we'd read, things we liked. It struck me as odd that she'd
never heard of classics like *Dr. Zhivago* or *Lawrence of Arabia*,
but she did like Mark Twain and Ernest Hemingway. She said
she found *Les Miserables* too long.

Ah well.

To change the mood Agnes suggested we go for coffee at a
quaint place in Buda up near the old castle. For a Communist
country, Hungary sure had some upscale joints! The place reminded me not so much of the cafés of Paris, but of the chic
places home on the Upper West Side, though I'm sure the
owners here paid lower monthly rents. We ordered designer
coffee and talked more about life.

I found Agnes fascinating. I could tell her gray-flecked eyes
explored my face to see if I was really sincere, or just some
condescending prick-bastard American. When she asked me
about my life, about the girl friends I'd had and what I was
looking for in a romance, I stammered and didn't know what
to say. Then I thought: sure, I'm as fucked up as the next
person. I've got Danette back home, waiting for me with open
arms, and here I am in Europe screwing around with Josephine
and flirting my ass off with various available women all along
my route.

I didn't want to say these things aloud, but with a stranger,
and not in those precise words . . .

Well, I guess upon hearing all this Agnes decided I was a

condescending prick-bastard American because she suddenly clammed up and asked to leave. Her eyes, formerly so sad and weary, were suddenly ice cold and girded for battle. I had no intention of pressing any interests, sexual or otherwise, but she seemed thoroughly braced for a conflict, and the mood of two lost souls wrapped in deep philosophic conversation abruptly ended. A rhapsody by Liszt came on the café's stereo, and I paid the check.

We took a brisk walk along the white stone monument called the Fisherman's Bastion. At night, overlooking the flat, illuminated city of Pest, the view was dazzling. The air was crisp, snow was still gently falling, and as we strolled along the ramparts of what resembled a fortified battlement, various kissing couples scattered from the shadows.

We came upon a short line of young people dressed in last year's American-style party clothes, standing outside a small wooden door cut in the wall of the battlement. A tiny rope hung at waist level, and two girthy gentlemen in suits one size too small stood guard. Western rock music blared from behind them, and a spiral staircase descended into a dark Dantesque environment. I heard George Benson singing, "The Lights On Broadway," from what was clearly a goddamned rock club.

I was shattered. A rock club in the middle of Budapest. Even worse, as part of a historic monument! The fact that the song playing was one I associated with an old black-and-white Radio-Free-Europe TV commercial back home was a cultural artifact I couldn't get Agnes to understand.

Our evening was truly over. Agnes used a public telephone to make a call, and suddenly she grew anxious and tired. A *fortaxi* pulled up, we got in, and I dropped Agnes off at a house in the Buda hills she said she recently inherited from her grandmother.

I knew we'd never meet again.

Back at the hotel I was too wound up, still reeling from the presence of a rock club inside a national monument, to go to my room, so I stayed downstairs at the bar and had a large bottle of East German beer.

I was sitting in the deep, plush chairs surrounding the bar, overlooking the moonlit Danube, watching as tram cars rumbled by, when I looked around and noticed a beautiful woman with dusty hair, thick lips, wide, deep eyes, high cheekbones and just the hint of a sarcastic smile. She was shamelessly flirting with me from across the bar, and I had to admit that I loved it. My resolve not to involve myself with any more members of the opposite gender was dissolving under the steady influence of malt, hops and barley. She was sitting with a scruffy guy with a poorly knotted tie who looked like a loser, and while it was nice to think what might have been, I was beginning to have doubts about where I should go sticking Major Tom.

All decisions were taken from me when her scruffy male companion abruptly paid the bill, took her by the arm and dragged her off. Our eyes locked for a final glance, I felt a cliched stirring in my loins (as it were), she smiled at me and then was swallowed up in a crowd of tourists as they banged their way in through the entrance. I chugged the rest of my beer, totally disgusted with the vagaries of life, feeling cheap and shallow and eminently seedy.

Upstairs in my room I opened my journal and wrote down the first line of a short story I hoped to write someday. It would be about the effect women have on men and the subsequent loss of rational thought when the right male-female combination is achieved. One haunting, promising, intimidating, vulnerable, whatever look from the right female and—whammo—a guy becomes Silly Putty.

"It's always the eyes" was the line I wrote.

It sure is.

I fell asleep with my clothes on and woke at six to realize I hadn't been called. I phoned the front desk, but they said I had not received any messages.

By ten I was showered, shaved and ready. Still no call. Was something wrong? Had something happened? What was I supposed to do, sit in my room all day and help the maid clean up?

I went through the pockets of my windbreaker and found the slip of paper Anne had given me three weeks earlier with the phone number I should use in case of emergencies. She asked me to memorize and destroy it.

Yeah, right.

I picked up the phone and got an outside line. I dialed the various digits and let it ring. I heard someone pick up.

"Hello, hello?"

"There is no need to shout," said the voice, a deep, basso profundo.

"This is Cliff Dan—"

"We know who you are. Why are you calling?"

"I was supposed to get a call last night. I thought maybe—"

Whoever was speaking covered the phone with his hand. When he came back on line it was with a more apologetic tone. "We are sorry. Things have been quite hectic. Last-minute changes. Someone will meet you in the lobby of your hotel in two hours. His name will be Sandor." He pronounced this "Shandor." "He will take you to us. Please pack your bag and take it with you, but do not check out."

"I won't be coming back to the hotel?"

"No."

"Oh."

Sandor met me in the lobby and seemed known to the concierge as a local tour guide. He was tall and thin with short dark hair he kept closely cropped. Parked in front of the hotel was his silver Audi hatchback, though it was old and needed work.

"Where are we going?" I boldly asked as we left the city.

"To my uncle's house," he said, not taking his eyes off the road.

Sandor turned on a cassette deck and popped in a tape of

Michael Jackson's *Thriller,* tapping the steering wheel in time
with Quincy Jones's studio-produced beat.

"Would you mind if we turned that off?" I asked.

"What?"

"I have a headache."

He turned it off.

The land surrounding Budapest was gorgeous, blanketed in
fresh snow, with low-sloping hills rising up in the distance on
either side of the narrow highway. We drove through small
towns, passing farming villages, tiny churches and old, filthy
factories. At one point a convoy of military trucks rumbled by,
heading back toward the city with jeeps, weapon transports and
armored tanks in rigid formation.

"Russians," spat Sandor.

"You don't like Russians?"

"We hate Russians. Russians make us learn Russian, yet we
never get the chance to visit Moscow. All Russians are concerned with is themselves, and stealing from Hungarians. That
is why Hungary no longer is as rich as it was, everything now
going more to Mother Russia"—this said with heavy sarcasm—"than to farmers and workers right here."

"What do you think of Americans?"

"I like only some of them," he said slyly.

"Which ones are those?"

He turned and smiled. "The ones who hate Russians."

We drove a few more hours, stopping at a roadside café for
a lunch of spicy fish soup, during which time we spoke more
about the weather than anything else. Sandor seemed anxious
to discuss politics, but wasn't sure what he could say to a
stranger from America, and though I assured him I hated the
Russians with equal fervor, after his initial outburst he kept his
chatter to a running travelogue concerning local sights and
forgettable history.

A few hours into early afternoon, we arrived in Sopron.
Sandor kept driving through the quaint baroque town until

once again we were in the countryside, only this time he pulled off the main road and onto a narrow, gravel path that led deep into a thick forest. The gravel became dirt, the car made its way slowly through the trees around a tiny ice-covered lake, crunching twigs and rocks beneath its tires, until at last we came to a clearing. Up ahead, shrouded in bright fresh snow, I saw a large, apparently deserted red brick house, three stories high with tall, shaded windows and a dark slate roof. It looked more like an apparition from a Chekhovian drama than any proletariat architectural nightmare built since World War Two. A few econo-box East European cars were parked in front.

Sandor took my bag and ushered me into the building. Inside I was greeted by the same old man with the veiny nose, ruddy complexion and rheumy eyes I'd met in my cab ride from the airport. The *fortaxi* driver was there, too, as were a group of forty or so men and women. For some reason they all seemed glad to see me, smiling and nodding at me as Veiny Nose led the way to a large room that once must have been used as a banquet hall. Now it was cold and damp, and our footsteps on the wooden floor echoed against the aging walls of plaster. It was immediately apparent, as I looked around, that the house was abandoned, but from the file cabinets, hanging wall maps, hurricane lamps, aluminum desks, portable computers and telex machines scattered around, I saw it had been recently commandeered by a group of well-financed and dedicated people with more pressing concerns than creature comfort.

I was led to a plush Morris chair in front of the largest aluminum desk, which was situated in front of a huge picture window like the throne of a corporate wizard. Veiny Nose sat behind the desk, folded his pudgy, hairy hands and smiled, simply smiled, at me like a proud parent. The others gathered around, waiting I suspect to see if I'd flap my wings and fly to the moon.

"Is this where the Funhouse Police enter and spray me with seltzer?" I said to break the tension.

Veiny Nose unfolded his hands and placed them flat on the paper-strewn table. "My name is Victor. Welcome to our headquarters."

Ah hah! Revelations at last!

"Headquarters? Whose headquarters?"

"We do not have a fancy name, we simply refer to ourselves as the Organization. Names are not important. Our actions, our work, that is what drives us."

Another one with a name fetish. "And those actions are? . . ." I asked.

"Soon, soon. First, I am happy to say you were not followed to Budapest. Nor was anyone following you last night. Agnes saw to that personally."

I looked around and noticed the tawny waif I'd dined with the previous evening.

I smiled.

She didn't.

"That's peachy," I said, turning to Victor. "And where, exactly, is here?"

A beautiful woman who looked exactly like Anne only younger, came over and handed me a cup of coffee just like Wendy always did when I visited Sam's office. Was Victor an agent too? Though I smiled at the woman and nodded thanks, she just turned and walked away.

"Is Anne all right?" I asked, suddenly remembering the condition I left her in.

The young woman stopped and turned, looking into Victor's now-concerned face. "Why should she not be?" she asked.

I said, "Well, when I last saw her she was badly wounded in a shoot-out with some thugs from the Opposition, whoever they may be."

A quick conference took place between Victor and a few of his men. The young woman tried getting closer, but was yelled at by my airport taxi driver, whose name I heard was Laszlo. Victor rested a reassuring hand on the young woman's shoulder, then she followed Laszlo, Sandor and two men into an adjoining room.

"A phone call will be made at once. It is good you said something, Mr. Dandridge."

"Is somebody going to tell me what the hell's going on?"

The others in the room took seats on the floor, on chairs or on boxes, wherever there was space, in anticipation of a performance. Victor stood. Slowly pacing in front of the picture window like a duck in a shooting gallery, and speaking with his hands and a variety of facial gestures, he launched into a discussion of the realities of life.

"Do you know what fascism is, Mr. Dandridge? Nazism? What about communism? All the euphemistic *isms* of hate and repression and death. Do you? Do you know any of them? Do you know what it is to live in a tiny country whose grave geographical misfortune has caused her to be overrun for centuries by warmongering peoples from the east and west? Do you know what it is to stand and watch as your people are torn apart in war after war, revolution after revolution, to be forced to submit to the will of dictators, whether imperial or Nazi or Communist, since one and all are they the same? Do you?"

Was I supposed to answer?

"Of course you do not," continued Victor. "America is isolated by its oceans, its arrogance, its malignant indifference. Willing to let the little countries of the world suffer beneath the boot of totalitarianism until the damage becomes so profound world opinion and the exigencies of international commerce force it to become involved, diplomatically, economically, ultimately militarily."

"Am I going to be tested on this later?" I asked. " 'Cause if I am I'd like to take notes."

It was a tough room: no one laughed.

"I am a man without a country, Mr. Dandridge," continued Victor, "as are all those sitting around you. Some were born when Hungary was free, the older ones when it was part of a once glorious but morally corrupt empire. The younger ones"—he smiled at Agnes—"well, they were born in a godless, decaying, ill-conceived Communist state. We saw our families and loved ones slaughtered by the Czar, by the white hate of anti-Semitism of our fellow countrymen, by the Nazis and their Final Solution, by the wholesale rape of our land by our Soviet liberators, by the rigged elections that produced an illegitimate Communist government, and by the needless, bloodthirsty invasion of the Russians and their Mongolian mercenaries in 1956, when our people tried to win back freedom from slavery."

"I bet you'd be marvelous on television."

"Forgive me, Mr. Dandridge, for being so polemic. I am an old man given to ponderous verbosity. It is an affectation of my youth, spent as a university scholar and a rabbi to my people."

"You're Jewish?"

"Are you surprised?"

"It's just that, I guess . . . Nazis, Eli Sternberg, Jesus." I slumped into my chair.

"He's one of ours, too. Though much of the world tends to forget." Victor smiled and sat back down. I finished my coffee and put the cup on the floor.

"All right, Victor, I get the drift, I think, of your angst. You hate the Nazis and Commies for ruining your lives. Who wouldn't? They've ruined much of the world. Planet Earth hasn't been the same since Yalta. But what's that got to do with me? I mean, please, tell me what's going on? Who is Eli Sternberg? Why am I being followed? Who is Anne, if that's her real name? Tell me anything else relevant I've forgotten about already."

Victor smiled wearily, disappointed that I'd cut off his sermon but resigned to the fact that there were more pressing matters to discuss. I saw his eyes focus on the past. "To begin at the beginning. A few years ago one of my people became involved in the hunt for a former Nazi SS officer who had survived the war and avoided Nuremburg, changed his name and eventually infiltrated a European government. Which government is currently of no matter, as you shall see. When that man was found and smuggled to Israel for trial, my agent was then secretly contacted by a freelance businessman who offered to sell him a list of names purportedly documenting who and where almost four hundred other Nazi SS and concentration camp officers could be found."

"So it's just another hunt for old Nazis," I mumbled softly.

But Victor heard. "I am sorry if the slaughter of six million Jews and three million other Europeans is a disappointing tale."

"It's just that I've seen too many documentaries about people who still believe the Nazis are behind every conspiracy to conquer the world."

"Books tend to minimize reality, creating in the collective consciousness a kind of misinformed tolerance. According to their argument, if we speak enough of the tragedy, perhaps it won't seem so tragic. I assure you, Mr. Dandridge, it was. I lost my wife to the Nazi camps. Every one in this room lost someone close to them. Joke if you must, but do not despair if no one laughs."

I made a silent vow to shut the fuck up and let Victor get on with it.

"This list, according to the man who claimed to possess it, included the names of Nazis who had infiltrated other governments, democratic, Communist and otherwise, and who have risen steadily in power and influence, awaiting the day they could seize power and redirect history toward their own hate-filled goals. Nazis, Communists, renegade Socialists, Fascists, national fronts, whatever name you like. Of course, like you just now, we were skeptical. *Four hundred dedicated Nazis in positions of power in governments around the world?* But after checking the man's bone fides, we were able to draw conclusive evidence that indeed there *is* a circle of men—and women—who are at or very near the seats of power around the world, ready to unleash their despotism on an unsuspecting public.

After so many years and careful planning, a kind of international Fourth Reich is about to be born."

Laszlo the taxi driver burst in and urgently whispered something in Victor's ear.

"Excuse me." Victor turned to me, wiping the performance from his eyes, "I will have to finish this later. There is trouble."

"With Anne?"

"Yes, with Anne." Victor was up and moving to the adjoining room. By the door he stopped and said, "I am sorry, Mr. Dandridge, but I am very worried. You see, to answer one of your questions, Anne *is* her real name. She also happens to be my daughter."

He and the taxi driver walked out.

As night fell Victor and his chief associates were wrapped in a powwow. Listening to bits and pieces of shouted instructions around the old, cold house, I learned that Anne and her Parisian friends, two young men who were part of a small underground cadre of fighters battling these Nazis, were missing, presumed kidnapped or dead. Victor and the others preferred to assume the former, thus giving them hope, however slim.

After dinner I tried talking with Agnes, but I'd obviously revealed too many truths about myself the previous night; she wished no further contact with me.

Fine. Play with me, then drop me cold. Be that way. I can handle it.

I wandered outside the building while the other members of the Organization met and planned. I sat down on a rusted swing and stared up at the clear night sky, wondering how in hell I'd gotten this far and how in hell I'd get home in one piece, when the young woman who looked like Anne came out to find me.

"Mind if I join you?" she asked.

"I'd say it's a free country, but I guess you know better."

"You should not make fun."

"It's what I do when I'm nervous. I can't help it."

"My name is Catherine."

"I've been waiting in the moors for you all my life."

"What?"

"My name is Heathcliff."

A beat. "So?"

"Wuthering Heights?"

She just looked at me.

"Never mind." Oh well. "Sure, Catherine, please join me. You know, you look a lot like—"

"Anne. Yes, I have been told. We are sisters."

"You're sisters?"

"Do you hear properly?"

"And Victor is your dad?"

"Igen."

"Huh?"

"Igen is yes in Hungarian. *Nem* is no."

"I'll remember that."

"No, you won't. But Anne is my sister and Victor is my father."

"But your mother died during World War Two, and you don't look a day over twenty-five."

"I am thirty-five, actually, and thank you. But that was not my mother. That was Victor's first wife. He has had three. My mother died during the uprising, and he has since remarried again."

"That ol' fox."

"He is not so bad. But you must help us, Heathcliff, we need you."

"Will *you,* at least, explain what's going on?"

She got up and walked through the snow, kicking at it lightly, deciding what to do. She dusted a large boulder clear and sat down on it, shivering from the sudden contact with cold. I walked over and stood facing her, waiting to see what she'd do.

"This is what I know," she said at last. "Anne was sent to find Eli Sternberg and get the list of secret Nazis Papa was talking about from him. Sternberg was the businessman who had contacted one of father's overseas agents. Sternberg led us to believe there was a dangerous man living in New York who was following him, and in exchange for protection from that man, Sternberg would get us the Nazi list. Through our contacts, we discovered that there was in fact a man following Sternberg, and he lived in your apartment building in New York City. That is why we put Anne there, across from your house, to watch for him."

A coincidence? A genuine coincidence?

"I know it sounds ridiculous," said Catherine, "but that is what happened. And when someone succeeded in killing Sternberg with a time-delayed poison—"

"That went off when Sternberg was in the museum?"

"Yes. Anne thought you were, in fact, the killer."

"That's two coincidences for the price of one."

"What?"

"It's something your sister said, about nothing being a coincidence."

"My sister is a good field agent, Heathcliff, but she is sometimes melodramatic. She takes after our father."

"And you don't."

"There is no time. The young sometimes see things more clearly than their elders."

"Yes, but the wisdom of age sometimes outweighs the impetuosity of youth."

"You are very strange, Heathcliff."

"That's what my friends keep saying."

She looked at me with dead seriousness and shook off whatever comment she was about to make.

"Please, we do not have time. You are our only link now, you must cooperate."

"Why is that?"

"There are people following you who think you know all about the Nazis and where they have infiltrated."

"I'm being followed by *Nazis?*"

"They think you stole the letter Sternberg was going to give my sister. They also fear Sternberg might have told you more about them, about who was following him, and why."

"But I know nothing. I never even got any list of names."

"They do not know that."

"What do you need me for?"

"As bait. To lure them out of hiding, so we can catch them."

That's two people who needed me as bait. I turned to Catherine. "Catch who? The people who knew about the list, the people on the list, the people who want the list?" I paused. "What the hell am I talking about?"

"Heathcliff, there are people in the United States who are on that list. People in important positions in your government in Washington. As well as in Moscow, London, Paris, Bonn . . . even Jerusalem. Their lives and careers and plans are threatened until everyone who knows of their existence and works against them is silenced. The men chasing you?"

"The two goons?"

"They are American FBI agents who we suspect are sympathetic Nazis. Anne did not tell you this because she did not wish to alarm you."

"Remind me to thank her."

"We, and you, must find that list of names and publicize it before it is too late. Before the world is overrun by hate."

"I think it's too late for that, but all right, what the hell, I'm game." What was I thinking? I didn't know the first thing about tracking down Nazis. Aside from a few receptionists and development people in the film business, I'd never even met any. Yet even if I didn't believe these people, didn't care about their crazy, paranoid conspiracy theories, there were malevolent forces after me, on two continents already, who seemed to know where I lived.

If there were a club for card-carrying paranoids, I suppose I deserved to be signed up.

202 ADVENTURES WITH DANGEROUS WOMEN

I said to Catherine, "It doesn't look like I have much to lose now and the only way I'm going to get you people off my back is to cooperate, right? And maybe we can help Anne. I feel I owe it to her, God knows why." Her life was at stake, that's why, schmuck. "I mean, she got me involved in this in the first place."

Catherine was looking at me, revealing nothing behind her poker face. With that look she reminded me of her sister. I'd have to get close to see if she smelled the same. "All right," I said, "you have me. Now what?"

At that moment Victor, Laszlo, Sandor, Agnes and the others appeared from behind the trees and began applauding.

"Well I'll be damned," I mumbled.

"Thank you" was all Catherine said. She took my arm and led me, stupefied, back into the house.

She smelled absolutely nothing like her sister.

PART THREE
The Sun Also Comes in From the Cold

THIRTEEN

With phony travel documents and tremendous precision, I was smuggled across the border into Austria a few days later, where a private car was waiting to take me to Vienna. Victor wished me good luck, Agnes ignored me totally, and Catherine hoped I would find peace and Anne, though not necessarily in that order. Once in Vienna there was no time to rest, since my flight to New York was set to leave before lunch. I was permitted to once again use my own passport, which had been miraculously, no doubt illegally, stamped with an entry visa for the Austrian Federal Republic. The flight home was long and uneventful, which allowed me to reflect on what was happening.

I didn't like it.

Still, I was alive. Thank heaven for small favors. With any luck, I'd be able to draw out whomever was after me, find Anne, get the list of names, hand it over to Victor and his cohorts, save the world from a group of Nazi lunatics and be done with it.

Of course there was still Oren to deal with, since he had gotten me involved with French smugglers, one of whom was dead, and now the French police, in the form of Inspector Lonsdale, was after my ass for skipping town without so much as a kind *au revoir.* And if Lonsdale was to be believed, there was Marcel Coloute, formerly of Haiti, current whereabouts unknown, also looking to turn me into human waste material.

And let's not forget darling Danette, bless her heart, awaiting with open arms and a heavy guilt trip, desirous of matrimony, or at least a reasonable explanation as to what I'd been doing for over a month.

A month? Jesus, and I hadn't called Sam in the last three weeks. But why worry? He'd have some patented excuse as to why nothing was happening in my career, why I'd have to continue having patience, and why I'd become his "number-one priority" since I was the client most likely to default on life and our contract.

If nothing else, it wasn't a promising reality to go home to. There was Rick, who'd be pissed that I caused him to go to jail in Paris, though I was sure he'd make it sound worse than it really was. I mean, after all, what did he really know about life and death anyway? Huh? When was the last time he was smuggled out of Eastern Europe by conspiracy-minded Hungarian Jews?

What am I saying? If I had any brains at all I'd disappear for good. I'd parachute out of this plane right now and make my way to some backwater monastery in some remote Austrian village and learn to etch on parchment, make pretzels and brew the best-tasting beer in creation.

Beer!

When was the last time I'd quaffed a cold one? Here I'd been in Europe and somehow (aside from a few Kronenbourgs and a nameless East German one) neglected to sample some of the most obscure local libations known to man. It often puzzled me why monks were so adept at making beer, cloistered in those huge, ancient, stone cold monasteries, where "pick up the soap" was more than a mere catch phrase for a good time in the shower. But I suppose I'd have to return someday on another sojourn to find out.

And that word: *sojourn.* Makes me recall the initial purpose of this excursion. Hemingway? Fitzgerald? The Lost Generation?

What did they know?

Drunken fistfights in the street, timid bullfighting, a few quick tosses in the hay with assorted floozies, unspoken sexual doubt and spurious literary ambition?

Let me ask you: were they running away from the same things I was?

Well, were they?

I'll tell you this—they never had it so good.

Boy, did I have a headache. . . .

The stewardess (or in-flight hostess or customer-service representative or airborne cocktail waitress, whatever) rolled up with a cart of fluids and I asked for a beer. She gave me a Heineken, which I chased with generic whiskey that burned as it went down. It tasted like woodshavings.

I ordered another two.

I soon fell asleep, alone with my demons, and didn't wake up until Queens.

New York and home, always synonymous, always there. The hustle of the international crowd at the airport, the accents, the wealthy Arabs, the cosmopolitan Europeople—who, though born in America were slaves to Continental fashion—the surly local employees barking in Queens and Brooklyn dialect, the frustration of waiting to collect your bags from the luggage carousel, of dealing with bored, menacing customs agents who, if you look like a jerk or a professional businessperson, will generally leave you alone, since they're only looking for the fear in your eyes as a tip-off to more sinister nondeclared items in your suitcase, all this, part of a reassuring ritual that somehow feels less classy, more working-class, in New York than in any other major Western international airport.

Yet there's a unique feeling of cyclical completion that accompanies me every time I come home. Not quite a Poe-like feeling of returning to the womb, more like a mythic ending to the wanderings of a legendary prodigal. Kind of a "lost sensation" that, regardless of how many newspapers you've read, how much television you've watched, life in the world has changed and you've missed it and you're no longer the same. I'm not talking about the specific and personal chaotic events of my recent past. I'm referring instead to a feeling that means a traveler returning from foreign soil must re-enter his home culture and reacquaint himself with the the Feeling of Life in America before he can resume a normal rhythm. There's a certain change of pace, loss of knowledge, alteration of spirit, that slows the pulse and eases the mind, even after the most exhilarating of trips, so no matter how the body and mind resist getting back "up to speed," whether you've been to Paris or Borneo or Cairo, there is that half-time, like twilight, that your mind must cross before you can really *return home.*

Usually I like to dwell on this feeling, let my body savor what feels like sexual afterglow, since to me a good traveling experience is as rewarding as good sex.

Unfortunately, this was not to be.

As soon as I handed my passport to the weary, bifocaled, overweight customs officer, a pair of beefy airport security guards came over and whisked me through an unmarked side door, down a long, empty linoleumed corridor into a private office with heavy soundproofing on the walls and ceiling. There was an aluminum table covered in puke green Formica, a smattering of beige, uncomfortable steel folding chairs, a water cooler, some paper cups. Air vents sucked out the stale odor, since the three-bladed ceiling fan seemed to be on the fritz.

All that was missing was a lone bare light bulb, a circling insect, and the Gestapo.

The latter soon appeared, however, in the guise of two well-built women. One, shaped like Winston Churchill, with a similar scowl, took a seat in the corner, nodded to the airport security guards, who left, and assumed a position to stare.

Churchill wore a nondescript dress, neither flattering nor in keeping with current fashion, and sensible shoes.

The other woman, tall and black and too muscular from working out with too many weights, was not unattractive, but was obviously cocky as hell. She moved with the same kind of self-assurance usually found in a gang of ghetto kids circling a lone man whose car has broken down in Harlem at four in the morning.

I cleared my throat. "I don't suppose—"

"Shut up." The tall black woman barked in my face.

I complied.

She continued moving, eyeing me, smirking with a shit-eating grin. Churchill sat motionless in the corner, breathing with difficulty; a clear sign she was more fat than muscle.

"Welcome to America, Dandridge. Been having a good time in Europe?" The tall black woman sat on the tabletop, revealing a pair of legs made of perfectly shaped ebony.

"Well I—"

"I could really give a shit."

Gulp.

She continued. "My name is Agent Dahlia. This is Agent Gompers. Pardon me while I whip this out." She immediately produced her identification badge, as did Gompers, but removed it before I could check its authenticity. I thought: just like on television.

"Agents of what?"

"Shut the fuck up, Dandridge, understand? Or have you been in Europe so long you forgot the mother tongue?"

This was one bad ass momma. Probably suffering PMS.

"Time to explain the ground rules," said Agent Dahlia. "I will do all the talking, you will do all the answering when I give you permission. You will refrain from smart-ass mouthing off, and you will tell me everything I want to know without heaping it with bullshit. Do I make myself clear? You may speak."

"Yes, ma'am."

"Don't play frightened white boy with me. I've had a shitty week and don't feel like mothering you for information."

Agent Gompers tittered in her chair, beads of sweat breaking on her brow.

Agent Dahlia continued. "Now, as we have already demonstrated by producing our badges, we are FBI Agents. Agent Gompers and I are in the midst of conducting an investigation, and it has come to our attention you know proportionally way too much for a man of so little consequence. You found yourself mixed up with people in something far out of your usual minuscule realm, so your candor in responding to our questions will be most appreciated."

"Do I have any rights?"

Agent Dahlia couldn't decide whether to kick out my eyes for speaking without permission or to actually answer my sheepishly asked question. She smiled like a Cheshire and craned her neck closer. "You are in the international zone of this airport. For all intents and purposes you are nowhere. A stateless person with all the rights pertaining thereto. Meaning zilch. Are we clear on that?"

Didn't sound right, but I was in no position to argue.

"Good." Agent Dahlia stood up, walked around the table and took a seat opposite me. Since she didn't produce any notebook, I could only assume our conversation was being recorded. Or maybe it wasn't, and this was not all it seemed. "Enough about me, let's talk about you." She pulled out two black-and-white studio portraits of middle-aged bureaucrats. I recognized them immediately. "Familiar? You may speak."

"These are the two men who were chasing me. First in New York, then in Paris."

"Good boy, Dandridge. That is exactly right. But could you please be more specific?"

I told her everything. It occurred to me she probably knew it all anyway and was hoping to catch me in a lie. Either that, or she was using my account to verify certain details. Nevertheless, I told her what I knew, and an hour later, after mentioning my sortie into Hungary, though not mentioning the fact that Anne had been kidnapped, I finished.

"Agent Gompers, bring Dandridge some water." I was handed a smudged paper cup, wet on the outside from Gompers's sweaty grip.

"I hope I didn't bore you," I said after I finished the water.

"Nonsense. And you told it so well. Shame you haven't had more success as a writer."

Agent Dahlia was up and leaning against the wall, munching on a bag of what looked like a Trail Mix bought in a health-food store. "Look, you've been straight with me, so I will be straight with you." Agent Gompers tittered again, causing Agent Dahlia to shoot her an ice-cold glare.

"I'd appreciate any enlightenment you could offer," I said to break the tension.

Agent Dahlia turned on me. "Enlightenment, Dandridge, is an eighteenth-century term describing rationalist thought popularized by Voltaire, Rousseau, Montesquieu and Hume, to name a few. It is not something I can offer you now, but if you like we can sit down when all this is over and discuss it."

"Like rational human beings?"

"Not bad, Dandridge."

I bowed.

"This is the horrible truth," said Agent Dahlia. "You've been authorized by my superiors to hear it, because—"

"Don't tell me you need me?"

"Score another one for the white boy. Keep this up and we'll make you an honorary junior spy."

"I'll pass if it's all the same."

Agent Dahlia slipped into ghetto-ese. "You ain't got no choice, man. You done messed wid da big boys and gots to play by dere rules."

Agent Gompers spoke for the first time in a soft, wheezy voice. "Can we get on with it?"

Agent Dahlia was not pleased with the interruption, but let her anger pass. She turned to me with a helpless expression. "Before I went to college, Dandridge, I grew up in Georgia. You know the rest. My family was so poor, etcetera etcetera. I put up with a lot, joined the bureau because I liked playing bitch with a badge, and the police force didn't offer enough room for advancement. Now with this case I can advance all the way to Go and collect two hundred dollars, and you are going to help me."

Agent Dahlia then explained that the two men who were following me were indeed bad-apple FBI agents, rogues more interested in selfish gain than serving their country. People who took the good name and reputation of Hoover's bureau and sullied it, all in the name of obeying some higher authority. It had been discovered, said Agent Dahlia, that a cadre of Nazis had penetrated the bureau and were working from within, trying to take it over. They could be working for themselves, they could be working for someone else, they could be working for the Soviets. This, she said, no one knew. What was known by a trusted few was that for some absurd joke of the universe a few of these Nazi fanatics were after Heathcliff Dandridge, perhaps because he knew damaging information. That he had managed to stay alive all this time was a testament to his natural abilities or his luck, which made him useful as bait to draw out the bad guys, catch them doing something dirty and bring them to justice.

Bait again. This was getting tedious.

"What about the black man who was with those men chasing me in the Paris zoo?"

"You a closet racist, Dandridge?"

I didn't dignify that.

Agent Dahlia took out a pad and pen and wrote something down. "We didn't know about that, to be honest. Monroe and

Madison were chasing you on their own, or so was the popular wisdom in Washington. I'll look into it."

I played my trump. "Could he have possibly been connected to this Marcel Coloute?"

"I said I'll look into it." She wrote down some more notes, though I could see her eyes start to shine.

How a former member of the Haitian Tonton Macoute could be wrapped up with subversive Nazis agents of the FBI and for what purpose, I could not fathom. But I was willing to buy anything.

"I love my country and I love the bureau," said Agent Dahlia.

"Though not necessarily in that order," I offered.

She looked like she wished she could swat me. "And I don't intend to see either sullied by a gang of renegade agents out for themselves. Do I make myself clear?"

"May I speak?"

"You may."

"Yes."

A smile crossed her face, and for a moment I thought she appreciated my style. The moment quickly passed. "You're free to leave, Dandridge. Go home, unpack, take a shower, eat your Wheaties. We'll be in touch."

I stood to shake hands with Agent Dahlia, and though I'm almost six feet tall, she towered over me and crunched my hand in her grip.

Agent Gompers handed me a business card. "Don't leave home without us," she wheezed.

It was great to be home and in New York, even if home was on the Upper West Side. I noticed that in less than a month two long-term merchants had been closed; one replaced with a boutique cookie store, the other with a sign advertising the place as "For Rent," which, if current local trends were to continue, would remain vacant for years, costing the landlord more money than if he'd kept it rented to the old merchant who'd been there and popular. You could walk up and down the Upper West Side and see high-rise luxury condominiums sprouting up like concrete weeds, stretching skyward, offering cubicle apartments the size of roach motels to the Europeople and brokers who could afford it, forcing out the flavor and character that originally made the neighborhood great. Fancy dogs of unpronounceable breeds, designer clothing stores for infants, overpriced restaurants offering rabbit-sized portions of old-world recipes that wouldn't feed a flea, everyone dressed for success, or if you'd already made it, dressed to appear downwardly mobile, unconcerned with appearance, and consequently chic. Style over substance, a crying shame bankrupting the city.

In the shadow of all this, at appropriate corners where foot traffic was heavy, like outside the twenty-four-hour cash machines, scattered homeless went through their individual rituals, panning for gold from the passing throng. There was the crying screamer who sat on the sidewalk and shouted "Help me please!" the obese woman standing draped in an oil-stained drop cloth quietly asking for change, the thorazine-riddled outpatient who stood at attention with his head hanging down and his arms outstretched in front, holding a begging cup, asking for nothing, expecting less, and the old grandmotherly-looking woman with the vacant eyes who parked herself inside a bank's money machine area, quietly asking if anyone could spare a cup of coffee. Many times people, including myself, offered her one, but she wouldn't take it. Instead, she just kept muttering if anyone could spare her a cup.

Ah, New York! Where life rubs you and slaps you in the face every day of your life. At least it keeps you honest. At least it keeps you in touch with reality as it is and not as the Madison Avenue image brokers process it.

I was wired and couldn't sleep, despite the change in time

zones, yet I was a little put off when Danette didn't want to make nooky. She came over as soon as I called, but after the initial embrace, the welcome home wet one, and a warming pair of cocktails—during which I briefly described the travelogue aspects of my trip—my psychosexual radar detected that something was amiss.

"I suppose you want to know what I've really been up to for the past month."

"No."

"Huh?"

"I mean," she said, fingering a loose thread on my sofa, choosing not to look at me, "you'll tell me what you want when you want to."

"Well, I certainly want to hear all about what you've been doing."

"You do?"

"Yup."

She faced me. "What if I said I didn't want to tell you?"

"Then I'd throw you on the floor and fuck your brains out until you changed your mind." I smiled.

She threw her drink at me.

"You asshole!" she screamed.

Hmm. I'd stepped into something I had to scrape off immediately. "Danette, I'm sorry. Come on, it's me, I'm a jerk sometimes. I thought a little intimate language would break the ice." With a finger I wiped the residue of her drink off my face and licked it. "An interesting way to drink Chivas."

"There you go again!" She pounded my chest in anger, so I grabbed her arms.

"Look," I said in all honesty, "I was hoping this reunion would be a lot better than it's going."

"Sorry." She didn't sound it.

"Let's start this all over."

"I think it may be too late for that."

"I don't understand."

"If you weren't so selfish, so worried about yourself all the time, maybe you would." Clipped, harsh, sarcastic.

"Where did this come from? Huh? I thought we understood each other? I thought when we spoke before I left, it was with the understanding that things were going to be better when I got back? That we'd talk about moving in together or something?"

"Or something."

I reached out to hold her, but she flinched, got off the sofa and disappeared into the kitchen. I sat alone for a few seconds in numbed silence. Not what I was expecting, none of this. I was prepared to tell her the bulk of my experiences, give or take a fact or two, but not this, not face the Wrath of Hell.

I finally got up and went into the kitchen and saw Danette was crying, sitting at the kitchen table, playing with an empty book of matches, crying her eyes out. "Get out of here" was all she said.

Back on the sofa I waited another ten minutes until she reappeared, eyes dry but red, her manner more composed. She'd apparently confronted her demons and selected her plan of attack. "Heathcliff, I'm not so foolish to expect you to have been monogamous while you were away, and neither was I. We're two grown, mature, single, sexually active adults, and that's life. But your insensitivity is driving me insane. Your life is in danger and you call me twice in five weeks? You pop home unannounced and expect me to rush over and welcome you with open arms and a blow job? What about me? What about what we were supposedly building? What about—oh, just forget it, fuck it, this isn't what I wanted to talk about."

Thoroughly confused by her scattershot emotions, I looked on helplessly as Danette came over and hugged me. It was more maternal than sexual. We leaned back on the sofa and stayed hanging on to each other, breathing slowly, softly, steadily in the darkness of my apartment.

It did occur to me that Danette seemed to suggest she had an affair while I was away, but now wasn't the time to inquire further. In any event, as we sat there, hugging each other for dear life, I fell asleep. When I awoke, the sun was up and Danette was gone.

FOURTEEN

I went down to the corner and bought a copy of the *Times* and the *News*. I wasn't in the mood for Stella D'Oro, so I grabbed a croissant and coffee from the corner deli that used to be owned by two old Jews but was now operated by a family of Pakistanis who were friendly and seemed to selectively understand English (they knew how to make change, but could never understand what you wanted on your sandwich).

On my way back I noticed that the burned-out building directly across the street had been boarded up, and a frayed orange police line had been draped across the walkway leading to the entrance. I pitied the people who were forced to move, pitied the old lady who lived there whom I used to help with bags at Gristedes, and wondered what would have happened had I not met Anne.

It suddenly dawned on me that there was still someone living in *my* building involved in all this. It was a mistake that I'd become involved, but Anne, wherever she was held right now, had originally taken up residence across the street to watch *someone else.*

But who?

I entered my lobby and stood gazing at the row of mailboxes. I didn't think I could match names with all the faces, but I did think I knew what everyone looked like. There were assorted elderly people, with accents from all over the map. There was the old guy who always seemed drunk, but courteous and helpful to all the young ladies in the building. There was the family of five who lived in a two-room apartment, and who supposedly converted their walk-in closet to a baby's room. There was a divorced woman who gave guided tours at the United Nations and who always seemed to be entertaining exotic men from around the world. There was a German banker, a Swiss pilot, an Italian television executive, a bunch of young and old actors and actresses in various stages of success, a few struggling musicians, a piano teacher, a couple of other writers, assorted business people, a drug dealer, a few retirees. Overall, I'd never been friendly with any of them, at least not any more than to say hello when passing in the street or on the stairway. The man involved with the death of Eli Sternberg and the list of Nazi names could have been any of them.

I opened my front door and noticed my answering machine in the process of taking a message. I ran to pick it up.

"Hello? I'm here! Hang on."

"Cliff?"

"Yeah? Hold on, let me turn this off. Who's there?"

"A close and personal friend of Inspector Lonsdale of the Paris Police." I immediately recognized it was Rick.

"When did you get back?"

"About two days ago. Cliff—"

"I know, I'm sorry. I really had no choice. You've got to understand that I didn't want to get you more involved."

"Involved? What do you call flying to Paris on a moment's notice?"

"Total self-interest."

"Yeah, well . . . let me tell you I had to fight for my life in that French prison for twenty-four hours. I don't understand a word of French, but I assure you, there are some things universally understood."

"You don't mean—"

"It was close, but I managed to maintain my virtue."

Silence for a few seconds. Rick didn't sound mad; I knew he really wouldn't be. Friends in time of crises generally understand and measure up. Still . . .

"So tell me what happened." I said.

"I paid the bill and figured you'd been kidnapped, so I went back to Lonsdale, who kept me euphemistically in protective custody for my own safety. My friend at the American Embassy arrived and got me out, and Lonsdale said I'd be safer in New York. I didn't feel compelled to question that wisdom, so I split."

"Then you're not mad that I suddenly cut out?" I asked hopefully.

His brain was deciding what to say. "Look, you're still alive, aren't you?"

"Yeah."

"I guess, then, I'm a little disappointed."

"Fuck you too, pal."

"Fuck this, Cliff."

Same ol' Rick. I briefly clued him in on what subsequently happened to me.

"Listen Cliff . . . you seen or spoken to Danette yet?"

Odd question coming from Rick. "She was here last night."

"And?"

"And what? Since when are you interested in the details of my sex life? I'm not running for president. You writing for a newspaper now?"

"No. But everything's still fine between you two? I mean, well . . . what'd she have to say?"

"What was she supposed to say, Rick?"

"Nothing. Look, I gotta get back to work. I'm glad you're home. Let's grab some brews and you can fill me in on everything. I'll come uptown."

"Make it seven at the All State unless I have to cancel. I gotta track down my job pimp and Oren the Human Scumbag."

"That's a ten-four, good buddy. Catch you on the flip-flop."

"Well, if it isn't the European traveler, come home from the wars!" Sam got up and came around his desk, shaking my hand and closing it in both of his. "Have a seat. You thirsty? Dorothy'll get you something."

"Dorothy?"

"My new assistant. Started last week."

"What happened to Wendy?"

"Don't ask." He sat down and a grave look descended over his face. He must have asked Wendy to run away with him and she declined. Good for her. She'd probably go far in this business.

"So?"

"So what, Cliff? You didn't call me in so long, I forgot the sound of your voice. I don't know how to tell you this, but everything I was working on fell through."

"What?"

"The series in L.A., the book deal, there was even an M.O.W. I was cooking up but didn't want to raise your hopes on in case it didn't pan out so I didn't tell you but now I am so you see how hard I work."

I thought, *Where can I find a chain saw at ten o'clock in the morning?*

"Sam, what do you mean? Don't you have any work for me?"

"I mean, Cliff, that I do not now have any work for you. If you'd have called, say, Tuesday, I could have told you to get on a plane and come straight home. But those *goniffs* couldn't wait, and went with somebody they knew they could get right away. That's the book deal. The series, well, the folks in 8-1-8 got all nervous about using a New York writer. You know how they think out there, they need you to be a breakfast away. If they can't see you at Hugo's for oatmeal, they don't want to know from you."

"Sam, I don't believe this. My life was supposed to be going gangbusters when I got back. Everything was falling apart and looked shitty, so I left. And now you tell me all these things have slipped away?"

"Like sand in an egg timer."

We argued a little more, and Sam promised he'd get right back on the stick, poking around to see what he could line up. He suggested I seriously consider moving west, where all the action was. I said get me work and I'm there. He asked me how the research was going for my new book and could I tell him what it was about so maybe he could feel around and see if any publisher would give a damn.

I told him I hadn't the foggiest idea what the book was about anymore.

Back home I put on some John Coltrane to soothe and relax me while I laid down on the sofa to sort out the direction of my life. It was two in the afternoon, making it eight in Paris. What the hell. I lowered the music, found my address book, reached for the phone. It was early enough, so there was still a chance she'd be home.

"*Allo?*"

"Josephine? It's Cliff."

"CLIFF? You are all right? I was so worried, I—"

At least *somebody* had the right response. "I'm fine, I think. I just got back."

"Back? Back where? Where are you calling from?"

"Home. I'm back in New York."

Silence. All I could hear was the intermittent thumping of the transatlantic connection.

"Josephine? You still there?"

"I thought you were coming back to Paris." A simple, declarative statement.

"I planned to. I wanted to. I—"

"Claude gave me your message. Addressed to Emma Bovary from Gustave Flaubert. Cliff, I thought we would again spend more time together. More time to—" She sounded hurt, confused, unsure whether to hate me or hang up. "I was so worried, I couldn't work."

"Josephine, let me try to explain. I thought you'd—"

"Understand? I do, Cliff." I could almost see her weary smile. "I don't mean to be like this. It is not like me at all. It is just that . . . this is so . . ."

"Josephine, I'm sorry. I am. I hoped we would've been together longer."

"Me, too."

Why is it I feel as though I've been spending my life having these elliptical conversations on the phone and not in person where they probably go better?

"Look, it's really very complicated. Anne, that woman I told you about, she was in trouble, I was in trouble, there were people chasing me, as you know, but more again later, shooting at me in the zoo . . . Christ, this sounds fucked up. Are you still there?"

"*Oui.*"

"I had to go on such short notice, Josephine, to Hungary, where this secret group of people smuggled me back through Vienna to New York. There wasn't any time . . . I feel like such a shit."

"Please Cliff, enough. I believe you, all of this, only it is hard to understand. I am trying, you know. Really, this is not like me. . . . I keep saying that." She mumbled something inarticulate in French. "And I miss you. I didn't want to."

"I miss you, too."

I heard fumbling on the other end and thought we'd lost our connection. "Josephine? Hello?"

"I am here . . . Cliff, we will see each other again?"

"I promise. I'll try and get back to Paris as soon as I can, as soon as I get another assignment. I'm a little short of funds at the moment. All this international intrigue. I'm just hoping I can pay next month's phone bill to call you."

I heard a little laugh and then what I thought were sobs. Maybe not, I wasn't sure. "I must go now, Cliff."

"Good-bye, Josephine."

"*Au revoir,* Gustave."

I put the phone down and sat there staring at it, feeling for some reason as though my stomach had been kicked in.

Risa, my nymphomaniac-nurse-ex-girlfriend, sent me a post-card from the Yucatan, where she'd been climbing Mayan ruins and young Americans on holiday. She missed me and said she wished I were there with her to explore our personal "Aztec roots," whatever that meant. I had no idea she'd even left the country, nor when she'd be back, but boy would I have a story to tell her.

If I survived.

I came up from the basement with a basket of fresh laundry to find agents Dahlia and Gompers standing in front of my door.

"Nice to see a man doing his chores," snapped Agent Dahlia.

"Good afternoon, ladies. I don't suppose this is a social call."

"Our duty requires that we see you again, Dandridge. Don't lip off or I swear I'll fuck you up."

"Charming invitation, that."

"At the risk of sounding cliche, we need to take you down-town." Agent Dahlia was casually looking at the laundry in my basket as we entered my apartment.

"See anything you like?" I asked.

"Figured you for a jockey shorts man, and I was right."

"They teach you that at the bureau?"

"Grab your coat and cut the crap. We have to make the world safe for democracy."

I saluted, dropped the laundry on my bed and followed them out.

Downtown—which was actually midtown, a fact I pointed out to deafening silence—Agent Dahlia and Agent Gompers escorted me into a plush, wood-paneled amphitheater that looked like a Hollywood screening room.

"Sit," barked Agent Dahlia.

Agent Gompers disappeared through a tiny door behind the last row of seats, below what I noticed was a projection booth.

I said to Agent Dahlia, "You're not going to give me any *Clockwork Orange*–style torture tests, are you? You don't have Beethoven all cued up against a series of war footage or anything kinky like that? You're not going to pry my eyelids open with toothpicks?"

Agent Dahlia stood behind a podium on the tiny stage. "Seems you forgot my little lecture from yesterday."

"And that—"

"Shut up, Dandridge. Speak only when spoken to. I have no time to deal with your breed."

"Breed?"

She glowered at me with eyes so dead I felt sorry for her. I stared right back, but blinked first. This brought a smile to her eyes. "We did some more checking on what you told us," she began. "You'll be happy to know your suspicions were correct."

"Gee, that's swell. What suspicions?"

"We already established that you were being chased by agents Madison and Monroe. The black man you described with them has been identified as one Huntley Toussaint, Haitian refugee living illegally in Paris. He was known to the French as an operative working for Marcel Coloute."

I raised my hand for permission to speak. It was granted. "Did they pick him up for questioning?"

"Oh, they picked him up all right, but not for questioning. They picked him for an autopsy."

"What?"

Agent Dahlia was literally beside herself with mirth. "Seems the coroner reported cause of death was as a result of beatings from a tire iron. Now, let me ponder how that could have happened. . . ."

I feigned ignorance. "You mean I killed someone?"

"Looks that way, son, don't it?"

"Shit."

"Exactly. Fortunately, Agent Madison survived. He's a vegetable, but at least he don't wet himself. Serves him right, disgracing the bureau like that."

"So, what happens now?"

"Well, therein lies the crux. An illegal Haitian refugee living and dying in France, a known operator of Marcel Coloute, working with bad agents, Nazi crazies, of the esteemed Federal Bureau of Investigation? And you, responsible for the man's demise? Possibilities are endless, Dandridge. Seem that way to you?"

I didn't know what to say.

"Speechless for the first time?"

"What am I supposed to say?"

"Well, first-time killers usually worry about the form of sentence they can expect to face. Life in prison, death by lethal injection, that sort of thing. Though I don't know how they do these things in France."

"You're not serious?"

"As serious as a stroke, Dandridge. They've been talking extradition all morning long."

"Wait a second, you still need me, right? I mean, now we've got a link between your Nazi crazies and this Marcel Coloute. Don't you think you ought to find out who, how and why that's there? Don't you think if they still think I know the names on their master list, that they'll try coming after me, and don't you think you'll be able to follow them to their leader, cut things off and save the day for peace, justice and the American Way?"

"I like you when you get nervous, Dandridge. Humbling experience, but on you it wears well."

"Come on, Dahlia."

"Agent Dahlia, asshole!"

"Sorry."

"Settle down, Dandridge, and listen up. Aside from agents Madison and Monroe, and the woman you describe as Anne, there were no witnesses, so your life is somewhat safe. It does intrigue the shit out of my superiors that this Coloute would be involving himself in bureau affairs, with Nazis and Tonton Macoutes."

"So start looking for Coloute."

"You're pretty stupid for a white boy. Coloute had plastic surgery, so say the files, and we have no idea what he looks like anymore, or where he makes his headquarters."

"Do you know anything about him?"

Like a game-show host she shouted enthusiastically, "I am glad you asked that question, Heathcliff Dandridge! Roll 'em, Gompers."

The lights dimmed and a series of images flashed on the movie screen at the front of the amphitheater. The first image was a grainy, jumpy silent film of the streets of a very poor city. There were goats and chickens wandering in the street, old women sitting curbside next to sheets covered with baskets, T-shirts, and assorted useless junk, hoping for a lucky sale. Some men were carrying baskets of fruit and vegetables, stopping to barter with anyone who passed, stepping over the open sewers and gutters.

"That's Port-au-Prince, Dandridge, capital of Haiti, poorest nation in the Western Hemisphere."

The images of poverty were interrupted by a parade of three black Mercedes limousines racing at top speed down the street.

Mercedes number one knocked over one of the men carrying fruit, and as the second Mercedes turned the corner, an old woman was run down, her legs clearly flattened beneath the weight of the car.

"Run that back at slow speed, Gompers. Now Dandridge, pay attention to the passengers inside the cars."

The cars backed up and the two old people popped up like marionettes. At slower speed the three Mercedes returned. Agent Dahlia spoke. "In the first car you can see, not too clearly, Jean-Claude Duvalier, his pudgy little face enjoying a candy bar as his car passes over the old man. Doesn't even phase him. In the next car is a short, stocky, bull-faced little thug with tiny round eyes. That was Marcel Coloute in 1984. Okay Gompers, normal speed."

There followed a stunning series of footage that included widespread violence on the streets of Haiti, in towns with names like Cap Haitien, Les Cayes, Gonaives, Ouanaminthe, wherein armed guards cut people down in the street with machine guns and machetes. Army vehicles rammed right over tiny shacks of corrugated steel and rotted wood, exposing the inhabitants to the ruthlessness of the Tonton Macoute, their weapons and their dogs.

Agent Dahlia said, "Most of that was back in '84 when a fictitious Communist threat gave Duvalier enough of an excuse to arrest whomever he wanted. In 1985 he proclaimed himself President-For-Life, just like his good ol' dad, the late Papa Doc. In January of '86 the government shut down the schools and forbid the radio stations to report any news of the growing unrest. Martial law was declared and all hell broke loose. Coloute was supposedly using this time to consolidate his network of hatchet men in case Duvalier abdicated. Then in February '86 when Duvalier fled and Army Chief of Staff General Namphy seized power, Coloute fled with money and men to South America, then Africa, and finally to Paris."

The next set of clips came much faster, containing more brutality. It was like watching an instructional tape on organized violence. Airport ticket counters, strewn with corpses and debris from terrorist bombings, a plane wreck in France, another in Texas, still another in Florida, body parts scattered on trees, shrubs, other body parts. A hospital room full of decapitated babies, a voting booth riddled with bullets, a candidate and his wife almost unrecognizable beneath reddish blue viscera. There were scenes of confiscated trucks containing heavy artillery, drugs, high-tech computer equipment. A highway bridge in New York blown apart, with dozens of cars and corpses lying crashed hundreds of feet below. There was a homemade video of a very nervous man in a blindfold, shaking and perspiring. The blindfold was removed by some unseen hand and the man stared directly at the camera in horror. The face looked familiar for some reason, like a man I'd seen somewhere on the news, but not after a machine gun was placed against his temple and his brains were splattered out on the wall behind him.

I shot out of my seat and Agent Dahlia pointed the way to the toilet.

When I returned, feeling faint, the lights had come on and the film, thankfully, was over.

"Sorry about that Dandridge."

"Why did you show me that?"

"Everything you saw was a crime attributed to Marcel Coloute and/or his operatives. Coloute seems to operate with impunity throughout the Third World, and is clearly one of the world's most dangerous men, though his motives aren't well known so the publicity usually goes to some sun-dried Arab or half-drunk Irishman. Anyway, I wanted you to know what we're facing. No games here, Dandridge. If this shitstain on the face of humanity is in some way working with my fellow agents, I'm personally going to use his dick for a paperweight."

Gompers returned from the projection booth and added in her wheezy voice, "At least you now see the dimension of his madness."

Agent Dahlia turned on Gompers, "Been reading again, Gompers?"

There was something going on between these two, a dynamic I couldn't quite place my finger on, not that I wanted to. I did have some ideas.

"Go home, Dandridge," said Agent Dahlia. "Get your life straight, drink a six-pack, watch the playoffs. We'll keep an eye on you so you don't end up dead or dismembered."

"Thanks." I stood up, a bit shaky.

"Don't it just make you all warm inside knowing all this?" said Agent Dahlia with a grim smirk.

And I thought *I* had a twisted sense of humor.

FIFTEEN

"**O**pen this door you ignorant fuck!"

The heavy metal panel slid aside and Oren graciously welcomed me in. "There's no need to shout," he said softly.

"It's been almost a month, Oren! I'd kill you if I could get away with it. What the fuck did you get me involved in?"

"Easy, Cliff. If you just take it easy everything in life will work itself out." He was wearing a white kimono with a red sash around his waist, his long black hair was tied in a ponytail, and he was smoking a joint in an old-fashioned cigarette holder. The remnants of dozens of candles stood in tiny dishes all around the loft, as did assorted party hats, paper plates and plastic cups. A dull, acrid haze hung in the air, reflecting in the afternoon light that penetrated his Levolors.

Oren walked toward a counter in his kitchen area. "You missed a great party last night. If you were home, you should have called. This Teamster brought in some fresh powder from Bucaramanga, Columbia. Some guy's private plantation high in the mountains. Guy supposedly gave up growing coffee for El Exigente to realize a better margin on his investment."

Pow! I knocked Oren in the face, sending him assbackwards to the floor. I was too frazzled to put up with any more of his bullshit.

231

"You prick! You scum! I don't want my brains blown out by any assassins, goddamn your ass! All this is your fault!"

Oren simply said, "You'll have to work on that right if you're thinking of turning pro." He stood, so I swung at him again. He was too chicken, or too mellow, to fight back, so he ran around the loft, throwing chairs and party streamers in my face. "Take it easy, Cliff."

"How can I take it easy when you get me involved in smuggling? When you get me mixed up with some goddamned Third-World Haitian terrorist? When half the fucking police of Paris and New York are after me?"

"I only got you involved partially, Cliff."

"Partially?"

Oren was standing to the side of his beloved bowling alley, where a few balls were resting in the return. I picked up the balls and began throwing them at the pins. I was a lunatic unhinged, picking up pins and smashing them on the lane.

I wasn't pretty.

Soon Oren was on my back, wrestling the pins out of my hands, smacking me in the face. I kicked him in the groin and he rolled over in pain. My nose was bleeding, I was panting like a madman, but the release felt good. I threw some more pins.

Oren was moaning on the floor as I stood over him like Ali over Liston. "Partially, huh?," I roared. "Partially involved? How partial? How fucking partial? What was in those goddamned cornices?"

"Peace, okay? Peace?" Oren stood slowly, clutching his kimono. He gingerly stepped back into the kitchen, poured himself a cup of coffee from a pot on the counter and sipped it. He sat on a stool near the butcher block and looked at me. "You're not going to like what I have to tell you, Cliff. But believe me I had no choice and didn't think any of it."

"Start 'splainin'," I said, a la Ricky Ricardo.

"Well, I don't know if I ever told you, but I still have family in Poland. Aunts, uncles, first and second cousins. People I've known my whole life, but who I haven't seen in ten—what is it?—twelve years. Anyway, we used to write, then I stopped hearing from them when the government got tense and closed down Solidarity. My uncle was a big deal in the union, used to eat breakfast with Walesa, met the Pope, that kind of heavy."

"This family biography has something to do with why my life is in grave danger?"

Oren winced. "Sometimes, Cliff, you get so melodramatic."

"Sue me."

He sipped more coffee. "About two years ago a group of people came to me one night and showed me pictures of my uncle in prison. He wasn't alone, his wife was with him. Cliff, they looked like shit. Beaten and thin, in a cold cell with black steel chains around their wrists and ankles. It looked like something out of a fucking movie, man. But these people, these visitors who came here, they spoke Polish like natives but with a terrible accent, well they said my family wouldn't be hurt if I did a few things for them. They said that in a few days time they would deliver a package to me, and all I had to do was get it to Europe. They didn't care how I did it, but since they knew I was involved in the film business they figured I could smuggle things overseas in a supply case or a film can or whatever. I said if they knew how to do it, why didn't they do it themselves. This, they didn't answer. They just sat there staring at me, looking mystical and ominous and very, very heavy."

Oren walked over to the stove and tried relighting the tip of a joint on a gas burner. No luck. He immediately found a pair of eyebrow tweezers, clipped the roach and frantically tried lighting it with a stove match. Again, his hands were too unstable to get either object to connect. I helped him light it, figuring it'd be the only way he'd continue with the narrative. He nodded his appreciation, finished his smoke, then sat back on a stool near the kitchen counter.

"Where was I?"

"You were telling me about the Polish Gestapo."

"Right, so they said if I did deliver their packages, then everything would be all right. Well I did it once, twice, the third time was about a year ago, and my aunt and uncle were released. Or so they said, but I had no choice and was forced to believe them. Then about five weeks ago one of the guys from the initial group who I hadn't seen in over a year came back by himself, showed me my uncle all over again in prison, with a handwritten note from my uncle begging me not to cooperate anymore. My aunt had died, said my uncle in the letter, he was all alone now and did not care anymore. Of course the letter had the opposite effect on me, and I felt I had to help anyway I could. The Polish guy, whether he was a secret agent or a terrorist or the Devil's messenger I have no idea, he said that soon there would be another package he needed to get to Europe. He said it was going to Raphael Arnot, a friend of mine. Actually, Raphael was more an acquaintance, someone I'd met, heard about, dealt with, more for his access to stimulants than his skills as a designer. He's a real shitty designer, into blending so many styles he loses all sense of perspective. Did some lousy Italian horror movies just to pay his dealers. He's a much better source when you need drugs. I didn't like Arnot, but felt, fuck it, I'd deal with him to save my uncle. Then I got that job doing the science fiction film, which turned out to be a real piece of shit but I got paid, so what the hell, right? Life's little karma. Anyway, I couldn't get away, and you said you were going to Paris on some literary expedition, so I thought I'd take advantage of your kind and generous disposition and let you carry the package for me. You did, and soon I got another letter from my uncle saying he'd been released." Oren finished his second coffee and put the cup in the sink. He stood there with his back toward me. "Sorry I used you, man. I didn't think anything of it."

"That's pretty clear."

Oren just stood there, staring at the mess in his sink.

I said, "Did you ever think that the whole thing was a setup, that your uncle may already be dead and they're just writing letters and concocting pictures to push your buttons to get you to help?"

Oren turned and looked at me as though the idea never occurred to him. Then he pulled his shoulders back and said, "What choice did I have? I couldn't take the risk. It's like lady and the tiger. Behind one door is a ferocious tiger, behind the other a beautiful lady. I was hoping I'd chosen correctly."

"Just maybe, Oren, behind both doors there were only tigers."

He paused. "I'm sorry, Cliff. I hope everything else works out. But you've got to understand I had no choice."

"No choice? To use your friends like that? Without even telling them?"

"Would you have done it if I'd have told you what little truth I knew?"

I couldn't believe Oren still didn't see how he'd done wrong. I bent down and picked up a bowling ball that had rolled to my feet.

"Look at the big picture," said Oren. "We all have to look out for ourselves in this world. Sometimes it isn't pretty, but that's the core of existentialism. I hope you'll understand, Cliff. And I hope this won't ruin our friendship."

He reached out to shake my hand. I picked up the bowling ball and hurled it dead center onto his granite coffee table, smashing it into a zillion pieces.

Oren shrugged. "I guess I had that coming."

Rick was sitting at the bar in the All State Café on West Seventy-second Street when I arrived. It was a dark and cozy place a few steps down from street level, where the food was good, the fireplace blazed in winter, and the people weren't obnoxiously Yupper West Side. The waitresses were also a lot of fun.

I noticed as I sat that Rick had already polished off a scotch and soda, which I hadn't seen him do in a long time. My suitcase—the one Inspector Lonsdale had confiscated—lay by his feet.

"Thinking of doing a remake of *Lost Weekend?*" I asked, indicating the scotch.

"Cliff, man, hey. . . ." Rick's voice was a bit slurred, making it clear he'd finished more than just the one glass resting on the bar.

"I see you brought my suitcase back," I said. "Thanks."

"Cheers." He tossed back his head and finished the last of his scotch. He waved toward the bartender, who came over and took our orders. I asked for an Anchor Steam, about the best domestic bottled beer around.

"So why the bender, Rick? You don't usually need so much booze to behave like a jerk."

"Jerk this, asshole. I'm just in the mood to give my palette some diversion."

"Ah, we're in our wise costume this evening."

He squinted at me in the dark. "How come you got a bloody eye and a puffy nose?"

"I went for pizza in the wrong neighborhood and wound up at Oren's instead."

"You two had it out?"

"Let me put it this way, he won't be asking any of us over for a bowling tournament for quite some time."

"Whew," said Rick, who seemed eminently impressed with whatever he thought I'd done. Our drinks came and we clinked glasses.

"May the best days of our past be the worst days of our future," he said.

We drank and ordered another round. I briefly recounted the events that had transpired since I scooted out on Rick in Paris, and we each ordered a hamburger. Nat King Cole sang Christmas tunes over the jukebox, and suddenly I remembered it was less than a week until December 25. I hadn't even shopped for anyone, so wrapped up was I in my own situation. Jose Feliciano came on to sing "Felice Navidad."

"Were you happy to see Danette?" asked Rick, as the bartender sang along with Jose at the other end of the bar, ("I want to weesh joo a Merry Chrees'mas . . .").

"Sure. I guess so. I mean, why not? A month away is a month away. That's enough time to miss your girl friend."

"It's not as though you weren't getting any," said Rick, avoiding my eyes.

"Meaning?"

"Meaning I saw those pictures Lonsdale took of you and that razor-cut brunet with the nifty bone structure in Paris."

"Josephine," I said more to myself than to Rick. "Well, these things happen, Rick. Come on. You sound like you object. What're you judging me for all of a sudden?"

"Me? Judging you? Furthest thing from my mind."

"Look Partridge, it's not as though we had anything special. It was a traveling romance, that's all." Did I sound convincing?

"Would you see her again?" he asked.

"I don't plan on visiting Paris in the near future."

"Would you see her again if she came to New York?"

"As I don't see how that's possible—"

"Just answer the fucking question."

"Not so hostile, Rick, okay?"

He held up his hands. "I'm not hostile. I'm a lawyer. Sometimes it comes out that way."

"Well, since we're not in court—"

He seemed hurt. "Fine, all right, be that way."

We proceeded to munch our burgers. Brown hamburger juice slid down my wrist and under my cuff; I started to wipe it clean with a napkin when Rick blurted out, "I think I'm in love with Danette."

"Huh?"

"I said I think I'm in love with your girl friend."

"She's terrific, that's for sure."

"I'm serious, Cliff."

"Serious what? What do you mean you think you're in love with Danette? What kind of thing is that to say?"

"I mean I think she's terrific and I don't think I can stay celibate any longer."

Now, Rick was a friend in good standing, one of my closest confidants, the man to whom I would turn (and have turned) in time of crisis. Furthermore, as my attorney he was privy to many of my most personal secrets, and if I ever got married, he'd be the one to handle the prenuptial agreement.

But this?

"Is this the booze talking, Rick, or have you seriously lost your mind?"

"Remember when I said I went with someone to the Jets-Miami game?"

I did.

"It was Danette."

"She hates football."

"I made it interesting for her. Taught her the rules, got her a wool hat, took her to a tailgate party before kickoff, these lawyers I know with a Winnebago and—"

"So you went with her to a football game. She didn't tell me that. Big deal."

"Then we went back to her place and I stayed until breakfast."

Ooh boy. My head swam. The bar seemed to move away. I felt shaky and angry and wanted to rush out for air.

"What happened, Rick?" I looked him in the eye. "You got so hard up you go after my girl?"

"Let's not talk in the possessive, my good Cliff. Danette is a bright and lovely young woman who belongs to no one at the moment."

"That's not how it is, Rick. She and I have been together for a while."

"That was preseason. The games all count from now on."

"I don't believe we're having this conversation. I don't believe this at all. Rick, this is my girl friend we're discussing here!
I mean, I know—I guess—it was strange when I called from
Europe and she said she'd spoken with you. You two seemed
friendly, but that's just, well, friendly . . ." Rick sat there staring
at me, letting me work this through all by myself. "And then
last night," I continued, "she said, or seemed to say, that she
wasn't entirely alone the whole month I was gone, but I never
figured it—Shit." I signaled the bartender. "I think I'll have a
scotch like my friend here."

"So we're still friends? That's nice."

"I'm not so sure." My drink came and I gulped it. "Where
do you two stand?"

"I have no idea."

"What?"

"I mean we saw each other a number of times before I went
off to Paris—"

"You knew then and you didn't say anything?" I couldn't
believe this was happening.

"I thought it wasn't my place, Cliff."

"I trusted you, Rick. I guess I fucked up."

"I didn't hurt you, Cliff. All I did was offer Danette another
option in her life. You don't have any monopolies on women,
pal. Not in Europe, especially not in New York."

"Monopoly this, fuckface."

He ignored our ritual banter. A bad sign. "She's a gentle and
loving woman," said Rick, "who deserves to have attention. To
you she has to be a nursemaid and psychologist, giving you
space to travel the globe and work out your angst and prema-
ture midlife crisis. To be there when you need her, when you
want her, and never when she needs or wants you. You're not
happy with your life the way it is, Cliff, but Danette is, basically.
And even if I want to paint pictures or take photographs, that's
a hobby, not an alternate reality, and so I offer her a picture of

legal and financial stability, which is pretty hard for a sweet redhead from Babylon—"

"Quogue. She's from Quogue."

"—from Quogue to turn down."

"Has she?" I wasn't sure I wanted the answer.

"Has she what?"

"Turned you down?"

"No. But she hasn't said yes yet, either. I haven't given up. She's got a lot to think about, and she does care an awful lot about you, too, despite your obvious flaws."

"And I thought we were friends. . . ."

"Cliff, we are best of friends. This has nothing to do with our friendship. But a man's got to do what a man's got to do, and my right forearm was beginning to get larger than my left. I needed a *wo-man.*"

"And Danette sure is that." I sounded more wistful and defeated than I'd wanted.

"Hey, cheer up. Don't be so depressed. You do what you have to, I'll do what I have to, we'll leave the rest up to her."

"Pretty confident, aren't you?"

But Rick wanted to change the subject. "Look, forget it for now. At least you got out of Europe alive. Thank heaven for small favors."

Thank heaven.

This wasn't happening to me. I couldn't stand it. My best friend and my girl friend. On top of all the other bullshit. How was I supposed to cope? How was anyone in my position supposed to cope?

I was more miserable now than I was when all this began. At least when I was feeling totally anxiety ridden, completely dispirited with life, there was my girl friend to give me strength and support. But I suppose Rick was right. Maybe all I did was take and never give, expect and never anticipate. Everything was a one-way street in my romance with Danette, and she was too good to deserve me.

But that was crap, and I knew it. Rick, as a lawyer, was a bullshit salesman with a mouth full of samples, and whether or not Danette felt as he'd described, he certainly would paint a picture wherein he'd come out smelling like a rose. I couldn't let his smoke and mirrors blind me to the reality of my relationship with Danette, which I knew was good, which I knew had a future . . . even though we sometimes had nothing more in common than our sexual proclivities, even though when she was over the night before she was, clearly, upset about something and didn't seem all that interested in . . .

Goddamn-it-to-hell!

I was debating whether or not to treat myself to bagels and fresh sturgeon from Barney Greengrass, when Oren and a group of his friends appeared at my door, a bunch of green cloth sacks in their hands.

"What do you want?" I asked, closing the door in Oren's face.

"I'm here to make a peace offering. Let me in."

"Who's with you?"

"Just some friends."

"I don't want to know any more of your friends."

"Come on, man, let us in. I needed them to help me carry stuff."

"What stuff?"

"Open up and I'll show you. Come on, man, we got a truck double-parked."

I shut the door and ran to the window and looked outside to see a rented Ryder truck like the ones used to carry props when they shoot movies in the city parked on the street out front. I went back to the door and shouted, "What are you up to, Petrowicz?"

"A little something to help make you feel safer." I heard a few giggles from behind my door, and figuring "What the hell?" I opened it.

"Greetings and felicitations, Healthcliff. I won't bother introducing my friends, but suffice to say I felt obliged to offer you assistance."

A group of techies—people who schlepp props and set pieces in movies and television—began carrying what appeared to be a few heavy-duty green cloth bags full of stuff into the center of my apartment. Two guys carefully placed a wooden crate beside the bags, then all eight helpers left. Oren stood there, beaming.

"What's all this Oren?"

"Only part of it. There's more. You're going to love it, Cliff. Just love it." He sounded like Willy Wonka.

I went over to the bag and kicked it. My foot met heavy steel. I opened the bag and saw not one, two or three, but almost a dozen heavy-gauge machine guns, shiny from oil and individually wrapped, bound together with rope.

I turned and said, "You're out of your mind."

"That is a subjective opinion you are ill equipped to prove." I'd never seen Oren so delighted.

"Are they real?"

"As real as death and taxes. Go ahead, open the crate."

I did. It contained what looked like enough ammunition to aid the Contras.

Oren said, "That's real, too. You'd be surprised to know how easy it is to get that stuff in this town."

"You always said you were connected."

"It is a truth I am comfortable with," he said somewhat inscrutably. Just then the other eight men came in carrying army sandbags, some on their shoulders, some in wheelcarts. One beefy guy asked, "Where do you want the trench?"

"What?"

"Where do you think you'll want to sit, waiting for the

attack. Once we put 'em down, we don't move 'em." The seven other guys all laughed at this.

Oren took over and, designer that he is, began rearranging my furniture, ordering his friends to set up a round protective area of sandbags in the middle of my living room, directly between the front door and the window.

"Oren, what do you think I'm going do with all this?"

"Protect yourself. You said you didn't want to get your brains splattered all over creation and you said it was my fault your life was in jeopardy. I figured the best way to get myself back in your good graces and make amends was by designing a way for you to protect yourself. A few quick calls, and voila! Here is my plan designed especially for you."

"What am I supposed to do with these weapons?"

"Clean 'em, load 'em, aim 'em and use 'em." Oren was really enjoying himself.

"I haven't the foggiest idea how these things work."

One of the techies then tossed me a manual. "Operational instructions for the layman," he said. "Written in English and Spanish. Don't worry, you have more intelligence than ninety percent of the people who use these on a regular basis. It's mostly instinct, anyway. You'll figure it out."

With that, the eight schleppers marched out, chanting like they do in drills at boot camp. "Ain't no use in going on, Charlie got my girl and gone. Ain't no use in going back, Charlie got my Cadillac. Ain't no matter what we do, Charlie got my sister too!" They laughed and disappeared down the stairs.

"Well, Cliff, I suppose I'll be leaving you to your vices." Oren was rearranging a few sandbags as he moved toward the door.

"Oren, you fuck, this is insane. I mean, machine guns, sandbags! What if the cops come?" I held up one of the machine guns. It was lighter than it looked. "None of this is licensed, is it?"

"Tell them you're watching it for a friend. If they don't

believe you, open fire . . . " Laughing hysterically, Oren
slammed my door as he left. I ran out after him, but by the time
I reached the street he'd jumped onto the rear platform, effect-
ing his getaway a la the the Keystone Cops. I stood there, pissed
as hell, as the truck drove away, then realized I was still holding
the machine gun, so I ran back inside.

Okay, fine. Might as well make the best of it. Use Oren's
peace offering as a way of insuring my safety. So if the guy who
lives in my building and killed Sternberg should deign to visit,
there'd be no way in hell he'd mess with me. No, sir! I was
surrounded with paramilitary hardware on the third floor of an
Upper West Side brownstone, a supply of machine guns and
ammo at the ready, I easily had the element of surprise on my
side. Whoever came a-calling, whether the guy in my building
or someone sent by Marcel Coloute or the FBI Nazis, I'd
simply take them out . . . BAM-BAM-BAM!

Of course, if this were up in Harlem or the South Bronx the
opposition would probably storm my place wearing flak jackets,
tossing mace.

But this was the neighborhood of Mrs. Fields cookies, Sushi
bars and Zabars. What were they going to do: food me to death?

I was sitting in the middle of my sandbags, loading and
unloading the clips on a machine gun when Danette, using her
key, came in. She nearly jumped out of her skin when she saw
me with the ordnance, but calmed herself and put down a small
cardboard box on a nearby table.

"I was cleaning up my apartment and found a few of your
things," she said.

"You didn't have to return them."

She ignored this. She now also ignored the sight before her.
"A few books you loaned me, some tools, maybe you've been
looking for them?"

I climbed out of my trench and went to her. I put the ma-

chine gun down next to the cardboard box and said, "I think
we better have a talk."

"Look, Cliff, I'm sorry I didn't talk to you about it last
night."

"What's going on, Danette? Talk to me."

"This doesn't mean it's over. It only means I need some time
to think things through. Not having your stuff at my house
takes the pressure off."

"Pressure? I really don't understand any of this. What happened while I was gone? It was only a few weeks, I don't see
why you couldn't—"

"It had nothing to do with the short time you were away. It
only gave me some freedom to think clearly."

"And Rick, for God sakes. I mean, Dani, be real."

"Oh Cliff, it has nothing to do with Rick. He's sweet, a friend,
but he's not you. You're not him, either, but that's not the issue.
The issue is not even us. It's me. What do I need to make me
happy? I'm not even sure I know the answer. I love you, I think
I love you very much. But maybe it's the wrong kind of love.
Who knows? Certainly not me, not at this point. Just give me
a few days, maybe a few weeks. It's only fair. I gave that time
to you."

"And I thought we were considering moving in together now
that I'm back."

She eyed the sandbags. "Doesn't seem as though you have
any room here anymore."

"Dani, the sandbags are from—"

She held up her hand. "Don't say another word. It's your
business. I don't want to know. You said when you called from
Europe I'd be better off not knowing, so don't tell me. Let me
reside in blissful ignorance. I care about you Cliff, and hope you
come through whatever troubles, whatever emotional breakdown you're experiencing. But you don't need me, you need
professional help."

I thought: that's probably true, but not the same kind she's referring to. A skilled assassin, a military analyst, something like that.

"Me? I need something too, Cliff. Some help, probably. And some time."

"Don't we get to talk this over like adults?"

"Neither of us has been behaving like adults, why should we start now?"

This didn't sound like the Danette I knew, but I was probably different after all that had happened the past weeks, so it was only fair to assume she'd been changing as well. I said, "Danette, we have something special between us. Let's not throw it away so easily."

She walked up to me and held my hands in both of hers. With her big, round doe-eyes and burnt-red eyebrows and thick lips and porcelain skin she stared at me with a profound emotion that somehow transcended love. "Do you love me, Cliff?" she asked.

"What?"

"Do you love me?"

"Of course I—don't be silly."

"Then say it. Look me in the eye and say you love me and think this is all ridiculous."

"It *is* all ridiculous."

"Then just say you love me and this is ridiculous."

I looked her in the eye and squeezed her hands and said softly, "I love you."

"Bullshit."

"What?"

"Bullshit. You don't love me. You think you love me, or you may be *in love* with me, but it's not the same."

"It's not?"

"You may be in love with the idea of being in love, but not of being in love with me. You may be on your way to loving me, but you're not there yet."

"How can you say that?" Was she right? Did she know me better than I did?

"It was the way you said it. And the look in your eyes. You can't hide your eyes, Cliff. They're the windows of your soul."

"Danette, this is ridiculous."

"*That* is correct. *This* is. Oh Cliff, you're so sweet and confused and I really think we'd be good for each other, but we both need time to think this through. And I don't think while you were away you gave much thought to our relationship. You were too busy exploring and running away from reality."

"There is some truth to that, Danette, but not the kind you—"

"Enough!" She paced around my living room, circling the artificial trench of sandbags, so bewildered by it she seemed to shrug off making any comments. She stood for a moment, staring out the window.

"Danette, please, I—"

She turned and said, matter-of-factly, "No more words, Cliff. Let's just give it time." I moved closer, saw there were tears welling up in the corners of her eyes. She was fighting them, sniffling a bit, wiping her eyes to keep them from bursting over. Emotional woman, but strong, too. I'd never seen her like this.

I said, "Let's just both of us not jump too fast one way or the other, agreed?"

"Agreed."

Like business partners closing a deal, we shook hands. I held hers a bit longer, but she pulled it away and silently left my apartment.

That night, lying in bed, I was unable to sleep. My mind was a jigsaw puzzle of ten thousand pieces, all the same shape, all entirely white. "A Polar Bear in a Blizzard."

Eventually I must have dozed, because I had this dream. In it I was sitting at a conference table in Sam's office, listening to a group of people telling me why I was worthless, why I was going nowhere in my life and my career. Editors, agents, producers, directors, Sam, Rick, Oren, Arnot, Victor, Canadian Tim, Lonsdale and Swaim, all sat there offering up their wisdom, telling me what direction I should turn myself. Gradually their voices became a monotonous drone and their faces blurred as they changed. Next thing I knew I was surrounded at the same conference table by Danette, Anne, Josephine, Olga the hedonist, some other women from the French sex house, Ellen of the Valley, Agnes, the unknown woman from the Budapest hotel bar, Anne's sister Catherine, FBI agents Dahlia and Gompers, and the old woman who was run over by the black Mercedes in Port-au-Prince, Haiti. They were all yelling and jabbering and pointing their fingers at me, getting up out of their chairs and coming to surround me at the head chair. "Blah-blah-blah," they shouted.

"No more blah-blah-blah," I shouted back.

I couldn't take it: I was in a cold sweat. I wanted to scream. And I did, too . . . and I woke up.

"I can't take it anymore!" I yelled, banging my fist on the wall behind my bed.

"Go to sleep, asshole," I heard shouted through the wall from my neighbor next door.

If I only could.

I lay there for another two hours, staring at the ceiling, until I closed my eyes and finally fell asleep as the sun was coming up on another day in my life.

SIXTEEN

All right, that's it! No more of this sitting around with my finger up my ass!

I jumped out of bed, grabbed the phone book and rifled through till I found the name and address of the Augsburg House up in Germantown.

I circled it. Underlined it. Stared at it. Fine.

Now what?

Well, maybe someone there would know what's going on? Maybe someone would have some answers? It was ten-thirty in the morning, but I reached for the phone to dial the restaurant.

My phone rang instead.

I picked it up to hear Anne's voice on the other end. She was frantic and spoke quickly.

"Listen, Cliff. They do not know everything. Whatever happens, you must not tell—" But the phone was taken from her before she could finish.

"Anne! Are you all right?"

A man's voice answered. "Good morning, Mr. Dandridge." It was clipped, nasal, arrogant, reminding me of the kind of people at movie theaters and banks who bray at you to "Stand in line, *please!*" Nasal Voice continued, "Aside from a few minor scrapes, your lady friend is fine. And I'm glad she saved me the trouble looking up your number. It was on my list of things to do today. Seems you were on *both* our minds this morning."

"Okay, fine. Just tell me what you want, who are you, where—"

"Too many questions, Dandridge. Put it this way—you want to see your lady friend alive you'll bring me whatever Sternberg slipped you at the Whitney before he cashed in his chips. Can't possibly be any use to you, and it just may save the life of your dear, sweet, partially bruised ma'm'selle."

I didn't have the matchbook. In fact, I'd given it to Anne back in Paris. Obviously, she'd been able to keep it from whomever was holding her, and hadn't revealed the phrase written inside.

"Come on, Dandy. You know you have no choice. I better see you in less than an hour with the list of names that Jew gave you, or your lady friend here will be discovered floating past the UN, missing various parts of her anatomy." Nasal Voice let loose a high-pitched giggle.

"All right, all right." I gave in quickly, trying to sound desperate. "I guess I have no choice. But I'll need a little more time to visit my safe-deposit box"—I was making this up as I went—"to get what I need."

Nasal Voice laughed, grunted, then agreed on meeting at noon. He gave me the address, then added, "I don't suppose you'll be foolish enough to call for help on this, Dandy, since there really isn't anyone you can trust."

Unfortunately, that made sense. For all I knew, agents Dahlia and Gompers were in on this too. I dressed, loaded one of the machine guns, placed it in a gym bag, and took the subway south.

The *F* delivered me to Delancey, where I emerged streetside into the bustle of bargain hunters combing for last-minute Christmas gifts. The sleazy emporia were rundown graffiti-covered firetraps, but that didn't faze these folks, who wouldn't know better and couldn't afford it if they did. To an out-of-towner it would seem strange that this neighborhood shared an island with the wealthy chic a mile west, but that's life in a metropolis where real estate has become the equivalent of government handouts for the rich.

I walked east then turned south, entering a no-man's land of vacant lots, abandoned storefronts and half-burned buildings. Amidst the rubble and stench, the bodegas and shops advertising "Checks Cashed," stood a few red-brick public buildings erected at taxpayers' expense to serve the local community: solid, foreboding, visually uninteresting structures reminiscent of prisons. Why couldn't they put affordable housing in attractive buildings down here? Why couldn't they put a few pleasant parks for the children to play in? I thought: *Let's call Don Trump and see if he can do something about it!*

I got to the address Nasal Voice gave me. Or at least I thought so; it was an abandoned building set back from the street behind a vacant lot. I pushed aside a hanging piece of chain-link fence and slowly walked over beer cans, broken bottles, pieces of wood with exposed nails, concrete chips, rubber tires and twisted strips of metal, looking nervously for signs of life. A rat scurried ahead, burrowing under some crates, and I noticed someone sleeping in an empty refrigerator box.

A new plank of unpainted plywood served as the front door of the building. I entered, removing the machine gun from my bag, feeling for some reason a bit like Ollie North. The inner hallway was dark and dusty.

"Hello?"

A baseball bat slammed from around a corner, banging my wrists, knocking my gun to the floor. A strong white man with pale skin and a blond butch cut kicked the gun further away, then he poked the Louisville Slugger into my stomach as he took possession of my weapon.

"Pretty stupid of you," he said, waving the mouth of the gun in the direction of a staircase.

I was led upstairs to an abandoned railroad flat. In the front near the kitchen was a table covered with paper plates and Chinese takeout. There were three other men, similar in make and model to my escort, each equipped with Kalashnikov automatic rifles.

At the table finishing lunch was a tall, thin, muscular blond man with a bushy mustache and a thick neck. I recognized him as one of the struggling actors who lived in my building. I'd always thought he was just another gay actor, what with the bushy mustache and impeccable way he dressed, not to mention the way he walked without moving his upper body, but now it seemed that was all just cover.

Was *this* who Anne had originally set out to watch?

"Your expression means you recognize me." He was smug. "I don't think we ever had the pleasure, though you may know my stage name from the mailboxes. Jack Martinson. Forgive me if I don't introduce my friends." He waved theatrically to indicate the other men.

"Where's Anne? Is she—?"

"First things first. You bring the Sternberg list?"

"You won't get away with whatever you're planning." I was stalling.

"I won't?" He was amused.

"There are people who already know about you. The FBI isn't so stupid it doesn't know when its own people are Nazis and traitors."

"I wouldn't be too sure about that." This produced a chuckle in all five goons, who looked so much alike they could have been products of selective breeding. "And be careful who you call Nazi. You don't even know what you're talking about."

"I don't? Well, it just so happens I've been in contact with senior people in various agencies around the world who're on to you. They know you've infiltrated the FBI, as well as other secret services, in the hope of taking them over and instilling your own hate-mongering Fascists. They know the names of all your operatives and it's only a matter of time before they're rolled off the streets." I grinned, satisfied.

"Very melodramatic, Dandy. Files said you wrote for a cop show once, so I guess it's paid off. Nevertheless, I'm not worried whether anyone is on to us or not. My superiors tell me everything's under control. Besides, that list isn't proof, merely a guide. There *is* no proof, nor is there any way they can stop us. Destiny is on our side."

"Destiny? What destiny? You talk like a madman, Jack. And to think I was living in the same building with a nut job like you."

An Aryan goon swung the butt of his Kalashnikov into my chest, knocking the wind from my system.

Martinson resumed his speech. "Our agents are hand picked, Dandy, thoroughly dedicated, the best. Our leaders saw to that." He rose and began circling the room, seemingly desperate to impart his sense of destiny to anyone who'd listen. He spoke in that tone usually associated with clinical psychopaths. "Our leaders were trained by the best sons of the Reich, men who knew better than Hitler, who saw the only way to ensure a thousand-year empire was to train and prepare for the future. Suffer we did, and many have not lived to see their dreams go forward. But many survived, and the torch was passed to a new generation. Tell me, Dandy, how many men in governments and corporations around the world today do you suppose were dedicated Nazis both during and after the war? Do you have any idea? Would it surprise you if I said thousands? Men of industry, men of prestige, of importance. Trained, funded and secretly supported by a vast network of National Socialists, awaiting the day when we'll finish the work begun during the Putsch of '23. Defeat communism, defeat weakness, defeat intellectualism. And *finally* exterminate the Jews!" With the back of his hand he wiped saliva from the corner of his mouth. "Now, hand over that list!"

He was too melodramatic to succeed as an actor. "What makes you think I didn't make any copies?" I asked.

"Copies are unimportant. All we need to know is what your so-called friends know so we can prepare." He was playing with a pair of chopsticks on the table, poking around a white carton for a sparerib. He suddenly looked up at me, deep in thought. "Come to think of it, I don't think I believe you at all. I don't think I believe you've spoken with anyone in quote authority unquote, and I think you've had nothing but the misfortune of falling in with Anne and her ridiculous hysterical collection of pathetic little Jews."

"Is that what you think?" I batted my eyes.

"Besides, if the cretins who run the bureau already had the list of names, they'd have moved on it by now and we'd have heard about it."

"You don't seem to have much of an organization if this is your headquarters."

"This is just a way station, for meetings like this. To deal with nuisances like you."

I played a hunch. "If I'm stupid enough to have brought the list with me, you mean Marcel Coloute will be stupid enough to permit you to let me and Anne leave here alive?"

He looked at me like I was nuts. "Who is that? Marcel—?"

"Coloute. Marcel Coloute. Come on, surely he's your—"

Martinson nodded in my direction and two of the Aryans grabbed my arms while a third proceeded to beat last night's dinner out of my stomach. I doubled over and felt a fist fly into my jaw, knocking my head back, spraining my neck. Finally, I screamed.

"Cliff!" It was Anne, shouting from somewhere close.

"It was pretty stupid of you not to have brought that list," said Martinson as he walked into another room. "Bring him. Let's show him how uncomfortable we make our guests."

I was dragged through the apartment to a room at the rear, where I saw Anne lying naked on an old mattress, tied down with rope around her ankles and wrists in a humiliating spread eagle. Her clothes were piled in a corner. I turned my head, but one of the Aryan goons twisted my neck so I was forced to look. I shut my eyes, and my stomach was punched.

"Leave him alone!" she shouted.

"This *is* a touching scene," said Martinson.

"Sorry about this," I said weakly to Anne.

"Cliff, it is not your fault."

Martinson poked me with a steel rod. I noticed there was a small fireplace burning with a compressed artificial log, and I watched as he rested the end of the branding iron in the fire.

"You see, Dandy, the little filly here is a tough Hungarian Jewess who's chosen to keep her mouth shut instead of cooperate. Pity, since there have been other areas on her we've been able to explore—"

"You miserable sick fu—"

For that I was repeatedly beaten until I was permitted to collapse on the floor.

"Oh Cliff," moaned Anne, struggling against her restraints, beyond the point of embarrassment. "They did not know what to do with a woman anyway." We both smiled despite ourselves, but Martinson thought it was just a response to the pain.

I mumbled, "So this is the guy you were following, the guy who killed Sternberg?"

Martinson was rotating the branding iron, getting it hot. Without turning to us, he said, "I did not kill that thieving Jew. Though I would have welcomed the chance. I was trying to find him. I was going to contact him as a representative of the Federal Bureau of Investigation and convince him to cooperate.

Unfortunately someone else got to him and killed him first. Of course, we had to know what you found out from him, so a few of our dedicated agents were sent to track you down."

"Madison and Monroe," I offered.

Martinson looked at me with new respect. "So maybe you do know something. Big deal. You now know even more, and I can't let you or your lady friend here go away and tell." He lifted the orange-tipped branding iron out of the flame. "You may enjoy this, Dandy. Or maybe not." He walked closer to Anne, waving the smoldering iron over her stomach.

"Is this what you do with women?" I asked.

"It's what they're good for," he leered. "Oh don't worry, she'll pass out soon enough and won't feel it after a few minutes. Then things can *really* start."

He lowered the branding iron to Anne's inner thigh and she bravely fought back the urge to scream. I struggled to kick Martinson back but couldn't reach, and sat there flailing ridiculously with my legs. Suddenly, the window shattered as a smoke bomb landed in the room.

"My eye's cut!" shouted Martinson, dropping the branding iron, his eye apparently sliced by a shard of flying glass. Smoke enveloped us, so I dove for the branding iron and swung it in his face. He screamed bloody death as I pressed it into his cheek, burning an emblem into his flesh.

The sound of open warfare echoed outside in the vacant lot. The four other Aryan goons had gone to their respective posts in adjoining rooms, and after more glass was shattered, I heard them returning the gunfire.

I peered over the windowsill and saw several unmarked cars crowded in front of the lot, about a dozen armed people taking aim at the building. Downstairs, the front door smashed open and a thunder of footsteps stormed in.

I quickly untied Anne, gave her her clothes. Martinson was stirring, so I kicked him in the groin. He buckled over, then with the branding iron I smashed him in back of the head. He fell unconscious to the floor. I noticed his cheek now had the permanent dark circle of a cattle ranch.

"Come on," I said when Anne was dressed. We ran down the corridor behind the Aryans, who were too busy firing out their windows to notice. At the top of the stairs we stopped and leaned against a wall as Agent Dahlia and Agent Gompers came racing up.

"Well if it ain't the Black Dahlia," I said, genuinely thrilled to see her.

"See Gompers, I told you he was a racist." Agent Dahlia smiled. Then she and Agent Gompers resumed shooting behind us, as one of the Aryans opened fire. He fell dead in a heap.

"Ta ta," I said, making a tiny waving gesture as Anne and I fled the premises.

The agents and the Aryans kept shooting.

Later, Anne marveled at the sandbags and artillery in my living room.

As we ate pizza and drank oil cans of Foster's Anne described how she and her friends in Paris had been overrun by a group of men and were turned over to Martinson, who killed her friends and smuggled her to America. It seems Martinson badly needed to know how much Sternberg had found out, and how badly their rogue FBI cell of fellow Nazis had been exposed.

"But we don't have any list of names," I said. "We never had any list."

"Martinson's superiors didn't know that."

"Was Sternberg trying to tell us we could get it at the Augsburg House?"

"Possibly," said Anne. "I am sure he was afraid he was being followed that day, so he did not wish to openly give me what he held. Then when he felt himself dying he must have hoped the opposition would never look for the information on a total stranger. He had no time to think, and could not possibly know what would happen to the stranger. Unfortunately, that stranger was you."

"Not so unfortunately. Otherwise we would never have met."

With a warm smile Anne let that notion linger. Then: "What do you suppose was meant by the phrase you found in the matchbook?"

" 'The man in the sand with the plan is at hand'? Maybe it's a code we're supposed to use to get the list from someone else? Maybe someone at the restaurant?"

"That was a month ago," she said hopelessly. "I am sure we are too late. Whoever was going to help us must have realized something went wrong. Besides, Sternberg was making the arrangements. We have no idea if there was a set meeting time, what method of transaction we were to employ, what payment was to be made . . . "

I studied Anne's face for a long time. "Look, we've come this far, we have nothing to lose and maybe plenty to gain. If all those people are anything like Jack Martinson, we've got to stop them."

"And you suggest? . . . "

"I suggest we get dressed in our finest and haul ass to the Augsburg House and make ourselves as conspicuous as possible, throwing around the phrase that pays for all it's worth. Maybe some more Nazis'll come out of the woodwork and lead us to the next level."

Anne asked, "Why is it that you make everything sound like an American television gameshow?"

For clean clothes I gave Anne some of the things Danette kept in my closet. The fit was perfect. I guess I'm attracted to women of the same build.

"You know," she said as we were getting ready to leave, "you have saved my life twice. In China, there is a saying that if you save a person's life you must be their guardian forever."

"Is that so?"

"That is so," she said, leaning in for a little tongue sushi.

Just then the front door opened and Danette walked in. What she must have thought, seeing me standing there kissing a strange women wearing her clothes, I'll never know.

"I just wanted to pick up a few things I'd left behind" was all she said.

I pulled back from Anne and said, to no one in particular, "I wish people would call before they drop by."

"I see you're miserable without me, Cliff." Danette was in a mocking mood. "Glad to see you're not jumping too fast, *one way or the other.*"

I said, "Danette, it's not like that . . ." but Anne and Danette both looked at me. "Well, maybe it is . . . "

"You're a nice guy, Cliff, but I never suspected you'd be so popular with so many people." Danette turned to Anne. "I don't know who you are, but I hope you have better luck than I did keeping his attention." She threw her copy of my house key into the sandbag trench and stormed out.

"Danette!"

All was lost, I was on a sinking ship.

Anne turned to me and said in all seriousness, "High strung, isn't she?"

We both broke out laughing.

The Augsburg House was located in that part of the Upper East Side known as Germantown because years ago that's where all the German immigrants came to start life anew. This was before the two World Wars, and though the immigrants were often suspected of being fifth-column agents for their former homeland, they had by now established multigenerational roots and were about as American and New York as an Astor or a Vanderbilt.

The front of the restaurant was plain enough, with a white neon sign stating the name over a smoked-glass entrance. It was an old, established place with an unassuming manner, none of that ersatz Alpine decor to detract from what purported to be an authentic homestyle restaurant inside. The menu posted by the front door offered in both English and German a dazzling array of old-world specialties, with assorted German pastries displayed in a tall, rotating refrigerated glass case tempting passersby.

"Price is right," I said as I held the door open for Anne.

Inside it was dark. We walked through a front bakery shop then down a corridor to the dining room. It was early: the dinner crowd hadn't yet arrived. A short, elderly man in black slacks, white shirt and a faded gold waiter's jacket that made him look like a monkey in need of an organ grinder, pulled two menus from a rack and led us to a table at the back of the room.

"Your waiter will be here to take your order," he said with a slight German accent.

"I, ah—," I looked into his face, Anne nudged my arm, so I said, "The man in the sand with the plan is at hand."

The host looked at me without reaction. I repeated the phrase, and I guess he couldn't decide whether I was deranged or serious, since he bowed slightly and moved away from us without comment.

"Guess it didn't mean anything to him," I said, reaching for a breadstick.

"You never know," said Anne. "Maybe he went back to report our arrival? Maybe there is some procedure we are to follow?"

"For a professional you're pretty unsure of yourself," I said between munches.

"I am a veteran, Cliff, not a professional. There is a difference. I received no government training, and learned from real situations as we hunted down our enemies."

"Aren't we hunting down our enemies?"

"In the past it was just one lone old man, scared, broke. This is the first time I have had to deal with an organization."

A busboy filled our glasses with water. I asked Anne, "Didn't you once tell me you had someone in their organization? Someone who warned you to get out of your safehouse before they torched it?"

"We had someone in the bureau, Cliff. It was the bureau that set fire to that apartment. More precisely the group of Nazis within the bureau. Now we are looking for whomever controls that group."

"I think I understand that."

"Operatives working as genuine American spies can do what they want. They decide to burn down my flat, so they do. Anyway, the FBI was easier to infiltrate, they are not so paranoid as other private organizations."

Our waiter, another elderly gent, around sixty, spoke perfect German to someone across the room, then came over. I thought: *Where were you, pal, in 1943?*

"Ready to order?" he asked.

"Give us a few more minutes," I said. He left.

"You forgot to tell him the phrase."

"Sorry. Look, I was just thinking. Remember the day after Sternberg died? I seem to remember stepping out of the shower and getting a knock on the door and looking through the peephole to see you standing there. But when I opened the door you were gone. Why did you run off? I mean, if that was in fact you and I wasn't having a hallucination."

"No hallucinations, Cliff. Remember, I had already been watching your building for some time, and had seen you, among other people, come and go on a regular basis. Then when I saw you at the museum, though you did not recognize me, I was able to immediately place your face. It could have been a coincidence—"

"In fact it was a coincidence," I said with a proud smile.

"Yes, a coincidence." She reluctantly conceded the point. "But I did not know that then. Nor could I be sure you were not somehow involved, somehow the person trying to kill Sternberg. I thought it best to confront you on another pretext, perhaps as a new neighbor in the building, to see you up close and judge your character. To see if you were, in fact, a killer."

"And when I called out that I was coming?"

She hesitated. "I suppose I changed my mind."

"Why?"

The waiter returned, interrupted our conversation and took our orders. Before he left I said, "The man in the sand with the plan is at hand."

"Very good, sir," he said. "You still have time for your salad." He walked off.

"Maybe now we are getting somewhere," said Anne.

"That's well and good, but why did you change your mind?"

"What?"

"Back at my apartment. We were talking before the waiter came. Why did you change your mind?"

She paused, then thankfully dove into her salad when the waiter brought them over.

"Anne?"

She said softly, "I suppose I was not prepared to think you were a killer. I suppose I thought you were a nice-looking man. I did not want to believe you were involved."

"So you chickened out rather than discover I was a killer."

"What?"

"I'm kidding, I'm kidding. Guess I should be flattered. I guess I thought you were nice looking, too."

It was one of those awkward moments where two people look into each other's eyes, waiting for the music to swell and the wind to start blowing their hair.

Instead, we both noticed a few men and women at various tables stand and walk off through a side door. Our host in the gold monkey jacket came over and whispered, "The meeting starts in five minutes. Your dinner will be waiting when you're through."

"*Danke shoen,*" I said.

Anne and I rose and joined the crowd as it exited through

a side door and moved down a short corridor into a large room. The walls of the room were paneled in blond, knotty pine, the ceiling sported dark wood beams and a number of open-blade fans. There were enough folding chairs to seat fifty, and at the front was a stage with a long covered table and a central podium. Along the walls were portraits of men I noticed on closer inspection to be military figures from World War Two. And not just any heroes, no sir. These were pictures of Hitler, Himmler, Goering, Goebbels, Heydrich, Hess, Rommel, among others: the cream of the Third Reich. There were banners and emblems, war and propaganda posters, and behind the podium— you guessed it—a huge Nazi flag. Place felt like a junior Nuremberg.

Everyone took their seats, and a group of men with short haircuts and bad suits filed in to sit at the table onstage.

"Good evening and welcome," said a pudgy man with short hair and stupid eyes, sitting at the head table. He looked like Ed Meese. "Glad to see you could make our nightly meeting. I see we have some new faces, some old friends we haven't seen in a while, and a few regulars." Pudgy laughed, as did a few of what I assumed were the regulars. "Let's begin, okay?"

A scratchy recording of "Deutschland Uber Alles" played over a tiny loudspeaker, and everyone stood. Then for the next hour Anne and I sat listening to a series of saber-rattling, hate-filled diatribes, calling for, among other things, death to blacks, death to Hispanics, death to Communists, death to cripples, death to liberals, death to pornographers, and death, of course, to Jews. To facilitate yet another "New Order" there was to be a massive mobilization of secret collaborators around the globe who would rise up in their individual cells and take control of organizations they'd penetrated. Corporations like IBM, IG Farben, Shell Oil, Sony. Organizations like the FBI, the CIA, the KGB, MI5, SDECE, Interpol, even the Mossad. Not to mention the IRA, the PLO, the Red Brigade, Omega Seven, Action Direct and assorted, little-known but highly ambitious terrorist groups. Fund-raising was discussed, as was a need to continue recruitment of new members.

The meeting then broke into tiny work groups, like those found at academic conferences, and specific plans were discussed in detail. It made little sense to me, though it was horrifying to sit and listen as normal-looking men and women sat and confabbed with the calmness of corporate planners just how they hoped to subvert and take over the world.

Anne seemed to be taking it all in, and since all I was digesting was the basic gist—after all, this *was* overwhelming—I hoped she'd remember enough to pass on to the good guys when we left.

Pudgy invited everyone back for the following evening; sessions were held every night in the same place at approximately the same time. Donations were taken, pamphlets were sold, then everyone was asked to turn in their membership keys for a new one.

"What do we do now?" I whispered to Anne as a group of men worked the aisles with glass jars like movie ushers collecting for the Will Rogers Institute.

"Act as though we are through and walk slowly to the door."

Anne stood and I followed. We walked along the side of the folding chairs, and sitting in back I noticed an old man I'd recognized as yet another resident of my building, a banker or diplomat or something.

Did everybody live in my building?

He was an old, stooped man with a thick gray beard covering most of his pasty-colored face. His eyes were clear, deep, surrounded by dark circles and heavy eyebrows. He coughed into a handkerchief as he stared at Anne and me as we made for the exit.

"Stop them," he barked loudly, pointing at us with his cane.

A pair of beefy guards marched down the aisle as the other fledgling Fascists turned to look, clearing an aisle for Pudgy, who walked over to us and narrowed his scowl.

"You're new members?"

"That's right," I said.

"Have you turned in your keys?"

"Our keys? Well, no. We forgot to bring them. We'll bring them tomorrow. I swear."

Pudgy wasn't pleased, but he didn't seem to be the person really in charge. That was the old gray-bearded man, who shook his head "no" ever so slightly. A few more guards approached us, exposing saps and police nightsticks beneath their suit jackets.

Pudgy asked, "Who told you about the meeting?"

"He didn't tell us his name," I said, then I described Jack Martinson. "He did say to repeat, 'The man in the sand with—'"

"Enough," barked Pudgy. An assistant brought a thick folder over to him. "If you were properly recruited and cleared, your names will be on this list. Tell me who you are?"

Ooh boy.

"Ah, I'm Adolf, this is Eva. *Sieg heil,* everybody."

With that I grabbed a chair and swung it into Pudgy's puss. Like a bowling pin he fell into a few people, sending half the room onto the floor. Anne did a few moves I hadn't seen since Emma Peel, God love her, kicking over two Nazis, clearing the door.

We sprinted down the corridor back through the restaurant with a group of angry Nazis hot in pursuit. In the bakery I grabbed the tall, rotating display case of cakes, heaved it on its side, blocking the crowd behind us.

"Jesus F. Christ," I screamed as we reached the sidewalk.

"My feelings exactly," said Anne, swinging to her left and racing toward Lexington Avenue. "This way!"

We ran, just like they do in the movies, through the evening crowd on the Upper East Side. Stores were open late, so many people were busily shopping and carrying holiday packages. Poor folks, we knocked over so many we must have ruined a good many Christmas mornings. Behind us I could see we were still being chased.

I ran into the street and shouted, "Taxi!" Not surprisingly, not a single cab stopped. Even the empty ones. They saw me running and screaming and flipped on their off-duty signs.

"Fuck you!" I shouted, flipping them the bird.

But Anne grabbed me and pulled me toward the subway.

"Oh no, not again!" I didn't know if I could take this much stress. I mean my stomach still ached from the baseball bat beatings suffered earlier.

We ran down the steps and jumped over the turnstile, but no one seemed to mind, which started a trend, as a bunch of college kids hurtled the turnstiles right behind us.

"Hey man, this is fun! Merry Christmas!" they shouted.

The express pulled in and we climbed aboard. Most of the cars were out of service, so everyone had to crowd into one or two lit ones. There were so many people on the train there was no sure way to tell if we'd been followed, but with my recent history it was safe to assume the worst.

The crush of people produced a horrible smell. To compensate for the cold outside the train was overheated, and with all the passengers packed like sardines in down coats and imitation leather, it created a moist odor not unlike a high school locker room after calisthenics. Mercifully, the train pulled into a midtown station and Anne and I were able to fight our way out before the doors closed and trapped us in the rumbling fumeatorium.

But a few of the Nazis had followed us and were making their way down the platform.

"Is there any place you can go?" I asked Anne as we ran up the escalator.

"I have the address of another safehouse."

"Great. Go there, I'll try and lose the Hansi brothers. Leave a message on my machine, I'll beep in from somewhere when I'm safe."

Anne was too experienced to argue with the wisdom of this plan—which disappointed me, somewhat—but we split up and she disappeared into the crowd on Fifth Avenue.

The Avenue itself was mobbed with holiday shoppers and out-of-towners in to see the Christmas tree at Rockefeller Center. I wove in and out of tourists gaping at Sak's window and the front of St. Patrick's Cathedral, and ran up toward Fifty-seventh Street.

And then I saw Trump Tower.

All right, Don, can your building do something useful for the common folk, like save my ass?

I ran in and took the long escalator up, overlooking the courtyard restaurant and the hoity-toity sippers and snackers. Back behind me I saw the two Nazis enter and head toward the foot of the escalator, pushing people out of the way. Fortunately there were some serious New Yorkers there who wouldn't stand for being shoved around, and the Nazis got into a verbal altercation with four old ladies carrying Bergdorf bags.

I hopped over the center divider and immediately took the down escalator as the goons were carried by the crowd and forced to go even higher.

I waved and ran out of Trump Tower. Thanks, Don.

Soaked from sweat and thoroughly winded, I ran north and saw a young couple wheeling a brand-new ten-speed out of FAO Schwarz.

"Excuse me, can I buy your bike?" I asked between gasps.

The woman started dragging her mate away, but the man said, "Easy honey, the guy looks desperate. Go ahead, make me an offer."

"Marty," whined the wife, "we waited two hours on line for that bike. Mindy'll be so upset—"

I interrupted. "Whatever you paid for it."

"Not enough." Marty was a negotiator and proud of it.

I took out my wallet. Pretty empty. "I've got the equivalent of one hundred and forty dollars in French and Hungarian currency, plus about forty-eight bucks US. How's that?"

"Well . . . "

"C'mon Marty, I don't have all day."

"I don't know . . ."

I turned and saw the Nazis running up Fifth. "For Christ's sake, man, take my Amex card and have a good time. I need this bike." I threw my wallet at a stunned Marty and he quite easily let me take the bike from his mitts.

It was a girl's bike, too small for me by far, and there was wrapping paper around the handlebars. But I didn't have time to quibble. I dodged through clogged traffic around Grand Army Plaza, ripping off the paper, and headed into Central Park. The two Nazis just stood and watched me disappear.

I was free, I was exhausted, I was sweating, it was freezing. But I'd lost the Nazis and was pedaling furiously up Park Drive East. It was closed to traffic at this hour, so thank God for that.

Where to now? At the southern tip of the Mall I veered right and headed north. It'd been so long since I rode regularly I didn't know how long I would last. Especially since I was in pain from the afternoon's beatings and still hadn't eaten dinner. But the cold rushed against my face and kept me alert.

The bike was, to be honest, a piece of shit, and if Mindy Whoevershewas was worth her salt, she'd have told her parents so in no uncertain terms. I probably did that family a favor. Still, I'd have to report my wallet stolen, so the most Marty could charge would be fifty bucks on my Amex card.

Damn it, what was I thinking about? My life was in danger, I still had no place to go. Great, so I could peddle my ass around Central Park in the dead of winter and work out my thoughts.

Near East Seventy-second Street I swung left and continued north on Park Drive, passing the Boat House Café as satisfied diners climbed aboard a fake jitney to be returned safely to the streets on either side of the park, away from the demons and villains that haunted the place at night.

How I envied those people!

I continued north, passing the Obelisk and rear of the Metropolitan. Another museum! That's where all this began.

Dear God, may I never walk into a museum again.

Along the reservoir I eased into a more relaxed mode afforded by the straightaway. Suddenly, near Ninetieth, a small gray car broke past the police barricade that closed the drive to vehicular traffic. The car turned on its high beams and came right for me. Gunshots fired everywhere.

Like a pro I shushed back and forth, using the maneuverability of the bike to avoid being shot. I peddled as fast as the shitty bike would go and pulled up to ride along the jogger's track surrounding the reservoir. The intermittent trees offered protection, so the shooter couldn't get a clear sight of me.

At the north end of the reservoir I made a sharp left and sunk into the mud of a bridle path. FUCK! I pumped and peddled until I broke free of the sludge and hit frozen dirt, which made pedaling more efficient, but the wheels had dented. Park Drive continued north so the car would have no choice but to follow it and swing down up around 110th, by which time I should have lost it in my wake.

Yeah, right.

The driver pulled right up onto the bridle path and came after me. I quickly cut over to a narrow, tree-lined footpath near the tennis courts, but that didn't stop whomever was driving, as he kept mowing down one tiny tree after another.

"You gotta have park!" I shouted as I rode on.

I dipped under the road and got onto another path, heading south. Where were the goddamned police when you needed them? The road sloped down, so I picked up speed and really flew.

But as I said, the bike was a piece of shit, and as I tried to avoid a pile of garbage lying in my path, the brakes locked and the bike twisted and buckled and hurled me skyward. I landed on my face, cutting it, bringing blood, smashing my legs and my knees.

I CAN'T TAKE IT ANYMORE! GODDAMN IT, I'VE HAD IT! I HAVE! I DON'T GIVE A DAMN ABOUT WHAT THESE PEOPLE ARE DOING! I DON'T CARE WHO DOES WHAT TO WHOM OR FOR WHY! PLEASE! I DON'T WANT TO PLAY ANYMORE!

I broke into uncontrollable laughter, but headlights suddenly washed over me and the car bore down from the north. I picked my miserable, self-pitying carcass off the snow and ran, stunned, dazed, emotionally drained, out onto the Great Lawn. All around me the lights of the great apartment buildings on Fifth and Central Park West mocked my hysteria. Blood oozed into my eyes from my forehead, but the car kept right on chasing me. I dodged behind a baseball backstop and raced over to the open-air theater used to present free Shakespeare in the park.

A HORSE, A HORSE, MY KINGDOM FOR A HORSE!

The car lost me in the winding thickets of the Shakespeare Garden. I paused to catch my breath, and to listen for my pursuers. Nothing, not even the idling of an engine. Slowly I crept up to the old Belvedere Castle, taking refuge in the corner of a gazebo off the main piazza.

I heard a cough, and in the moonlight was able to see a few homeless people wrapped in blankets, using the gazebo as a shelter. One man sat up and looked at me.

"This is my house, get outta here!" he shouted.

"SHHH!" I begged him.

"Go on, get out!" A few of his friends woke up, four people in all. They all started yelling at me to leave.

Dear God, PLEASE!

A flashlight shined in the faces of the homeless, then on me. I heard the click-click of a weapon being loaded, and a voice from behind the flashlight said, "Get out of here, all of you!"

A gunshot was fired into the center of the shelter, and the homeless scattered into the night. I tried scattering with them, but an arm grabbed and held me.

"Good run, Dandridge. But the race is over and you lost."

I was pulled onto my feet. My arms were tied around my body with twine, and I was marched to the top of the castle, a good sixty or so feet above a rocky cliff.

The voice said, "Seems, Dandridge, you learned way too much this evening. And from what I hear you been getting in everybody's way for quite some time. Can't let that go unpunished."

For my benefit the flashlight was shined over the side of the castle onto the jagged rocks below. Sure did look far.

"You have a choice. You can either jump, which means you'll first smack into the rocks and probably snap your neck. However, if that doesn't get you, then when you fall into the icy water below, it'll be pretty rough trying to swim with your arms and legs all tied up like that."

"What's my other choice?"

"The other choice? That's the one where you let me shoot you to death." The man laughed, and it seemed like there were two other men around who shared his mirth.

"Not much of a choice, is it?"

"No, I guess not." More laughter.

In the light of the night I saw the man lift and take aim with his gun. So this was it? This was where it was all going to end for Heathcliff Dandridge? And I didn't even have a great exit line.

Suddenly I heard a car drive up behind the castle. I couldn't make it out, but I was able to hear some words shouted from below. Reluctantly, the man who tied me up pulled me from the ledge and marched me down the stairs to the castle plaza. A few yards behind I noticed a parked stretch limo, it's rear door ajar. Faceless hands motioned me forward. I was pushed inside.

The door was closed and the car moved on. Sitting beside me was a Neanderthal-sized black man with a pistol aimed at my heart. Across from him, leaning back as if asleep, was the old, stooped man with the thick gray beard covering his white, pasty face, and clear, deep eyes surrounded by dark, sad circles.

He coughed into his handkerchief and said with a faint French accent, "It is indeed a privilege to meet you at last, Monsieur Dandridge. Since you will not be alive long, permit me an introduction. I am Marcel Coloute."

SEVENTEEN

It was like being trapped in a bad episode of *Mission: Impossible.*

The windows on the limo were so dark I couldn't see where we were going. Beside me, the old white man who claimed to be Marcel Coloute removed his leather gloves and cracked his individual knuckles.

"It would have been a shame letting you die before we met," he said as he placed a brown briefcase across his lap. "Uther sometimes is overanxious to please. It is fortunate I arrived in time. I really did wish to meet you." He clicked open the briefcase to reveal a collection of tubes and glass jars and a round vanity mirror. Ever so carefully he reached beneath his neck and began rolling the white flesh forward under his chin, peeling back what was apparently a latex mask, pulling the rubbery substance over his mouth, along his nose, around his eyes, until finally removing the whole thing with a puckered snap. Revealed was a face black and thick, just as I remembered it from the film Agent Dahlia had shown me. After storing the mask in its case, he reached up and pulled off his wig. His own short black hair showed not a trace of gray.

"So there was never any plastic surgery," I suggested.

"None whatsoever," Coloute answered with pride. "This is easier and more efficient and much more adaptable to specific situations. I employ four of the best makeup artists from Hollywood, California."

Another one in love with show business.

"So, how long have you been living in my building?"

"There will be time for answers later, *mon cher.* I look forward to explaining everything to you. You've been most persistent following me, and have done quite a good job. You're the first and only person to get this far."

"A miserable coincidence, I assure you."

"Ah, *mon cher!* But I do not believe in coincidence. The invisible spirits are responsible for all that transpires."

"Sure. But what about—?"

With a friendly smile—was this the face of a killer?—he held up his hand seeking silence. Then he leaned back and closed his eyes.

I turned to see if the doors were locked, but the man with the gun aimed at my heart grunted and waved his pistol. I, too, leaned back and nervously awaited our destination.

Who was I to argue with a gun?

The limo stopped and Coloute easily moved his thick body from the car. The man with the gun ushered me forward. We'd parked in an empty lot surrounded by a chain-link fence topped with circles of serrated steel. By the angle of the New York skyline, I figured we were somewhere in the uncharted wilds of Brooklyn.

An entourage of alert black men in slick suits led the way into a warehouse. The windows were concealed behind sheets of metal, and an old sign advertising an electronics manufacturer was covered with streaks of red and black spray paint. The whole place looked abandoned.

Yet once inside, as our feet echoed off the concrete, I noticed a group of men in faded clothes, lounging around rattan mats with apparently nothing to do. They seemed listless: their movements were slow and labored. As Coloute passed they struggled to stand in homage, but their efforts were pathetic. I smiled and nodded as I followed, but the men were already more interested in returning to their mats, so ignored me completely.

One of Coloute's lackeys opened another door, and I swear we entered *The Twilight Zone.* It literally looked like that, since we'd apparently landed inside an enormous Gothic mansion. Polished wood floors, ornate hanging tapestries, fine porcelain vases. The foyer was straight out of *Gone With the Wind,* with dashes of Tennessee Williams thrown in for good measure. The opulent antiques and furnishings seemed authentic enough, but then again I'm a poor schmuck who lives in a hovel on the Upper West Side, so what do I know?

I did, however, recognize, on top of a fine oak sideboard, two wooden cornices with tiny gargoyles smiling stupidly up at me. There were places for four, yet two remained. I don't have to tell you they were identical to the ones I'd smuggled for Oren to Paris.

"I can see, *mon cher,* you are pleased. *D'accord,* as it should be. A man like me, forced to live in shadows, must be surrounded with beauty to make life more bearable, do you not agree?"

"You've come a long way," I said, "since your murdering days in Port-au-Prince."

"I detect moral outrage. A pity. But you do not understand. Still, make yourself comfortable. I believe we both missed our dinners this evening." He coughed into his handkerchief. "Justin will see to our needs."

At this, a large, linebacker-sized thug with dreadlocks shuffled off with two listless men at his feet.

I was getting restless and wanted to get on with it. "So did you bring me here for an evening's entertainment, or are we going to discuss what's been happening and why you saved my life?"

"I saved your life because you intrigue me. Of all those who've been searching for me, you're the only one to have come this far. I wanted to see what you were like."

"Well here I am, take a look. I got a bus to catch in an hour."

Coloute was not amused. "So you are the man who has been chasing me across two continents, who has been disrupting my plans, who has been making a nuisance of himself, who has killed my friend—"

"Killed? I never killed—" I stopped, remembering the Paris zoo.

Coloute said, "Ah! I see you remember poor Toussaint."

"If that was his name."

He mumbled something in a language I didn't recognize, then said, "He was a true and dedicated believer."

"Wait a second. That jerk was coming at me with less than friendly intent. He was waving a crowbar at me, for God's sake. What was I supposed to do, stop and offer him scones? It was an act of self-defense, an accident, a—"

"Silence!" he shouted, sounding for a moment very much like the great and powerful Wizard of Oz. "There is no such thing as an accident!"

Yeah, right.

Coloute led me into a dining room, where he sat at the head of a long banquet-sized table. I took a seat beside him. "Accidents, coincidences," he said, "mere words and concepts, nothing more! The *loa* guides all movement in this earthly realm!" Then, like a rollercoaster, his mood zoomed down, and he spoke low and slow. "Your appearance at the Whitney that day was the work of the *loa*. An act of the invisible spirits, *les invisibles,* to bring us together, to help me in my struggle to serve God and attain religious purity. To ready me and my followers for our divine destiny. The everlasting death of Toussaint was, therefore, necessary."

I looked at him. "Right, absolutely. Think of it as a favor."

"Tell me, *mon cher,* soon after you witnessed the death of Sternberg, you went to Paris to the home of Raphael Arnot. Why?"

"I heard he knew the name of a good place to eat."

Coloute looked bored. "Save your levity for someone else. You're at the end of your days, *mon cher.* It can be speedy or it can linger, but only your cooperation will assure an easy death."

"Well, if you put it that way . . ." What was I supposed to do? Clearly, I was in the company of a dangerous lunatic, but by the very size of this illusory mansion and the scope of his international reputation, well, I didn't want to mess with him too much.

"So?"

I sighed and said, "I went there delivering a package."

"A package? And who gave you this package to deliver?"

"Oren Petrowicz, infamous art director and international drug fiend." Fuck Oren, I thought. He'd sell me to hell for a six-pack.

Coloute smiled, then laughed, filling the room with his joy. "As I suspected." He sipped from his wineglass. "And you and I lived in the same building, *mon cher.* And we dealt with the same people. This is too much. It is clearly the will of *les invisibles* that we meet."

"If you insist."

"The *djab,* the most evil *baka* of them all, the spirit of the underworld, the devil, has brought us together as sure as we're sitting here talking."

"Would you mind telling me *what* we're talking about?"

Coloute mumbled again in that strange language, then looked up as though he'd just noticed me for the first time. "Not at all, *mon cher.* But first, we eat."

The man called Justin returned with his listless factotums, carrying trays of stews, rice and bread. The stews were heavily spiced with peppers and onions and reminded me of Cajun cooking. As we ate, Coloute launched into his own take on the Horatio Alger story, Caribbean style.

"I was born to a poor family that lived in the remote hills of Haiti, far from the grand cities of Port-au-Prince or Cap Haitien. The tiny roadside village where I grew up was typical in that it was a diseased and poverty-stricken place with a deeply religious people. The religion, of course, was *vodoun.*"

"Voo-doo," I nodded sagely. "That explains everything." I looked around for Justin. "My check, please."

Justin grunted and pushed me back into my seat.

Coloute continued. "Before Dr. Duvalier rose to power, I worked the beaches of the early tourist hotels, offering trinkets, excursions into the hills, boat rides round the island, anything a customer would want. Naturally that included voodoo dolls and zombie potions."

"Naturally."

"I developed a charming personality for the tourist trade," he said, throwing his arms into the air. "I would shout, 'The man in the sand with the plan is at hand,' and they'd swarm around to buy what I offered. They wanted to believe I sold authentic potions and powders. Who was I to deny them that pleasure? I would walk up and down the sun-drenched beaches, playing the ignorant native islander who spoke poor English, and the arrogant rich from Europe and the Americas would be too busy drinking and enjoying themselves to notice otherwise. They'd be too busy to notice the poverty just beyond the hotel fence. I hated them with a passion, *mon cher.* But it was necessary that I see their wealth. It was *necessary* that I grow to hate them. I did not understand that then, but thanks be to God, I do now."

"If you say so," I said, munching my stew.

While it was easy resenting the foreigners, said Coloute, their money was needed "to put food in our stomachs and tin on our rooftops. I swallowed my pride and befriended many of them, gradually developing a network of friends all over the world. I learned how to deal with foreigners, with *blancs,* how to talk to them, and eventually earned the trust of some of the world's most notorious individuals."

I had no idea what he was getting at, but that didn't matter since I was suddenly feeling nauseous from the spices. I drank some water.

"It's surprising, *mon cher,* how easily a stranger will confide in someone with a kind face." For a moment he looked like a TV preacher, brimming with evangelical warmth. "Within four years I had a list of names that included some of the most dangerous men living on the planet, including a large number of former Nazis on the run or in hiding."

Despite my growing nausea, I marveled at how dispassionately he told his story, taking time to translate certain phrases into English. For instance, he said that throughout the time he built his network he continued his religious studies, becoming a full-blown *houngan,* or voodoo priest, learning the secrets of the various *vodoun* deities, the *loa,* becoming fully conversant with all the toxic chemicals required for the *coup poudre,* or magic powder, that turns men into zombies.

I spit out my wine. "Zombies?"

"Finish your meal, *mon cher,* and I'll tell you all about them."

I suddenly lost my appetite and threw down my spoon. Coloute grinned, and Justin cleared my place.

He continued. "By the time Duvalier introduced his *Volontaires pour la Securite Nationale,* the Tonton Macoute, I realized the best way to serve God and help my beloved country was to secure great power and enormous wealth."

"A nice, simple, greedy religious fanatic," I observed bitterly.

"Greed is not the sole province of Caucasians and Orientals, *mon cher.* Greed can be black as well."

With the aid of friends in his local *bizango,* or secret society, Coloute enlisted in the Tonton Macoute. A group of ruthless, savage, sadistic men who served at the whim of Papa Doc, the Macoute were drawn from the various secret societies that truly ruled Haiti. "There is official law, and there is effective law, and the *bizango* offered the latter. Still, the secret societies had no money, their only power was fear and the use of zombies, so I had to be modern, you see. I had to be modern." It was through the Macoute that Coloute established his reputation as a ruthless—"some would say barbaric, *mon cher,* but they miss the point"—killer.

As for the secret societies, they were based on the tribunals found in ancient Africa, recreated by the Haitians when they were slaves to enforce laws relevant to their lives. To judge their own, according to the will of the *loa,* and to issue punishment in accordance with ancient practice, that was the purpose of the *bizangos.* To *punish.* The Macoute exploited the people's fears, and the zombies, the living dead that roamed the hills of Haiti, were often said to be the punished political enemies of Papa Doc.

Lost in reverie, Coloute continued. "The years passed, and through extortion and killing I was able to amass quite a fortune. Not as much as the Duvaliers"—he coughed again into his handkerchief—"but enough. With careful overseas investments and the encouragement of my friends, I built an international network of contacts, all equally as greedy, as you put it, as I."

He had power, albeit in the world's poorest nation, but it was a start. By carefully introducing the more fanatic of his international contacts to each other, he began to exploit their hate and greed by convincing them they were part of an international movement poised to take control of the world. "And I called my movement ICE."

"Ice?" I asked, feeling suddenly light-headed and woozy.

He spelled it out. "I-C-E. The International Conspiracy of Evil. Has a nice sound, do you not think?"

"Lovely."

"To manipulate my associates, to mete out justice as I saw fit, in accordance with the devout philosophy of the *vodoun*, I created ICE as my personal secret society. My own international *bizango.* "

So that was what Sternberg was trying to tell me. He knew he'd been poisoned, been double-crossed, and "Aaahhs" from the mouth of a dying man is as close to "Ice" as you could get.

I said, with as much sarcasm as my nauseousness would permit, "So what're you planning to do, *mon cher,* introduce voodoo around the world and cash in on the doll market?"

"Your flippancy disappoints."

"Yeah, well."

"Through ICE I have convinced these fanatics that they are working in concert with other like-minded individuals, dedicated to a cause. Slowly, these people—in many cases devoted Nazis, as you observed this evening—penetrated governments and companies, all in the belief that I would guide them to a glorious future. We would work together in a worldwide army of invincible, subversive ICE men and women. Of course, through their activities I found myself in a unique position to acquire great wealth. You see, history and experience show that right-wing fanatics are quite able to raise large sums of money, and by making these people think they were working toward eventual control of the world, I've been fortunate to become quite rich myself."

"So what about the list we've all been chasing? I guess it contained more than just the names of Nazis. It sounds like it must have contained the names of all the people in your ICE organization."

"You are very clever, *mon cher.* No wonder you've gotten this far."

Coloute stood and began circling the table. My eyes followed him as he walked, but a powerful ache began throbbing in my head.

"Eli Sternberg had indeed been given a list of names by a disgruntled associate of ICE, a man who suspected that I was using all the money he'd raised for our cause exclusively for my personal ambition. He was right, of course, and has since been appropriately dealt with. In fact, he was one of the living dead you saw so pathetically lingering outside the mansion."

"Don't tell me he's a zombie?"

"All right, I won't." He laughed at his own feeble joke. "Anyway, when I learned Sternberg had the list I arranged to meet him, pretending to be a disgruntled Nazi from the group you met this evening. I promised to give him an even more detailed list than the one he had. In the process I stole the authentic list from him, slipped him a delayed poison, then substituted the authentic list with a phony one. I burned the real list, then slipped a fake one into one of those,"—he pointed to the wooden cornices—"and had the whole package taken to a group of Polish members of ICE with instructions to get it to Europe. And to accomplish their task it seems these dedicated ICE men gave the package with the list to Monsieur Oren Petrowicz."

I thought: *Oren, that lying bastard.*

Coloute saw my expression. "Oh, don't worry. He had no idea he was working for ICE. Anyway, there you were again, involved with the list. Papa Legba and Baron Samedi clearly were working their *vodoun* on you."

"Clearly."

"You took the phony list to Paris, where Justin retrieved it from Monsieur Arnot, another member of ICE who had become greedy and had to be disciplined. You see, *mon cher,* I have no patience for people who are not loyal."

I opened my mouth to speak, but found I couldn't produce any sound. I grabbed my throat, which felt like it was suddenly constricting. Saliva began foaming in my mouth. I was unable to spit. My pulse rate shot up through the roof.

"*Mon cher,* I wanted to test the devotion of my followers, to see how truly loyal they were. By letting it be known there was a list of names that threatened to bring ICE down, I wanted to see how far they would go to ensure the safety and secrecy of their organization, of *my* organization. Naturally there would be enemies seeking to gain control of the list, since they had no way of knowing it was fake, and as these enemies surfaced, I needed to see if my people were loyal enough to risk their lives. That is why the existence of the list became so, so public. Therefore, you see, you and your friends have been chased by my followers in a test. Some have passed, others have . . . well, the *loa* work in strange ways."

I struggled to speak, but barely got out a raspy whisper. "People have died for your test!"

"Ah, *mon cher, c'est la vie.*"

"You evil—," but I was unable to finish, as I was suddenly wracked with dry heaves.

"Oh, some people have died permanently, that is true." Coloute made a sign of the cross. "Others have merely been reprimanded, while others have been severely punished, condemned to a new life of mindless servitude, a new life as the living dead . . . a new life as zombies."

I tried standing, but fell off my chair, unable to move. Coloute came and stood menacingly over me, all traces of his kindly demeanor were gone.

"And you, my friend, shall soon be joining them!"

I awoke from a groggy sleep and found myself in a tiny room decorated with feathers, beads, candles and the black-and-red flag of Haiti. I was no longer dressed in my own clothes, but instead wore a ragged pair of pants that barely covered my legs. My naked chest and bare feet were numb.

Coloute was standing in front of a mirror, carefully primping in a long, purple robe.

"Welcome to my *bagi, mon cher.* The private temple of the *vodoun* priest. I trust you are rested for the big day?"

It was hard to talk. "Where are we? What—?" I tried sitting up, but found I still couldn't move.

"It's Christmas day all over the world, and you are in the *houngan*'s inner sanctum. Through that door over there"—he pointed with the end of a strange-looking whip—"is the *houn-four*. The voodoo temple."

"What's happening?" I asked, but I don't think he heard me.

"You are about to witness a rite seldom seen by members of your race."

From outside I heard the faint, rhythmic beating of drums. A cowbell rang once, twice, three times, the drums beat rapidly to a climax, then all was silent.

Huh?

Coloute continued primping, gathering assorted feathers, carefully painting his face with white lines. "You have served my loyalty test well, *mon cher,* but too many people have begun looking for me, and it is all your fault. At first I thought you were working with those paranoid Hungarian Jews, then I imagined, incorrectly again, that you were an agent of the FBI, the CIA, or the KGB, something like that. I see you were simply a victim of *les invisibles.* Their divine power brought you to me for judgment, and I have not failed. You have been the catalyst that helped determine who among my flock was most devout, but unfortunately you know too much and must not be allowed to interfere with my plans any longer."

I hoarsely whispered, "I don't even know what your plans are."

He turned and glared at me. "Why I thought that was obvious. To amass a huge fortune and return in glory and triumph to liberate the people of Haiti."

Ta da!

I thought: *That's it?* "All this, just to become ruler of Haiti?"

"Have you no sense of national patriotism?"

"Well, sure," I croaked. "But, I mean, we're talking about Haiti, not the breadbasket of the world."

"My people have suffered enough! It is time for them to have a leader of piety and vision!"

"That's you, I take it?"

"You disappoint, *mon cher*. I can see I will have to persuade you."

"Don't go to any trouble on my account," I said, trying to stand. I rolled onto the floor and Coloute laughed.

"Someone so eager to follow danger must assuredly crave death. Soon you will have your wish."

I was carried from the *bagi* into another part of the warehouse designed like a church. Large and airy, it was filled with dozens of men and women standing in makeshift pews, all wearing elaborate disguises that made them look like mythical beasts. Men with horns, women with beaks. Heavy kettle drums beat a steady rhythm, and six young women with tambourines swayed lyrically on either side of a front altar.

I was being held upright by two men, one of whom looked like Justin, but my vision was becoming blurred so I wasn't sure; we were standing at the rear of the center aisle, directly facing the pulpit. Intricate white chalk marks covered the floor, and a rooster dressed in top hat, trousers and tails was suddenly released from a cage, its wings flapping and fluttering as it strutted down the aisle toward the pulpit. The crowd cheered, then began chanting in a language I didn't understand.

Four old men in suits and ties entered through a side door, carrying overhead a tiny box shaped like a child's coffin. They made a circle in front of the pulpit, and for the first time I noticed that Coloute was standing on the platform, his head tilted down, his eyes shut, his lips mumbling as if in a trance. He snapped open his eyes, cracked his whip, and in a deep and powerful voice intoned, "In the name of the Father, and of the Son, and of the Holy Spirit, let this ceremony begin!"

Beside him a large, fat black woman, dressed all in white, pranced across the pulpit like a Sumo wrestler, hands on her hips, hair filled with twigs and small bones and feathers and what looked like the carcass of a dead mouse.

The crowd suddenly shouted, *"Danse, Mambo Calinda, Danse, Mambo Calinda! Boudoum, boudoum, boudoum!* Send away evil, bring only good!"

Coloute swirled his robe and approached the pulpit. He shouted, "The Catholic goes to his church and speaks about God. But the *vodounist* dances in the temple and becomes God!"

Jets of fire spat out of tiny gas spigots on either side of the pulpit, and the possessed young women with tambourines began gyrating back and forth over the fire. The fat woman, Mambo Calinda, leapt off the stage and ran toward a table covered with opened bottles of rum. With frantic energy she began spilling the liquid over the devotees seated in front. Then she drank the rum and sprayed it between her teeth onto the four old men, the tiny coffin, and the twirling women.

Coloute was chanting furiously. The drums, the cowbell and the tambourines made a deafening but precise musical sound. Candles and torches were lit around the room.

Two of the old men opened the tiny coffin and removed a live black cat. An iron cauldron with boiling water was carried front and center and placed on a contraption over a jet of fire, then the screaming cat was forced, head first, into the water. A young man, deep in a trance, spun up from his seat, removed the drowned cat from the cauldron, and danced wildly with the carcass. Without hesitating he bit the cat's throat, spraying its blood over himself. He then began shredding its skin with his teeth. I wanted to look away, but the muscles in my body wouldn't respond.

"Merry Christmas! Merry Christmas!" shouted the crowd. Sleighbells rattled from somewhere, and another large coffin was brought forth and placed near the table of rum bottles. The coffin lid was raised, and Coloute reached inside and removed a long, black snake. He handed the snake to Mambo Calinda, who draped it over her tremendous body, then he accepted two steel machetes. Scraping them together, he barked in that bizarre language, and the crowd fell silent.

"Children of Guinea!" he shouted. "Children of Africa! I bring you the goat without horns!"

I suddenly felt myself being lifted and carried down the center aisle of the church. The crowd roared its approval. Then I was picked up and lowered, face up, into the wooden coffin.

I couldn't breathe. I couldn't move. Not a single muscle would respond. I could hear what was happening, but my eyesight had disappeared and I could no longer feel a thing. Like I was dead, physically dead.

But I was conscious. And I could hear everything being said.

"An evil man, judged an enemy of our people." It was Coloute. "For his crimes and for his transgressions, for his acts against the spirits and for his interference with our dreams, *this man has been condemned!*"

Everyone began cheering, and the music continued wildly for what seemed like a year. I found it increasingly harder to breathe.

"Can you hear me, *mon cher?*" It was Coloute, very close, whispering over me. "I know you can. I know that you are alive, though to my followers you appear quite dead. Even now they are passing beside your open coffin, dropping *gris-gris* onto your body. Can you not feel it? *Gris-gris* are good luck charms. If your death satisfies the spirits, everyone who places *gris-gris* on your body will be assured good things. Now, you are covered with cat bones and feathers, snake skins and maggots, frog legs and pointy stones. Ah, someone has just placed a live spider on your stomach. But you cannot move. You are dead, *mon cher.* Everyone here can see that for themselves. You are dead and do not move, you do not breathe and you do not feel. Soon we will nail shut your coffin, and the magic powder poisoning you will vanish. You will wake up, *mon cher,* alive and well and buried beneath six feet of earth . . . And no one will hear your screams!"

Coloute moved away, and all I heard was more music.

I couldn't believe this was happening. But it was and there was nothing I could do about it. My mind raced. I couldn't understand this. I didn't have the intellectual capacity to accept my own death.

I mean, how could I die in some bizarre voodoo ritual in a warehouse in goddamned Brooklyn?

Let's be real. Was this the last act of my life? Was this the way it was destined to end for Heathcliff Dandridge, struggling hack scenarist and international bon vivant?

More than that, was the whole time I was running through New York and Paris and Budapest, running for my life, running to help people, a miserable, sick joke? A mere game, a test, concocted by a religious madman who'd stolen money from Nazis and right-wing fanatics to finance his personal salvation through the liberation of Haiti?

The horrible truth was that I supposed it was.

Still, there *were* real Nazis out there planning to take over the world. Now they would be stopped. Anne was on to them, and she would tell her friends, and they would work with Agent Dahlia and Agent Gompers and Inspector Lonsdale and—

What the fuck was I thinking? I was dying!

But I wasn't ready to die!

Maybe Coloute was right. Maybe someone who'd craved danger like I did was eager to face death? Maybe I deserved it? Two months ago I was feeling lonely and miserable and hated my life and all it stood for. I easily related to the notion of artistic martyrdom. Hemingway, Van Gogh. They were old pals. I thought, *Yeah, well, maybe life really did suck and maybe I'd be better off catching the program on the flip side.*

But not this way!

Besides, what was my epitaph going to be? That he suffered

a midlife crisis in his early thirties, went off in search of adventure, found more than he bargained for, and wound up buried alive by voodooists as a zombie?

Pretty pathetic. Like the cheap synopsis someone would use on a movie-studio reader's report of my life.

Christ! To be summed up in a reader's report . . .

Jesus in Heaven, it's Christmas! You can't let me die like this!

And I'd never even written my will!

My mind was full of disconnected thoughts. To be dying and not able to stop it. To never again struggle with an unfinished script . . . to never see a new head coach with the New York Jets . . . to never again sip café au lait in a Parisian bistro . . . to never again drink beer and share a laugh with my friends . . . to never again visit museums and see the great paintings and sculptures and photos . . . to never travel the world and sample the cultures of the seven continents . . . to never again ride a bike in Central Park . . . to never smell the exhaust fumes of a New York bus . . . to never take a weekend stroll with the woman of my dreams . . . to never see the fall foliage of Vermont . . . to never know the profound joys of marriage, fatherhood . . . to never again confront my agent over a lack of employment—well, even that would be something I didn't want to miss . . . to never again hear Benny Goodman play "Sing, Sing, Sing" . . . to never again eat fresh hot New York pizza, or bagels, or Chinese food, or Seventy-second Street hot dogs . . . to never again find joy in all the simple things that give life meaning . . . to never again walk down a street and feel the thrill of making eye contact with a single, attractive woman.

I mean women were what life's all about.

Dear God, women! Maybe I'm twisted, maybe I'm sick, but as I was lying there in my coffin, awaiting death, voodoo drumbeats filling my ears, all I kept thinking was that women were a damned good reason for wanting to stay alive.

Alive, damn it! Not dead! No more of this feeling sorry for yourself. No more! Life is for the living! For those who reach out and grab it, not for those who bemoan their fate. A quote from Shakespeare popped in, something about how wise men never sit and wail their woes, but presently prevent the ways to wail. Yeah! Damn right! Good ol' Shakespeare.

So what if the career I'd chosen wasn't working out? So what if I struggled? I had a roof over my head, friends I could call, women interested in me . . . Life was good! Life was fine! Life was worth living!

I heard someone raising a wooden plank, and someone else said, "Here's the hammer."

An image of Jimmy Stewart and *It's a Wonderful Life* flashed through my head. And I thought, *Help me Clarence, please. I want to live, Clarence.* I want to live.

Now or never, folks. I summoned all my strength and tried forcing movement into my arm.

And it worked! Dear God, it worked!

Like lint sucked by a vacuum, life refilled my body. I was free, able to move. Breathing came normally, vision was restored.

It was as if I'd never been poisoned at all.

I sat up in my coffin, knocking aside all the *gris-gris* the voodooists left on my body. Suddenly people were screaming. Panic set in.

Coloute shouted, "You!"

I said, "Is that any way to great an old friend back from the dead?"

I jumped out of the coffin, and Coloute's devotees scattered in fear. I was, after all, a zombie arisen; they didn't want to get too close.

Without thinking, I ran to the rum bottles and began spilling the stuff onto the ground, pouring it through the jets of fire. This spread rapidly, engulfing the entire church in flames before the followers could flee.

Coloute was running wildly, throwing robes and drop cloths

over the rising flames. He signaled for his followers to seize me, but they were too busy running for their lives to be concerned with a little ol' zombie like me.

Quickly, I jammed a few pieces of cloth into the tops of some rum bottles. I tipped over the rum, drenching the cloth, then held the bottle up to the fire. Heaving them like a pro, I threw about a half dozen Molotov cocktails all around the room, including one directly at Marcel Coloute himself, just as he was leveling a Kalashnikov in my direction. The Molotov exploded in his face, setting his body ablaze.

The entire warehouse had become inflamed, but my strength had fully returned and I was able to join the fleeing crowd and make my way out to the street.

It was a snowy Christmas day, and all I had on were the ragged pants and a couple of cat bones in my hair. Not even the flames that burned down the warehouse could keep me warm from the intense urban cold.

So I shivered.

It was a sensation I was overjoyed to feel.

EIGHTEEN

Agent Dahlia smoothed things over with the police. Since the incident at the tenement she'd been back and forth to NYU Medical Center checking up on Agent Gompers, critically injured in the shooting with Martinson's Aryan thugs. But she was able to get to the warehouse as soon as I called, and inside the Gothic mansion found a fireproof file cabinet with a complete list of names and bank accounts, fully documenting the worldwide reach of the late Marcel Coloute and his ICE organization. The bureau was braced for a purge of its Nazi fanatics, and Agent Dahlia, whose first name I never learned, assured me she'd circulate the information to her counterparts overseas.

"By the way," I said as she dropped me off at my apartment, "tell Agent Gompers I hope she feels better."

"What's she gonna care what a dumb shit like you has to say?" replied Agent Dahlia.

I spent the rest of Christmas Day recuperating. Ol' Risa had just returned from her travels and was loving and attentive and brought over a doctor friend to check me out to see if I was fine. Neither commented on the sandbags or artillery still occupying the center of my living room, but the doctor did examine me thoroughly, and aside from a few bumps, bruises and a mild case of frostbite, he said I showed no signs of my ordeal. I didn't go into detail about the voodoo ceremony, but I did give a description of the physical symptoms I suffered at the warehouse, which apparently fascinated him. He chose to call a specialist.

The specialist listened, ooo'd and aah'd in all the right places, then asked me if I'd ever been to Japan.

"You see," he said, "over there they eat this delicacy called *fugu*. It's a blowfish that contains a very powerful nerve toxin. Chefs there have to be licensed to prepare it, but sometimes they miss and the eater dies. The poison's called *tetrodotoxin*. A slight taste can produce a chemical high, kind of like great cocaine. In the right doses, though, it relaxes a body's movements and makes a person look dead."

"That so?" I said.

"Yeah. Can either paralyze or kill, but sometimes it kind of naturally wears off. Rare chance of that, though. Usually fatal. I'd say you were lucky as hell. Tell me, what were you doing before you experienced those symptoms?"

That night the news reported the burning of an abandoned warehouse in Brooklyn. Many people belonging to a "local religious cult" were seen fleeing the scene, and a few neighborhood witnesses claimed the cult had been performing a bizarre African ritual that included the torturing of animals. More than a few people suggested to reporters that there was a zombie now on the loose in the borough.

One of the messages on my machine was from Sam, who'd been working overtime to give me a holiday present. Seems a local production company was interested in using me to adapt one of the books represented by Brisketsomething for a syndicated, made-for-TV movie. "I don't care whether you like the book or not, it's work. I want you to call the producer's new assistant on Monday for details," said Sam on my tape. "Her name's Ellen Jankowsky and she said she knew you and couldn't believe fate and was dying to work with you personally. She's cute, Cliff, so play your cards right and—"

I shut off the machine. Ellen Jankowsky? The girl from the train? She sure got home to a job in a hurry.

The next morning, Boxing Day in some parts of the English-speaking world, I phoned Anne at the number she'd left on my machine. She'd been worried about me, thankfully, but was disappointed that the list of Nazi names had fallen into the hands of the FBI. I assured her that in gratitude for my services Agent Dahlia would probably give her a copy.

"I hope so."

I described the bizarre events at the warehouse and told her how I was nearly buried alive, embellishing the bravery and heroism that led me to use Molotov cocktails, "made famous by freedom fighters from your country, you know," to burn down the warehouse and kill Coloute before he killed me.

"You Americans," she said, "are never subtle."

I couldn't disagree. She promised to come over as soon as she made some calls.

I followed her example and made a few calls myself. Oren was glad to hear things had worked out, and though he hated to bring it up, he did have to get the guns back to the guy they belonged to, so would I mind terribly if he sent some Teamsters over to moose the stuff out of my apartment?

"Anytime, Oren. Send them over."

"Does this mean we're still friends?"

"Don't push it."

"Me, man? It's *your* emotional space. You let me in when you're ready. I'm just glad to see you went out and faced the demons that were haunting you. Bet it made you appreciate your own life a little more."

"Good-bye, Oren."

"By the way, Cliffie, I got new pins. You want to bowl tomorrow night?"

* * *

"So, does your dick still work?"

It's the consistency in my friendships that I enjoy. "Since when did you care, Rick? Turn funny on me?"

"Funny this, pal. I just want to know if that numb drug numbed Mr. Peter."

"I haven't noticed any malfunctions."

Rick thought this over. "I hate to admit this, Cliff. Especially to you. But it looks as though Danette and me are *kaput.*"

I said nothing, just let the phone hang by my ear. I began sorting my bills.

"Cliff, you still there?"

"I'm here, Rick. What do you want me to say?"

"Nothing *to* say. I think she's still got the hots for you. You're all she ever talked about."

"That's how it should be. I'm that kind of guy."

"Yeah. Well, we had some laughs, you know. Some fun, stuff like that. She's bright, fun, sensitive. A real catch, Cliff. If she comes around, you ought to reconsider."

"I never *not* considered, Rick."

"Well, as your attorney I suggest you give her some more attention. She cares about you. She needs to feel you care, too."

"I'll take that under advisement."

"You know, *some guys* . . . Well anyway, as I said, we did have fun together. And she does give the best—"

"Gotta go, Rick."

"You're right. Talking out of school makes Ricky a bad boy. You'll never know what we did together."

"Did anyone ever tell you for a lawyer you're a scumbag?"

"Stand in line and take a number. Look, I'm glad you're back, glad you're alive, etcetera and stuff like that. . . . I'm not very good at this."

"The sentiment touches my heart. *Merci beaucoup.*"

We made arrangements to have lunch at MOMA and to watch the bowl games on New Year's Day.

"You know, Cliff, I knew I didn't stand a chance when Danette turned to me one night and said yours was bigger."

At last, I hung up on someone first.

The doorbell rang and I got up to answer it.

"*Joyeux Noel!*"

"Josephine!"

She was standing there with a shopping bag full of packages, and was personally wrapped in a gorgeous white fur jacket. She ran into my arms and we kissed.

"What're you doing here?" I asked when we came up for air.

"I was worried and I missed you. In fact, I have been in New York three days. I wanted to spend Christmas Eve with you, and thought you would be happy and surprised. But you were not home—I kept stopping here four times each day."

I marveled at how fresh and vibrant she looked, and that she was able to get a last-minute flight Christmas Eve.

"Money talks, bullshit walks," she said with her wonderful French accent.

She accepted as normal the military hardware in my apartment, and removed her fur jacket to reveal a cowl-neck white sweater that clung to her distinctive proportions.

"I just can't believe you're here," I said.

"Oh good. I am glad you are pleased."

"I never thought we'd see each other again."

"*I* never thought that at all," she said with a smile.

I fixed us some drinks and she began telling me how marvelous a city New York was, especially at Christmas, though she was disappointed at all the homeless and gave five-dollar bills to everyone she met. "Your dollar is so inexpensive, I perhaps should have given them more?"

The subways she thought were fascinating, and she bought all sorts of oils and incense from the Islamic salesmen set up in the various stations.

"I always wondered who bought that stuff," I said.

She rustled through her shopping bag and produced a paperback with an erupting volcano on its cover. "Cliff, tell me something. Is this Dianetics about sex?"

It was great seeing Josephine. Her dramatic reappearance in my life reminded me of Emma Bovary's heroic crossing of the fields to meet her true love. Was that what we had? I wasn't sure. But of all the women I'd met, she certainly was possessed of the most spontaneous, provocative spirit, and it certainly had its appeal. And while it was flattering to assume she'd come all this way out of amorous devotion, I knew she was no emotional child and wouldn't have traveled so far without some selfish motives of her own.

We spent about forty-five minutes exploring those motives.

As a welcoming memento, I found the snowy New York paperweight I bought at the airport and was still in my suitcase, and gave it to her.

"I shall treasure it always," she said with sincerity.

By midafternoon we were a little drunk and very tired, so she excused herself to use the euphemism. She wanted to freshen up before we ventured out to hunt for dinner. As I got dressed, the doorbell rang, and I opened it to see Anne standing there with a bag from Gristedes and a smile.

"I am sorry I took so long, Cliff. Everything now is fine. I spoke with your Agent Dahlia, a most unpleasant woman—"

"You have to get to know her," I suggested.

"Yes, I think that is so. But she gave me a copy of the list, which I already sent to Papa. He was grateful and happy to hear you were still alive. My sister, Catherine, also wishes you good health."

"That's nice," I said, wondering what to do next. I certainly was glad to see Anne, make no mistake. And her deep sense of loyalty, honesty and supreme bravery, not to mention her profound political convictions and bone structure, were powerful inducements. And though I suspected there were some strong emotional attachments developing between us, it occurred to me we'd yet to consummate them horizontally.

But Josephine was in the loo and had to emerge sooner or later.

Anne said, "I brought something for dinner. You are in no condition to leave, so I will just go into the kitchen and begin preparing."

"What did you bring?" I asked helplessly.

"Hungarian goulash, of course. And a desert *palinscinta* I will make that will drive you wild." She disappeared into the kitchen.

There was another knock on my door. I didn't think I could take any more.

But it was only two large men in overalls, the moose patrol I recognized from the day Oren delivered the guns and the sandbags.

"Here to pick up some military ordnance," said Moose Number One in a surprisingly high-pitched monotone.

"Help yourself, gentlemen."

Josephine came out of the bathroom, dressed and ready to go. "I thought I heard you talking to someone," she said, noticing the men lugging out the sandbags.

As Josephine sat on the sofa, watching the men carry out the weapons, and Anne puttered quietly in the kitchen, who should pop through the front door but dear, darling Danette.

"Cliff, I think we have to talk," she said, focusing on the activities of the Moose Patrol. "We have too much in common, too much shared history, to casually throw our relationship out the window. *Who* are you?"

She'd spotted Josephine.

"This must be Danette," offered Josephine.

"Ah, the French woman." Danette was unusually calm. "I

suspected there was a French woman. Whatever happened to the Hungarian?"

Just then Anne popped out of the kitchen, wearing my cooking apron. "Cliff, where do you keep your spices? Oh."

Welcome to my nightmare.

Josephine, bless her heart, noticed my inability to speak and took up the slack, playing hostess, making introductions. She was clearly the most comfortable dealing with this, having confronted untold bizarre situations in her lifetime, but Anne held up well too, since she and Josephine had, in fact, seen each other before. Almost immediately, Anne displayed the cool professionalism that had occasionally saved our lives.

As for Danette, well, it wasn't the scene she'd expected, but she did seem to take the benign view that if she was going to confront me about the future of our romance, having the various additional parties present wouldn't necessarily be a hindrance.

Yeah, right.

Danette said, "Cliff, stop standing around like a zombie. Why don't you get us some drinks?"

"Right, fine, of course." I stumbled into the kitchen and grabbed four bottles of Red Stripe. I don't think it's what the girls wanted.

"I have a better idea, Cliff." Josephine again, commanding the scene, taking the beers from my hand and placing them on the coffee table. "Why do you not let us girls discuss things ourselves? We know you, but we all know different sides of you." She winked at me. "I think it would be helpful if we exchanged our views and impressions. Go out for a little while and enjoy the nice fresh air."

"You haven't been in New York long, have you?" commented Danette, sarcastically, to Josephine.

"I think it is a good idea, Cliff," added Anne.

I went to my bookshelf and reached behind *Les Miserables,*

where I kept a few spare dollars. Like the Parisian poor of 1832, you never know when you'll be caught without. I still needed to report a stolen wallet.

I turned to Moose Number One, who was just wheeling out a handtruck with the last of the sandbags. "You guys want to grab a beer?"

"Never met a Teamster who didn't," replied the Moose.

I turned to the women. "I'll be at the All State. It's in the phone book. Call me there when you've sorted out my life."

"Relax, Cliff," said Josephine. "No one is going to harm you. We all care about you very much."

"Otherwise we would not be here," observed Anne the diplomat.

"What am I all of a sudden? Lady Brett Ashley, the whole world suddenly in love with me?"

"Don't push it, Cliff," Danette said archly.

"After we've spoken, we will know what is best," suggested Josephine.

Anne smiled at me, but seemed to be focusing on her own personal thoughts.

"Fine, wonderful, a great idea," added Danette who, quite remarkably for her, got into the spirit of things.

"Cliff, one of us will be here when you get back," suggested Josephine. The other women seemed to like that idea.

I was struck, speechless and immobile. The notion of the three women who knew me so well, yet so differently, discussing me like a class project, was frightening.

Josephine got up to lead me to the door. She whispered, "Whatever happens, even if you and I should not see each other for years and we marry and have families, I will always be there for you. That is a sacred promise." She kissed my forehead.

Anne was sitting, withdrawn and silent. She looked like she wanted to leave. Danette was chugging a Red Stripe, a wicked smile on her face.

I left with the two mooses. Or was it two meese?

* * *

I had the notion, sitting at the warm, dark bar, ignoring the chatter of the two Teamsters, that if I got through to New Year's I could change my life by selling my story to New York magazine. I mean, it had all the elements, and they could even kick in a little veiled racism by speaking haughtily of the corrupt nature of Brooklyn and the Lower East Side, with insider's travel tips. That is, of course, if they weren't planning a cover story on the gentrification of another ghetto, or voodoo hadn't become the flavor of the week along with Canadian restaurants and fever blisters. But then I thought, nah, no one would believe it, so why bother? I'd long since abandoned the notion of writing about today's Lost Generation. Who'd really care, anyway?

The Teamsters hoisted beer for beer with me until I could no longer keep the stuff down. You can only rent beer, not buy it, and seven trips to the toilet later, I still hadn't heard from the girls. My life had to be forfeit. The Teamsters thanked me for the brews, and said for a writer I wasn't too much of a jerk. I could drink beers with them any day. I paid the bill and thought I could probably drink with them for a month just to get back my money's worth.

I staggered around the Upper West Side. It was Saturday, and young couples were already fulfilling a ritual, shlepping bags from Zabar's and picking up the Sunday *Times*. They'd be home and in front of the VCR long before the bridge and tunnel crowd piled in to swamp the avenues. Saturday was singles' night on the Upper West Side, and with the exception of the Europeople who sought style over substance and who'd probably stay in SoHo, NoHo, TriBeCa or Chelsea anyway because there were fewer lights and the crowds didn't move in packs, all members of the Lonely Hearts Club would be out in force. It was dangerous to be alone. But there I was, a solitary free agent, a man without caste, wandering the cold, snow-blown streets.

I was hungry and drunk. I stopped in front of my building

and looked up into my apartment window, but couldn't see a thing, though the lights were on. I stood there, thinking about the three women slicing up my life. One was exciting, spontaneous, confident, but would probably wear me out inside a month. Another was intelligent, brave and headstrong, but perhaps too dedicated to her causes and would forever live on the short side of danger. I'd learned, coming within an inch of death too many times recently for a man of my breeding, that danger was for other heartier souls. The last, who was also the first, was loving and attentive, with a truly generous disposition, but even she'd shown some steel and I'd probably have to explain myself too many times. Eventually we'd grow bored and restless.

Clearly, I wasn't ready to settle down at all. But what could I do about it? I was weak, selfish, your basic male shit. Always drawn to the next unexpected female I'd hadn't yet met.

God, send me a sign. I know not what to do!

"Excuse me, I'm terribly sorry."

"What, what?" I was so wrapped up in thought I didn't notice what was happening.

"Boris didn't mean it. He's never like this, I'm really terribly sorry."

I turned and looked down and noticed a white poodle with a spiked collar standing astride my boots, grinning stupidly. A yellow puddle surrounded my foot in the snow.

"He's never done that to anyone. But you were just standing there, so quiet and still, he must've thought—I'm really very sorry."

"It's okay, these boots are water- and doggieproof. Forget it."

Boris's owner smacked him on the nose, then, though she tried not to, she started laughing. I started laughing too, and noticed that Boris's owner was very, very pretty. My kind of very pretty.

Heel, Heathcliff.

But there's no teaching an old dog new tricks.

"Listen," I asked, "you live around here? You want to grab some pizza or something? It's pretty cold, and I haven't eaten and—"

Before I knew it, Boris's owner had removed a can of mace from her purse and was holding it in my face. "Don't you come near me!" she shouted. "You just stay away or I'll scream! I swear I'll blind you, you motherfucker!"

I quickly ran around the corner.

When I returned, Boris and his owner were gone, so I went up to my apartment, thinking enough time had elapsed for the dangerous women in my life to have gotten to know one another. Maybe they'd come to some arrangement and we'd rotate for a while, kind of like a test?

But when I entered my apartment, they were gone. They'd apparently eaten Anne's Hungarian goulash, cleaned the dishes and split.

They left behind no note.

Well, maybe Anne or Josephine or Danette would call when they wanted to. All I could do was wait. All I could do was hope. I could call them, but what good would that do?

Maybe they were finally on to me. . . .

In any event, I went back out and bought some lox at Zabar's and bagels at H & H and picked up the *Times* on the corner. The Arab news vendor was friendly and wished me a "Ccheppy New Yir."

Back home, I settled in for a nice, quiet evening by myself.